The Pilot's Wife

— A Novel —

ANITA SHREVE

D0089572

BACK BAY BOOKS

Little, Brown and Company

New York   Boston   London

For Christopher

The characters and events in this book are fictitious. Any similarity to real persons, living or dead, is coincidental and not intended by the author.

Copyright © 1998 by Anita Shreve
Reading group guide copyright © 2008 by Anita Shreve and Little, Brown and Company
Excerpt from *Testimony* copyright © 2008 by Anita Shreve

All rights reserved. In accordance with the U.S. Copyright Act of 1976, the scanning, uploading, and electronic sharing of any part of this book without the permission of the publisher constitute unlawful piracy and theft of the author's intellectual property. If you would like to use material from the book (other than for review purposes), prior written permission must be obtained by contacting the publisher at permissions@hbgusa.com. Thank you for your support of the author's rights.

Back Bay Books / Little, Brown and Company
Hachette Book Group
1290 Avenue of the Americas, New York, NY 10104
littlebrown.com

Originally published in hardcover by Little, Brown and Company, May 1998
First Back Bay paperback edition, March 1999

Back Bay Books is an imprint of Little, Brown and Company. The Back Bay Books name and logo are trademarks of Hachette Book Group, Inc.

The publisher is not responsible for websites (or their content) that are not owned by the publisher.

Excerpt from "Antrim" by Robinson Jeffers from *The Collected Poetry of Robinson Jeffers,* Three Volumes, edited by Tim Hunt. Reprinted with the permission of the publishers, Stanford University Press. Copyright © 1995 by the Board of Trustees of the Leland Stanford Junior University.

Library of Congress Cataloging-in-Publication Data
Shreve, Anita.
    The pilot's wife : a novel / Anita Shreve. — 1st ed.
        p. cm.
    ISBN 978-0-316-78908-0 (hc) / 978-0-316-60195-5 (trade pb) /
978-0-316-78822-9 (mass market pb) / 978-0-316-30305-7 (special edition)   I. Title.
    PS3569.H7385 55   1998
    813'.54 — dc21   97-51647

10 9 8 7 6 5 4 3 2 1

RRD-C

Book design by Julia Sedykh

Printed in the United States of America

one

SHE HEARD A KNOCKING, AND THEN A DOG BARKING. Her dream left her, skittering behind a closing door. It had been a good dream, warm and close, and she minded. She fought the waking. It was dark in the small bedroom, with no light yet behind the shades. She reached for the lamp, fumbled her way up the brass, and she was thinking, *What? What?*

The lit room alarmed her, the wrongness of it, like an emergency room at midnight. She thought, in quick succession: Mattie. Then, Jack. Then, Neighbor. Then, Car accident. But Mattie was in bed, wasn't she? Kathryn had seen her to bed, had watched her walk down the hall and through a door, the door shutting with a firmness that was just short of a slam, enough to make a statement but not provoke a reprimand. And Jack — where was Jack? She scratched the sides of her head, raking out her sleep-flattened hair. Jack was — where? She tried to remember the schedule: London. Due home around lunchtime. She was certain. Or did she have it wrong and had he forgotten his keys again?

She sat up and put her feet on the freezing floorboards. She had never understood why the wood of an old house lost its warmth so completely in the winter. Her black leggings had ridden up to the middle of her calves, and the cuffs of the shirt she had slept in, a worn white shirt of Jack's, had unrolled and were hanging past the tips of her fingers. She couldn't hear the knocking anymore, and she thought for a few seconds that she had imagined it. Had dreamed it, in the way she sometimes had dreams from which she woke into other dreams. She reached for the small clock on her bedside table and looked at it: 3:24. She peered more closely at the black face with the glow-in-the-dark dial and then set the clock down on the marble top of the table so hard that the case popped open and a battery rolled under the bed.

But Jack was in London, she told herself again. And Mattie was in bed.

There was another knock then, three sharp raps on glass. A small stoppage in her chest traveled down into her stomach and lay there. In the distance, the dog started up again with short, brittle yips.

She took careful steps across the floor, as if moving too fast might set something in motion that hadn't yet begun. She opened the latch of the bedroom door with a soft click and made her way down the back staircase. She was thinking that her daughter was upstairs and that she should be careful.

She walked through the kitchen and tried to see, through the window over the sink, into the driveway that wound around to the back of the house. She could just make out the shape of an ordinary dark car. She turned the corner into the narrow back hallway, where the tiles were worse than the floorboards, ice on the soles of her feet. She flipped on the back-door light and saw, beyond the small panes set into the top of the door, a man.

He tried not to look surprised by the sudden light. He moved his head slowly to the side, not staring into the glass, as if it were not a polite thing to do, as if he had all the time in the world, as if it were not 3:24 in the morning. He looked pale in the glare of the light. He had hooded eyelids and a widow's peak, hair the color of dust that had been cut short and brushed back at the sides. His topcoat collar was turned up, and his shoulders were hunched. He moved once quickly on the doorstep, stamping his feet. She made a judgment then. The long face, slightly sad; decent clothes; an interesting mouth, the bottom lip slightly curved and fuller than the upper lip: not dangerous. As she reached for the knob, she thought, Not a burglar, not a rapist. Definitely not a rapist. She opened the door.

"Mrs. Lyons?" he asked.

And then she knew.

It was in the way he said her name, the fact that he knew her name at all. It was in his eyes, a wary flicker. The quick breath he took.

She snapped away from him and bent over at the waist. She put a hand to her chest.

He reached his hand through the doorway and touched her at the small of her back.

The touch made her flinch. She tried to straighten up but couldn't.

"When?" she asked.

He took a step into her house and closed the door.

"Earlier this morning," he said.

"Where?"

"About ten miles off the coast of Ireland."

"In the water?"

"No. In the air."

"Oh. . . ." She brought a hand to her mouth.

"It almost certainly was an explosion," he said quickly.

"You're sure it was Jack?"

He glanced away and then back again.

"Yes."

He caught her elbows as she went down. She was momentarily embarrassed, but she couldn't help it, her legs were gone. She hadn't known that her body could abandon her so, could just give out like that. He held her elbows, but she wanted her arms back. Gently, he lowered her to the floor.

She bent her face to her knees and wrapped her arms over her head. Inside her there was a white noise, and she couldn't hear what he was saying. Consciously, she tried to breathe, to fill up her lungs. She raised her head up and took in great gulps of air. As if in the distance, she heard an odd choking sound that wasn't exactly crying because her face was dry. From behind her, the man was trying to lift her up.

"Let me get you to a chair," he said.

She swung her head from side to side. She wanted him to let her go. She wanted to sink into the tiles, to ooze onto the floor.

Awkwardly, he placed his arms under hers. She let him help her up.

"I'm going to be —," she said.

Quickly, she pushed him away with the palms of her hands and leaned against the wall for support. She coughed and gagged, but there was nothing in her stomach.

When she looked up, she could see that he was apprehensive. He took her by the arm and made her round the corner into the kitchen.

"Sit here in this chair," he said. "Where's the light?"

"On the wall."

Her voice was raspy and faint. She realized she was shivering.

He swiped for the switch and found it. She put a hand up in front of her face to ward off the light. Instinctively, she did not want to be seen.

"Where do you keep the glasses?" he asked.

She pointed to a cabinet. He poured her a glass of water and handed it to her, but she couldn't hold it steady. He braced her fingers while she took a sip.

"You're in shock," he said. "Where can I get you a blanket?"

"You're with the airline," she said.

He took off his topcoat and his jacket and put the jacket around her shoulders. He made her slide her arms into the sleeves, which were surprisingly silky and warm.

"No," he said. "The union."

She nodded slowly, trying to make sense of this.

"Robert Hart," he said, introducing himself.

She nodded again, took another sip of water. Her throat felt dry and sore.

"I'm here to help," he said. "This is going to be difficult to get through. Is your daughter here?"

"You know I have a daughter?" she asked quickly.

And then she thought, Of course you do.

"Would you like me to tell her?" he asked.

Kathryn shook her head.

"They always said the union would get here first," she said. "The wives, I mean. Do I have to wake her now?"

He glanced quickly at his watch, then at Kathryn, as if considering how much time was left to them.

"In a few minutes," he said. "When you're ready. Take your time."

The telephone rang, a serrated edge in the silence of the kitchen. Robert Hart answered it immediately.

"No comment," he said.

"No comment.

"No comment.

"No comment."

She watched him lay the receiver back on its cradle and massage his forehead with his fingers. He had thick fingers and large hands, hands that seemed too big for his body.

She looked at the man's shirt, a white oxford with a gray stripe, but all she could see was a fake plane in a fake sky blowing itself to bits in the distance.

She wanted the man from the union to turn around and tell her that he had made a mistake: He'd gotten the plane wrong; she was the wrong wife; it hadn't happened the way he said it had. She could almost feel the joy of that.

"Is there someone you want me to call?" he asked. "To be with you."

"No," she said. "Yes." She paused. "No."

She shook her head. She wasn't ready yet. She lowered her eyes and fixed them on the cabinet under the sink. What was in it? Cascade. Drano. Pine Sol. Jack's black shoe polish. She bit the inside of her cheek and looked around at the kitchen, at the cracked pine table, the stained hearth behind it, the milk-green Hoosier cabinet. Her husband had shined his shoes in this room not two days ago, his foot braced on a bread drawer he had pulled out for the task. It was often the last thing he did before he left for work. She would sit and watch him from the chair, and lately it had become a kind of ritual, a part of his leaving her.

It had always been hard for her, his leaving the house — no matter how much work she had to do, no matter how much she looked forward to having time to herself. And it wasn't that she had been afraid. She hadn't been in the habit of being fearful. Safer than driving a car, he'd always said, and he'd had an offhand confidence, as though his safety were not even worthy of a conversation. No, it wasn't exactly safety. It was the act of leaving itself, of Jack's removing himself from the house, that had always been difficult. She often felt, watching him walk out of the door with his thick, boxy flight bag in one hand and his overnight bag in the other, his uniform cap tucked under his arm, that he was, in some profound way, separating from her. And, of course, he was. He was leaving her in order to take a 170-ton airplane into the air and across the ocean to London or to Amsterdam or to Nairobi. It wasn't a particularly hard feeling to sort out, and within moments it would pass. Sometimes Kathryn would become so accustomed to his absence that she bristled at the change in her routines when he returned. And then, three or four days later, the cycle would begin again.

She didn't think Jack had ever felt the coming and going in quite the same way she had. To leave, after all, was not the same as being left.

I'm just a glorified bus driver, he used to say.

And not all that glorified, he would add.

Used to say. She tried to take it in. She tried to understand that Jack no longer existed. But all she could see were cartoon puffs of smoke, lines drawn outward in all directions. She let the image go as quickly as it had come.

"Mrs. Lyons? Is there a television in another room that I could keep half an eye on?" Robert Hart asked.

"In the front room," she said, pointing.

"I just need to hear what they're reporting now."

"It's fine," she said. "I'm fine."

He nodded, but he seemed reluctant. She watched him leave the room. She shut her eyes and thought: I absolutely cannot tell Mattie.

Already, she could imagine how it would be. She would open the door to Mattie's room, and on the wall there would be posters of Less Than Jake and extreme skiing in Colorado. On the floor would be two or three days' worth of inside-out clothes. Mattie's sports equipment would be propped up in a corner — her skis and poles, her snowboard, her field hockey and lacrosse sticks. Her bulletin board would be covered with cartoons and pictures of her friends: Taylor, Alyssa, and Kara, fifteen-year-old girls with ponytails and long hair wisps in the front. Mattie would be huddled under her blue-and-white comforter and would pretend not to hear her until Kathryn said her name for the third time. Then Mattie would bolt upright, at first irritated to be woken, thinking it was time for school and wondering why Kathryn had moved into the room. Mattie's hair, a sandy red with metallic threads, would be spread along the shoulders of a purple T-shirt that said "Ely Lacrosse" in white letters across her tiny breasts. She would put her hands behind her on the mattress and hold herself up.

"What is it, Mom?" she would say.

Like that.

"What is it, Mom?"

And then again, her voice instantly more high pitched.

"Mom, what is it?"

And Kathryn would have to kneel beside the bed and would have to tell her daughter what had happened.

"No, Mom!" Mattie would cry.

"No! Mom!"

———

When Kathryn opened her eyes, she could hear the low murmur of the television.

She got up from the kitchen chair and walked into the long front room with its six pairs of floor-to-ceiling windows overlooking the lawn and the water. There was a Christmas tree in the corner that stopped her at the threshold. Robert Hart was hunched forward on the sofa, and an old man was being interviewed on the TV. She had missed the beginning of the report. It was CNN or maybe CBS. Robert looked quickly over at her.

"Are you sure you want to watch this?" he asked.

"Please," she said. "I'd rather see."

She entered the room and moved closer to the television.

It was raining where the old man was, and later they printed the name of the place along the bottom of the screen. Malin Head, Ireland. She couldn't picture where it might be on a map. She didn't even know which Ireland it was in. Rain dripped from the old man's cheeks, and he had long white pouches under his eyes. The camera moved away and showed a village green with pristine white facades of buildings fronting it. In the center of the row of buildings was a sad-looking hotel, and she read the name along a thin marquee: Malin Hotel. There were men standing around its doorway with mugs of tea or coffee in their hands, looking over in a shy way at all the news crews. The camera slid back to the old man and moved in close to his face. He looked shocky around the eyes, and his mouth was hanging open, as though it was hard for him to breathe. Kathryn watched him on the television, and she thought: That is what I look like now. Gray in the face. The eyes staring out at something that isn't even there. The mouth loose like that of a hooked fish.

The interviewer, a dark-haired woman with a black umbrella, asked the old man to describe what he had seen.

It were moonlight with dark water, he said haltingly.

His voice was hoarse, his accent so thick they had to print what he was saying at the bottom of the screen.

There were bits of silver falling from the sky and landing all around the boat, he said.

The bits fluttered like

Birds.

Birds that were wounded.

Falling downward.

Spiraling, like, and spinning.

She walked to the TV and knelt on the carpet so that her face was even with the old man's on the screen. The fisherman was waving his hands around to show what he meant. He made a cone shape and moved his fingers up and down and then drew a ragged edge. He told the interviewer that none of the strange bits had actually landed in his boat and that by the time he had motored to the places where it seemed the things had fallen, they had disappeared or sunk into the sea and he could not get at them, not even with his nets.

Facing the camera, the reporter said that the man's name was Eamon Gilley. He was eighty-three, she said, and he was the first eyewitness to come forward. No one else appeared to have seen what the fisherman had seen, and nothing had been confirmed yet. Kathryn had the feeling that the reporter wanted very much for Gilley's story to be true but felt obliged to say that it might not be.

But Kathryn knew that it was true. She could see the moonlight on the sea, the way it must have twitched and sparkled, the silvery glints falling from the sky, falling, falling, like tiny angels coming down to earth. She could see the small boat in the water and the fisherman standing at its bow — his face turned upward toward the moon, his hands outstretched. She could see him risk his balance to catch the fluttering bits, poking the air like a small child grabbing for fireflies on a summer night. And she thought then how strange it was that disaster — the sort of disaster that drained the blood from your body and took the air out of your lungs and hit you again and again in the face — could be, at times, such a thing of beauty.

Robert reached over and turned off the television.

"Are you all right?" he asked.

"When did you say it happened?"

He rested his elbows on his knees and folded his hands.

"One fifty-seven. Our time. Six fifty-seven theirs."

Above his right eyebrow, there was a scar. He must be in his late thirties, she thought, closer to her age than to Jack's. He had the fair skin of a blond and brown eyes with flecks of rust in the irises. Jack had had blue eyes, two different blues — one a washed-out blue, almost translucent, a watercolor sky; the other brilliant, a sharp royal. The unusual coloring drew others' eyes to his, made people examine his face as though this asymmetrical characteristic suggested imbalance, perhaps something wrong.

She thought: Is this the man's job?

"That was the time of the last transmission," the man from the union said in a voice she could hardly hear.

"What was the last transmission?" she asked.

"It was routine."

She didn't believe him. What was routine about a last transmission?

"Do you know," she asked, "what the most common last

words are from a pilot when he knows he's going down? Well, of course you know."

"Mrs. Lyons," he said, turning to her.

"Kathryn."

"You're still in shock. You should have some sugar. Is there juice?"

"In the fridge. It was a bomb, wasn't it?"

"I wish I had more to tell you."

He stood up and walked into the kitchen. She realized that she didn't want to be left alone in a room just yet, and so she followed him. She looked at the clock over the sink. 3:38. Was it possible that only fourteen minutes had elapsed since she had peered at the clock on the night table upstairs?

"You got here fast," she said, sitting again on the kitchen chair.

He poured orange juice into a glass.

"How did you do it?" she asked.

"We have a plane," he said quietly.

"No. I mean, tell me. How is it done? You have a plane waiting? You sit around waiting for a crash?"

He handed her the glass of juice. He leaned against the sink and ran the middle finger of his right hand vertically along his brow, from the bridge of his nose to his hairline. He seemed to be making decisions then, judgments.

"No, I don't," he said. "I don't sit around waiting for a crash. But if one occurs, we have procedures in place. We have a Lear jet at Washington National. It flies me to the nearest major airport. In this case, Portsmouth."

"And then?"

"And then there's a car waiting."

"And you did it in . . ."

She calculated the time it would take him to travel from Washington, which was where the union headquarters was, to Ely, New Hampshire, just over the Massachusetts border.

"A little over an hour," he said.

"But why?" she asked.

"To get here first," he said. "To inform you. To help you through it."

"That's not why," she said quickly.

He thought a minute.

"It's part of it," he said.

She smoothed her hand over the cracked surface of the pine table. On nights when Jack had been home, Jack and she and Mattie had seemed to live within a ten-foot radius of that table — reading the paper, listening to the news, cooking, eating, cleaning up, doing homework, and then, after Mattie had gone to bed, talking or not talking, and sometimes, if Jack didn't have a trip, sharing a bottle of wine. In the beginning, when Mattie was little and early to bed, they had sometimes had candlelight and made love in the kitchen, one or the other of them seized by a sudden lust or fondness.

She tilted her head back and shut her eyes. The pain seemed to stretch from her abdomen to her throat. She felt panicky, as though she had strayed too close to the edge. She drew in her breath so sharply that Robert looked over at her.

And then she moved from shock to grief the way she might enter another room.

The images assaulted her. The feeling of Jack's breath at the top of her spine, as though he were whispering to her bones. The sliding sensation against her mouth when he gave her a quick kiss as he went off to work. The drape of his arm around Mattie after her last field hockey game, when Mattie was sticky and sweaty and crying because her team had lost eight-zip. The pale skin on the inside of Jack's arms. The slightly pitted skin between his shoulder blades, a legacy of adolescence. The odd tenderness of his feet, the way he couldn't walk along a beach without sneakers. The warmth of him always, even on the coldest of nights, as though his inner furnace burned extravagantly. The images pushed and jostled and competed rudely with each other for space. She tried to stop them, but she couldn't.

The man from the union stood at the sink and watched her. He didn't move.

"I loved him," she said when she could speak.

She got up and ripped a sheet of paper towel from its holder. She blew her nose. She felt a momentary bewilderment of tenses. She wondered if time were opening up an envelope and would swallow her — for a day or a week or a month or possibly forever.

"I know," said Robert.

"Are you married?" she asked, sitting down again.

He put his hands in the pockets of his trousers and jiggled the change there. He had on gray suit trousers. Jack hardly ever wore a suit. Like many men who wore a uniform to work, he had never been a particularly good dresser.

"No," he said. "I'm divorced."

"Do you have children?"

"Two boys. Nine and six."

"Do they live with you?"

"With my wife in Alexandria. Ex-wife."

"Do you see them much?"

"I try."

"Why did you get divorced?"

"I stopped drinking," he said.

He said this matter-of-factly, without explanation. She wasn't sure she understood. She blew her nose again.

"I have to call the school," she said. "I'm a teacher."

"That can wait," he said. "No one will be there anyway. No one is awake yet." He looked at his watch.

"Tell me about your job," she said.

"There isn't a lot to tell. It's mostly public relations."

"How many of these things have you had to do?" she asked.

"Things?"

"Crashes," she said. "Crashes."

He was silent for a minute.

"Five," he said finally. "Five major ones."

"Five?"

"And four smaller ones."

"Tell me about them," she said.

He glanced out the window. Thirty seconds passed. Maybe a minute. Again she sensed that he was making judgments, decisions.

"Once I got to the widow's house," he said, "and I found her in bed with another man."

"Where was this?"

"Westport. Connecticut."

"What happened?"

"The wife came down in a robe, and I told her, and then the man got dressed and came down. He was a neighbor. And then he and I stood in the woman's kitchen and watched her collapse. It was a mess."

"Did you know him?" Kathryn asked. "My husband?"

"No," he said. "I'm sorry."

"He was older than you."

"I know."

"What else did they tell you about him?"

"Eleven years with Vision. Before that, Santa Fe, five years. Before that, Teterboro, two years. Two years Vietnam, DC-3 gunships. Born in Boston. College, Holy Cross. One child, a daughter, fifteen. A wife."

He thought a minute.

"Tall," he said. "Six-four? Fit."

She nodded.

"Good record. Excellent record, actually."

He scratched the back of one hand with the other.

"I'm sorry," he said. "I'm sorry I know these facts about your husband yet didn't know him at all."

"Did they tell you anything about me?"

"Only that you're fifteen years younger than your husband. And that you'd be here with your daughter."

She examined her feet, which were small and white, as if the blood had left them. The soles weren't clean.

"How many were on board?" she asked.

"A hundred and four."

"Not full," she said.

"Not full, no."

"Any survivors?"

"They're searching. . . ."

Other images intruded now. A moment of knowledge — what knowledge? — in the cockpit. Jack's hands at the controls. A body spinning in the air. No. Not even a body. She shook her head roughly.

"I have to tell her alone," she said.

He nodded quickly, as if that were already understood.

"No," she said. "I mean you have to leave the house. I don't want anyone to see this or hear this."

"I'll sit in my car," he said.

She slipped off the jacket he had given her. The telephone rang again, but neither of them moved. In the distance, they could hear the answering machine click on.

She wasn't prepared for Jack's voice, deep and amiable, a hint of Boston in the vowels, with its familiar message. She put her face into her hands and waited for the message to be over.

When she looked up, she saw that Robert had been studying her. He glanced away.

"It's to keep me from talking to the press, isn't it?" she said. "That's why you're here."

A car rolled into the driveway and crunched on the gravel. The man from the union looked out the window, took the jacket from her, and put it on.

"It's so I won't say anything that might make them think pilot error," she said. "You don't want them to think pilot error."

He lifted the telephone receiver off its hook and laid it on the counter.

Lately, Jack and she had hardly ever made love in the kitchen. They had told themselves that Mattie was older now and might come down to the kitchen looking for a snack. Most nights, after Mattie had gone up to her room to listen to her CDs or to talk on the phone, they had just sat at the table reading magazines, too exhausted to put away the dishes or even to talk.

"I'll tell her now," she said.

He hesitated.

"You understand we can't stay out there long," he said.

"They're from the airline, aren't they?" she asked, looking through the kitchen window. In the driveway, she could just make out two shadowy shapes emerging from a car. She walked toward the bottom of the stairs.

She looked up the steep incline. There were five hundred steps, at least five hundred. They stretched on and on. She understood that something had been set in motion and was beginning now. She was not sure she had the stamina to make it to the top.

She looked at the man from the union, who was moving through the kitchen to answer the door.

"*Mom,*" she said, and he turned. "What they usually say is *Mom.*"

THE GLARE OF THE SUN, REFLECTED FROM THE occasional passing car, moves along the back wall of the shop like a slow strobe. The shop seems airless today, suffocating in the heat, the air thick with dust motes floating in the shafts of light. She stands with a rag in her hand inside a maze of mahogany and walnut tables, of lamps and old linens, of books that smell of mildew. She glances up at him as he walks in. She has a brief impression of someone official on an errand, of someone lost and looking for directions. He has on a white shirt with short sleeves that stick out from his shoulders like thin white flags. Heavy navy blue trousers. He wears old man's shoes, black shoes that are weighty and enormous.

— We're closed, she says.

He looks quickly behind him and sees the OPEN sign on the inside of the door. He scratches the back of his neck.

— Sorry, he says, and turns to leave.

She has always marveled at the speed with which the mind makes judgments — a second, two seconds at the most, even before anyone has moved or said a word. Early thirties, she guesses. Not stocky, exactly, but large. He has broad shoulders, and she thinks at once that there is nothing anemic about him. She is struck initially by his jawline, which is rectangular and smooth, and by his somewhat comical ears, which stick out at their tops. She thinks there might be something wrong with his eyes.

— I'm taking inventory, but if there's something that you're looking for, that's fine, she says.

He moves into a tube of sunlight that comes from a round window over the door. She can see his face clearly.

There are tiny wrinkles at the corners of his eyes, and he doesn't have perfect teeth. His hair is cut short, a military cut, dark, almost black, and would be curly if it had any length. There is a dent in his hair, as if he had a cap on earlier.

He puts his hands into his trouser pockets. He asks her if she has any old checkerboards.

— Yes, she says.

She begins to walk through the maze to a far wall, apologizing for the mess as she goes. She is aware of him behind her, aware of her gait and posture, which suddenly seem unnatural, too stiff. She has on jeans, a red tank top, and a pair of old leather sandals. Her hair is loose and sticky on the back of her neck. She feels as though the heat and the humidity, combined with the dust she has been kicking up, have created a kind of dirty film all over her. In the mosaic of her reflection in an antique mirror on the wall, she catches a glimpse of soggy tendrils of hair on either side of her face, which is shiny with perspiration. Her bra strap is showing, a white flash under the red, and there is a blue stain on the tank top from something that bled in the wash.

The board is lying against the wall with several old paintings. The man moves in front of her and crouches to get a better look. She can see the strength of him in his thighs, the length of his back in the crouch, the place where the belt dips in the back with the strain. She notices the white epaulets on his shoulders.

—What's this? he asks, his eye caught by a painting beside the checkerboard. It is a landscape, an impressionistic rendering of a hotel out at the Isles of Shoals. The hotel is old, nineteenth century, with deep porches and a long smooth lawn in the middle of a rocky seascape.

He stands and shows her the painting, which she has never paid much attention to before.

—This is pretty good, he says. —Who's the artist?

She tilts her head and reads from the back of the painting: — Claude Legny, she says. — Eighteen ninety. It says here that it came from an estate sale in Portsmouth.

— It's like a Childe Hassam, he says.

She doesn't respond. She doesn't know who Childe Hassam is.

He traces the wooden frame with his fingers, and it seems to her as though someone were trailing his fingers up and down her spine.

— How much is it? he asks.

— I'll look it up, she says.

They walk together to the register. The price, when she finds it, seems staggeringly high. She feels embarrassed to name such a sum, but it is not her shop, and she should try to make the sale for her grandmother.

When she tells him the price, he doesn't even blink.

— I'll take it, he says.

He gives her cash, and she hands him a receipt, which he sticks absentmindedly in his shirt pocket. She wonders what he does in the military, why he isn't at his base on a Wednesday afternoon.

— What do you do? she asks, looking again at the epaulets on his shoulders.

— Cargo transport, he says. — I have a layover. I borrow a car from a ticket agent at the airport and go for drives.

— You fly, she says, stating the obvious.

— I'm like a truck driver, only it's a plane, he says, looking at her intently.

— What's in the plane? she asks.

— Canceled checks.

— Canceled checks?

She laughs. She tries to imagine an entire plane filled with canceled checks.

— Nice shop, he says, looking around.

— It's my grandmother's.

She crosses her arms over her chest.

— Your eyes are two different colors, she says.

— It's genetic. It's from my father's side of the family.

He pauses.

— The eyes are both real, in case you wanted to know.

— I did, as a matter of fact.

— Your hair is beautiful, he says.

— It's genetic, she says.

He nods his head and smiles, as if to say *touché*.

— It's . . . what color? he asks.

— Red.

— No, I mean . . .

— It depends on the light.

— How old are you?

— Eighteen.

He seems surprised. Taken aback.

— Why? she asks. — How old are you?

— Thirty-three. I thought . . .

— Thought what?

— That you were older, I don't know.

It lies there between them, the age difference, the fifteen years.

— Look, he says.

— Look, she says.

He puts a hand on the register.

— I was born in Boston, he says, — and grew up in Chelsea, which is a part of Boston you don't want to know about. I went to Boston Latin and to Holy Cross. My mother died when I was nine, and my father had a heart attack when I was in college. I had a low lottery number and was drafted and learned to fly in Vietnam. I don't currently have a girlfriend, and I've never been married. I have a one-bedroom condo in Teterboro. It's too small, and I'm hardly ever —

— Stop, she says.

— I want to get this part over with.

She understands then, in a way she has seldom been allowed to know such things in her eighteen years, that she holds it all in her hand at that moment, that she can wrap her fingers around it and grasp it tightly and never let it go, or she can open her hand, lay open her palm and give it away. Just give it away, as simply as that.

— I know where Chelsea is, she says.

Ten seconds pass, maybe twenty. They stand in the hot gloom of the shop, neither of them speaking. She knows he wants to touch her. She can feel the heat from his skin even across the counter. She draws in her breath slowly and evenly, so as not to attract attention to the effort. She has a nearly overwhelming desire to close her eyes.

— It's hot in here, he says.

— It's hot out there, she says.

— Unseasonably hot.

— For so early in June.

— Want to go for a drive? he asks. — Cool off?

— Where? she asks.

— Anywhere. Just a drive.

She allows herself to meet his gaze. He smiles slowly, and the smile takes her by surprise.

They drive to the beach and go swimming in their clothes. The water is frigid, but the air is hot, and that contrast is delicious. Jack ruins his uniform and later has to borrow another. When she comes out of the water, he is standing with his hands in his pockets and a blanket rolled under his arm. His clothes are soaked and hanging off him, and his shirt has gone a translucent flesh color.

They lie on the blanket on the sand. She shivers against his wet shirt. He keeps the fingers of his left hand anchored, knotted in her hair, as he kisses her and moves his right hand under the tank top and along the flat of her stomach. She feels loose, loose limbed and opened up — as though someone had just tugged at a thread and was unraveling her.

She covers his hand with her own. His is oddly warm, and rough and sandy and abrasive. She feels happy. It is a pure and undiluted happiness. It is all beginning, and she knows it.

EVEN BEFORE KATHRYN REACHED THE TOP OF THE stairs, she could hear Mattie walking into the bathroom. Her daughter's hair had a lovely natural curl, but each morning Mattie would get up to wash her hair and painstakingly blow-dry it to straighten it. It always seemed to Kathryn that Mattie was trying to subdue her hair, as though wrestling with a part of herself that had emerged not long ago. Kathryn was waiting for Mattie to outgrow this stage and had been thinking that any day now her daughter would wake up and let her hair go natural. Then Kathryn would know that Mattie was all right.

Mattie had probably heard the cars in the driveway, Kathryn thought. Perhaps she had heard the voices in the kitchen, too. Mattie was used to waking up in the dark, particularly in the winter.

She knew she had to get Mattie out of the bathroom. Already she was thinking that it was not a safe place to tell her daughter.

She stood outside the door. Mattie had turned on the shower. Kathryn could hear her undressing.

Kathryn knocked.

"Mattie," she said.

"What?"

"I need to talk to you."

"Mom. . . ."

The way Mattie said it, in that familiar singsong tone, as if annoyed already.

"I can't," she said. "I'm having a shower."

"Mattie, it's important."

"*What?*"

The bathroom door opened abruptly. Mattie had a green towel wrapped around her.

My lovely, beautiful daughter, Kathryn thought. How can I possibly do this to her?

Kathryn's hands began to shake. She crossed her arms over her chest and tucked her hands under her armpits.

"Put on a robe, Mattie," Kathryn said, feeling herself beginning to cry. She never cried in front of Mattie. "I need to talk to you. It's important."

Mattie slipped her robe off the hook and put it on, stunned into obedience.

"What is it, Mom?"

A child's mind couldn't take it in, Kathryn decided later. A child's body couldn't absorb such grotesque facts.

Mattie flung herself down onto the floor as if she had been shot. She flailed her arms furiously all around her head, and Kathryn thought of bees. She tried to seize Mattie's arms and hold tightly onto her, but Mattie threw her off and ran. She was out of the house and halfway down the lawn before Kathryn caught her.

"Mattie, Mattie, Mattie," Kathryn said when she had reached her.

Over and over and over.

"Mattie, Mattie, Mattie."

Kathryn put her hands behind Mattie's head and pressed her face close to her own, pressed it in hard, as though to tell her she must listen, she had no choice.

"I will take care of you," Kathryn said.

And then again.

"Listen to me, Mattie. I will take care of you."

Kathryn folded her daughter into her arms. There was frost at their feet. Mattie was crying now, and Kathryn thought her own heart would break. But this was better, she knew. This was better.

Kathryn helped Mattie into the house and made her lie down on the couch. She wrapped her daughter in blankets and held onto her and rubbed her arms and legs to stop the shivering. Robert tried to give Mattie some water, which made her gag. Julia, Kathryn's grandmother, the woman who had raised her, was called. Kathryn was vaguely aware of other people in the house then, a man and a woman with suits on, standing at the kitchen counter, waiting.

She could hear Robert talking on the telephone and then murmuring with the people from the airline. She hadn't realized that a television was on, but Mattie suddenly sat up and looked at her.

"Did they say a bomb?" Mattie asked.

And then Kathryn heard the bulletin, in retrospect, the way one realizes that subliminally all the words have been heard and are there in the mind just waiting to be called forth.

Later Kathryn would come to think of the bulletins as bullets. Word bullets that tore into the brain and exploded, obliterating memories.

"Robert," she called.

He came into the living room and stood next to her.

"It's not confirmed," he said.

"They think a bomb?"

"It's just a theory. Give her one of these."

"What is it?"

"It's a Valium."

"You carry these?" she asked. "With you?"

Julia moved through the house with the stolid presence of a relief worker in an emergency zone: disrespectful toward death and seemingly unwilling to be cowed. With her matronly bulk and poodle perm — her only concession to age — she had Mattie off the couch and upstairs within minutes. When Julia was certain that Mattie could stand up by herself in a room alone and pull on a pair of jeans, she came back downstairs to attend to her granddaughter. She stood in the kitchen and made a pot of strong tea. She laced it generously with brandy from a bottle she had brought with her. She told the woman from the airline to be sure that Kathryn drank it down, at least one mug. Then Julia went back up to Mattie and made the girl wash her face. By then the Valium was kicking in, and except for small sudden bursts of surprise and grief, Mattie was winding down. Among other things, Kathryn knew, grief was physically exhausting.

Julia made Mattie lie down on her bed and then returned to the front room. Sitting beside Kathryn on the couch, she peered into Kathryn's cup to see how much tea she had swallowed, then told her to drink some more. She asked straight out if Kathryn had any tranquilizers. Robert volunteered the Valium.

Julia said, "Who are you?" and Robert told her, and then she asked him for a pill.

"Take this," Julia said to Kathryn.

"I can't," Kathryn said. "I've had the brandy."

"So what. Take it."

Julia didn't ask Kathryn how she felt or if she was all right. In Julia's way of thinking, Kathryn knew, there wasn't an alternative to being a certain level of all right. Nothing else would work now. The tears, the shock, the sympathy — all of that could come later.

"It's awful," Julia said. "Kathryn, I know it's awful. Look at me. But the only way to the other side is through it. You know that, don't you? Nod your head."

"Mrs. Lyons?"

Kathryn turned from the window. Rita, a small blond woman from the chief pilot's office, was sliding her arms into her coat.

"I'm going to go now, to the inn."

Rita, who wore oak-colored lipstick, had been in the house all day, since four in the morning, yet her face was oddly dewy, her navy blue suit barely wrinkled. The woman's partner, Jim something, also from the airline, had left the house hours ago; Kathryn couldn't remember exactly when.

"Robert Hart is still here," Rita said. "In the office."

Kathryn was studying the perfect part in Rita's straight hair with a kind of fascination. Rita, she was thinking, bore a striking resemblance to a certain newscaster on a station out of Portland. Earlier in the day, Kathryn had minded the strangers in her house, but she'd quickly seen she couldn't cope alone.

"You have rooms at the Tides?" Kathryn asked.

"Yes. We've taken several."

Kathryn nodded. She understood that the Tides Inn, which in the off-season was lucky to have two couples for a weekend stay, would be full now, full of the press and people from the airline.

"You're all right?" Rita asked.

"Yes."

"Can I get you anything before I go?"

"No," Kathryn said. "I'm fine."

It was an absurd statement, Kathryn was thinking, watching Rita leave the kitchen. Laughably meaningless. She would probably never be fine again.

It was not yet four-fifteen, but it was nearly dark already. In late December, the shadows started as soon as lunch was over, and all afternoon the light was long and stretched thin. It made soft, feathery colors she hadn't seen in months, so that nothing seemed exactly familiar anymore. Night would settle in like slow blindness, sucking the color from the trees and the low sky and the rocks and the frozen grass and the frost white hydrangeas until there was nothing left in the window but her own reflection.

She crossed her arms and leaned forward against the lip of the sink, looking out through the kitchen window. It had been a long day, a long, terrible day — a day so long and so terrible it had hours ago passed out of any reality Kathryn had ever known. She had the distinct feeling she would never sleep again, that when she'd woken early that morning she had emerged from a state of being that could never be reentered. She watched Rita walk to her car, start it up, and head out the driveway. There were four of them in the house now — Mattie asleep in her room, with Julia and Kathryn taking turns watching over her, and Robert, Rita had said, was in Jack's office. Doing what? Kathryn wondered.

All day, down the long gravel drive and behind the wooden gate, there had been people looking in and other people keeping them away. But now, Kathryn imagined, the reporters and cameramen and producers and makeup artists were probably all headed over to the Tides Inn to have a drink, tell stories, discuss the rumors, have dinner, and sleep. Wasn't this just the end of a normal workday for them?

Kathryn heard on the stairs a heavy tread, a man's tread, and for a moment she thought it was Jack coming down to the kitchen. But then she remembered almost immediately that it couldn't be Jack, it wasn't Jack at all.

"Kathryn."

The tie was gone, the cuffs of his shirt rolled, the top button of his shirt open. Already she had noticed that Robert Hart had a nervous habit of holding his pen between the knuckles of his fingers and flipping it back and forth like a baton.

"I thought you should know," Robert said. "They're saying mechanical failure."

"Who's saying mechanical failure?"

"London."

"They know?"

"No. It's just bullshit at this point. They're guessing. They've found a piece of the fuselage and an engine."

"Oh," she said. She combed her hair with her fingers. It was her own nervous habit. A piece of the fuselage, she thought. She repeated the phrase in her mind. She tried to see the piece of the fuselage, to imagine what it might be.

"What piece of the fuselage?" she asked.

"The cabin. About twenty feet."

"Any . . . ?"

"No. You haven't eaten all day, have you?" he asked.

"It's all right."

"No, it's not all right."

She looked over at the table, which was covered with dishes of food — casseroles, pies, entire dinners in separately marked plastic containers, brownies, cakes, cookies, salads. It would take a large family days to eat all of that.

"It's what people do," she said. "They don't know what else to do, so they bring food."

Throughout the day, individual policemen had periodically walked the length of the driveway carrying yet another offering. Kathryn understood this custom, had seen it happen over and over again when there was a death in a family. But it amazed her the way the body kept moving forward, past the shock and the grief, past the retching and the hollowness inside, and kept wanting sustenance, kept wanting to be fed. It seemed unsuitable, like wanting sex.

"We should have sent it back out to the end of the drive," Kathryn said. "To the police and the press. It'll just go to waste in here."

"Never feed the press," Robert said quickly. "They're like dogs looking for affection. They're hungry to be let inside the house."

Kathryn smiled, and it shocked her, that she could smile. Her face hurt, the dryness and the salt of the crying.

"Well, I'll be heading out now," he said, unrolling his shirt-sleeves and buttoning his cuffs. "You probably want to be alone with your family."

Kathryn wasn't at all sure she wanted to be alone.

"You're going back to Washington?"

"No, I'm staying at the inn. I'll stop by tomorrow before I go." He reached for his jacket on the back of a chair and put it on. He took his tie out of the pocket.

"Oh," she said vaguely. "Good."

He slid his tie through his collar. "So," he said, when he had knotted the tie. He gave it a small tug.

The phone rang. It seemed too loud in the kitchen, too abrasive, too intrusive. She looked at it helplessly.

"Robert, I can't," she said.

He walked over to the telephone and answered it. "Robert Hart," he said.

"No comment," he said.

"Not as yet," he said.

"No comment."

When he hung up, Kathryn started to speak.

"You go up and take a shower," he said, cutting her off. He began to remove his jacket. "I'll heat something up."

"Fine," she said. And felt relieved.

Upstairs in the hallway, she was momentarily confused. It was too long a hallway, with too many doors and too many rooms. Already the memories of the day had begun to taint the rooms, to overlay previous memories. She walked the length of the hallway and entered Mattie's bedroom. Both Mattie and Julia were in Mattie's bed, sound asleep. Julia was snoring lightly. Each had her back to the other, sharing the double bed's sheets and comforter. Kathryn watched the covers rise and fall over the humpy mound, caught the sparkle of Mattie's newest earring in the cartilage of her left ear.

Julia stirred.

"Hi," Kathryn whispered, so as not to wake Mattie. "How is she?"

"I hope she sleeps all night," Julia said, rubbing an eye. "Robert's still here?"

"Yes."

"He's going to stay?"

"I don't know. No. I imagine he'll go to the inn with the others."

Kathryn wanted to lie down with her grandmother and her daughter. Periodically throughout the day, she'd felt the strength in her thighs giving out and had been overwhelmed with the need to sit down. There was a hierarchy at work here, she thought. In Kathryn's presence, Mattie could be a child. In Julia's presence, Kathryn found herself wanting Julia's solace and embrace.

Downstairs, on a table in the hallway, there was a photograph of Julia, an evocative photograph from another era. In the picture, Julia had on a narrow, dark skirt that fell just below the knees, a white blouse, and a short cardigan sweater. There were pearls at her throat. She was long waisted and thin, and her glossy black hair was parted to one side. Her features were strong, what people meant when they said a handsome woman. In the photograph, Julia was sitting on a sofa, leaning forward to reach for something out of the frame. In her other hand she was holding a cigarette in the sort of pose that had once made cigarette smoking seductive: the cigarette held casually in slender fingers, the smoke curling around the throat and chin. The woman in the photograph was perhaps twenty years old.

Now Julia was seventy-eight and wore baggy jeans that were always slightly too short, loose sweaters that attempted to camouflage a prominent stomach. There was no longer any trace of the young woman with the glossy hair and slender waist in the woman with the thinning silver hair who was now with Mattie. Perhaps in the eyes there was a resemblance, but even there time had destroyed beauty. Julia's eyes were sometimes watery now and had lost nearly all their lashes. No matter how often Kathryn observed the phenomenon, she found it hard to comprehend: the way nothing could remain as it had been, not a house that was falling down, not a woman's face that had once been beautiful, not childhood, not a marriage, not love.

"I can't explain it," Kathryn said. "I feel as though I've temporarily lost Jack and I need to find him."

"You're not going to find him," Julia said. "He's gone."

"I know, I know."

"He didn't suffer."

"We don't know that."

"Mr. Hart was pretty sure."

"No one knows anything yet. It's all rumor and speculation."

"You should get out of here, Kathryn," Julia said. "It's a madhouse at the end of your driveway. I don't want to frighten you, but they've had to bring back Charlie and Burt to help keep everyone away from the gate."

Behind Kathryn, a cold slice of air slid through the crack of the opened window, and she breathed it in deeply, smelling the salt. She hadn't been outside all day except to bring Mattie back inside.

"I don't know how long this will take to die down," Julia said.

"Robert says it may take a while."

Kathryn inhaled deeply. It was like breathing in ammonia the way the air cleared the head, sharpened the senses.

"No one can help you with this, Kathryn. It's something you have to do by yourself. You know that, don't you?"

Kathryn briefly closed her eyes.

"Kathryn?"

"I loved him," Kathryn said.

"I know you did. I know you did. I loved him, too. We all loved him."

"Why did this happen?"

"Forget the why," Julia said. "There is no why. It doesn't matter. It doesn't help. It's done, and it can't be undone."

"I'm . . ."

"You're exhausted. Go to bed."

"I'm all right."

"You know," Julia said. "When your mother and father drowned, I literally thought I couldn't stand it. I literally thought I'd one day just burst apart. The pain was terrible. Terrible. Losing a son is — it's unimaginable until it happens. And I blamed your mother, Kathryn. I won't pretend I didn't. She and your father were lethal together when they were drinking, horribly careless and dangerous. But there you were, bewildered by the loss of these parents you hadn't even properly had. That's what saved me, Kathryn. Saving you saved me. Having to take care of you. I had to stop asking why Bobby had died. I just had to stop asking. There was no why. And there isn't now."

Kathryn laid her head on the mattress. Julia began to stroke her hair.

"You loved him. I know you did," Julia said.

Kathryn left Mattie's room and walked into the bathroom. In the shower, she turned on the water as hot as she could stand it and let it run over her body without moving. Her eyes were swollen and ached from crying. Her head felt heavy. She'd had to blow her nose so many times the skin between her nose and upper lip stung. She'd had a headache since early morning and had been swallowing Advil tablets without counting. She imagined her blood thinning out and draining away with the water from the shower.

There will be many days like this, Robert had said earlier. Not quite as bad, but bad.

She could not imagine surviving another day like the one she had just been through.

She could not remember the sequence of things. What had happened first or second or third. What had happened in the morning or in the afternoon, or later in the morning or earlier in the afternoon. There were bulletins on the TV, news-casters who spoke words that made her stomach kick and con-tract when she heard them: *Downed after taking off . . . Baby clothes and a floating seat . . . Tragedy in the . . . Ninety seconds for the wreckage . . . Shock and grief on both sides of the . . . The fifteen-year-old T-900 . . . Debris spread over . . . The continuing story of Vision Flight 384 . . . Reports indicate that . . . Early morning busi-nessman's . . . The jointly-owned British and American airline . . . Gathering at the airport . . . FAA maintenance inspection . . . Specu-lation that a massive . . .*

And then there were the images Kathryn doubted would ever leave her. A girl's high school yearbook photo that filled the screen; a vast plain of ocean with a helicopter hovering and flipping white slivers from the tops of the waves; a mother who held her arms out, palms pushing the air, as though she could ward off an unwanted flow of words. Men in complex diving gear, anxiously peering over the edge of a boat; relatives at the airport, scanning a manifest. And then, immediately after the footage of the relatives, three still photographs appeared, one above another, three men in uniform and in formal poses, with their names written underneath. Kathryn hadn't ever seen that particular picture of Jack, could not imagine for what purpose it had been taken. Not for this eventuality, surely. Not just in case. But whenever else did a pilot's face appear on the news? she wondered.

All day, Robert had told her not to watch. The pictures would stay with her, he had warned, the images would not leave. It was better not to see, not to have them, for they would come back, in the daytime and in her dreams.

It was unimaginable, he said to her.

Meaning, Don't imagine it.

But how could she not? How could she stop the flow of detail, the flow of words and photographs in her mind?

Throughout the day, the phone had rung continuously. Most often Robert had answered it or given it to one of the people from the airline, but sometimes, when they were watching the bulletins, he let it ring, and she heard the voices on the answering machine. Tentative, inquiring voices from news organizations. The voices of friends and neighbors in town, calling to say how terrible it was (*I can't believe it was Jack. . . .*), (*If there is anything we can do . . .*). The voice of an older woman from the union — businesslike, hard edged, demanding that Robert return her call. The union, Kathryn knew, didn't want it to be pilot error, and the airline didn't want it to be pilot error or mechanical failure. Already she had heard that there were lawyers scavenging. She wondered if a lawyer had tried to contact her, if Robert Hart had cut him off.

The divers, she knew, were searching for the flight data

recorder and the CVR, the box with the last words. She was afraid of the divers' finding the latter. It was the one news bulletin she knew she would not be able to bear — hearing Jack's voice, the authority in it, the control, and then what? It seemed ghoulishly intrusive to record the last seconds of a man. Where else but on death row did they do that?

She stepped out of the shower, toweled herself off, and then realized, in the way a woman might absentmindedly get into a car and remember that she had forgotten her keys, that she had not used any soap or shampoo. She turned the water on again and stepped back in. There were spaces between her thoughts now — dead air, cotton fluff.

She stepped out of the shower for a second time, dried herself off, and looked quickly around her for her robe. The shirt and socks and leggings she had had on all day were strewn over the tile floor, but she had forgotten her robe. She looked at the back of the door.

Jack's jeans were on a hook. Old jeans, faded in the knees. He would have worn these his last day home, she was thinking.

She pressed the jeans to her face. She breathed through the denim.

She took the jeans off the hook and laid them on the bathroom counter. She heard change in the pockets, the crinkle of papers. She reached into a back pocket and found a wad of papers, slightly curved, compacted from having been sat on. She extracted a fold of money from the papers, several ones and a twenty. There was a receipt from Ames, for an extension cord, a package of lightbulbs, a can of Right Guard. There was a pink dry-cleaning slip: six shirts, light starch, hangers. A receipt from Staples: printer cable and twelve pens. A receipt from the post office for a twenty-two-dollar purchase; stamps, she guessed, looking at it quickly. There was a business card: Barron Todd, Investments. Two lottery tickets. Lottery tickets? She hadn't known that Jack had played the lottery. She looked at one of the tickets more closely. There was a faint note scribbled in pencil. *M at A's,* it read. Followed by a series of numbers. Mattie at someone's? But what did the numbers mean? There were a lot of them. Another lottery pick? And then, unfolding the dense wad more thoroughly, she saw that there were two pieces of white lined paper. On the first was written several lines from what looked like a poem, written in ink, real fountain-pen ink. It was Jack's handwriting.

Here in the narrow passage and the pitiless north, perpetual
Betrayals, relentless resultless fighting.
A random fury of dirks in the dark: a struggle for survival
Of hungry blind cells of life in the womb.

Puzzled, she leaned against the wall. What poem was this, and what did it mean? she wondered. Why had Jack written it down?

She unfolded the second piece of lined paper. It was a remember list. Jack had made one every morning he'd been home. She read the items on the list: *Extension cord, Call gutter, Mattie HP color printer, Bergdorf FedEx robe to arrive 20th.*

Bergdorf. FedEx robe. To arrive 20th.

Bergdorf Goodman? The New York department store?

She tried to think, to remember the December calendar on the fridge. Today, despite its agonizing length, was still December 17. On the 20th, she was to have been in school, the last day before vacation. And Jack would have been home that day. Between trips.

Was this a reference to her Christmas present?

She gathered the papers in her hand, clutched them tightly. She leaned her back against the door and slid down its length.

Her exhaustion was bone deep. She could barely hold up her head.

THE CAR FILLS WITH OVERLY WARM AIR. HER stomach is so full from Julia's Christmas dinner that she has to flip the seat back to make herself more comfortable. Jack has on the cream-colored sweater that she knit for him their first winter together, the one with the mistakes in the back only she can see. He wears the sweater loyally each Thanksgiving and Christmas when they make the trip from Santa Fe. He has let his hair grow out some, and it curls slightly just behind his ears. He has on sunglasses, which he almost always wears, except on the grayest of days.

— You're good at this, she says.

— Good at what?

— Surprises.

Once there was a sudden trip to Mexico. Another time, during a Christmas visit, he took her to the Ritz for the weekend when she thought they were driving into Boston to see an orthopedist for his back. Today, after the meal at Julia's, he said only that he wanted to take a drive to pick up her Christmas present. Just the two of them. Julia would stay with Mattie, who, at four, would not be separated from her new toys.

They leave the town of Ely and drive toward Fortune's Rocks, where the summer houses are. As a girl, on her walks from the village to the beach, she used to imagine that these houses, which sit empty ten months of the year, had character and personality. This one proud and a little showy, and then, after a particularly brutal storm, a bit chastened. This one tall and elegant, an aging beauty. This one challenging the elements, pushing its face forward, foolhardy. Another too quiet, sullen, unadorned, as if unloved. Yet another separated from the others, self-contained, unruffled by the crush of summer people or the long, lonely nights of winter.

— I can't imagine what this present is, Kathryn says.

— You'll see.

In the car, she allows herself to close her eyes. It seems she dozes only a minute, but when she wakes, it is with a start. The car is in a driveway. A familiar driveway.

— You're feeling nostalgic? she asks.

— Something like that, he says.

She peers through the windshield at the house. It is, she thinks, as she has so often thought before, the most beautiful house she has ever seen. Sided with white clapboards, the house is two stories high, with a generous wraparound porch. The shutters are a dusty blue, the muted opaque of the ocean on a hazy day. The upper story is cedar shingled and long weathered, and it curves shallowly, as though someone had shaved a slice out. Perhaps it is a mansard roof — she has never been exactly sure. There are dormers in that upper story, evenly spaced, that seem to suggest comfortably sleeping bodies behind them. She thinks of old hotels, old oceanfront hotels.

Wordlessly, Jack gets out of the car and climbs the steps to the porch, and she follows him. The woven rockers and the wide floorboards have weathered to an ageless gray patina. She stands at the railing, looking across the lawn and down to the shore-line, where the water ebbs and flows over the rocks so that it seems it is the light itself that gathers and spills, gathers and spills, and then falls back into the sea.

In the distance, there is a haze on the ocean, a fresh, clean haze that comes only on fine days. She cannot precisely see the islands; they are there, then not, and then they seem to hover above the water. To one side of the lawn lies a meadow; to the other, orchards of dwarf pear and peach. By the porch is an overgrown flower garden oddly planted in the shape of an arched window, an oblong with a fan attached. In the arch is a white marble bench, now covered with vines.

A sudden east wind rises and blows across the porch, bring-ing with it a faintly damp chill, as it almost always does. In a minute, she knows, there will be whitecaps on the water. She hunches her shoulders inside her coat.

Behind her, Jack unlocks the kitchen door and enters the house.

— Jack, what are you doing? she asks.

Bewildered, she follows him through the kitchen and into the front room, a long space that runs the width of the ocean side of the house, a lovely room with six pairs of tall floor-to-ceiling windows. On the walls is a faded yellow paper, peeling at the seams. There are shades at the windows, rolled a quarter of the way down, that remind her of shades in old schoolrooms.

It has been four and a half years since the first time they tres-passed in this house, since they first made love in an upstairs bedroom. It was after they'd gone swimming in their clothes. She told him she knew about a house that was abandoned. She remembers the way he unbuttoned his shirt and let it drop to the floor. How different he looked without his shirt — years younger, looser, like someone from the mills she might once have gone out with. He crouched over her and began to lick the salt from her skin. She felt dizzy with the heat. Beneath her own lips, the skin of his chest was tangy, silky with fine hairs.

Jack passes through the front room and waits for her at the bottom of the stairs. The house is still unoccupied, has been for decades. It was once a convent, and then it belonged to a family from Boston who used it as a summer house. It has been for sale for years, and she wonders why the house never sells. Perhaps it is the dormitory effect of the many bedrooms, the single bathroom at the end of the hall.

He holds out his hand. She decides, as she climbs the steps with him, that he means to give her the present in the room where they once made love. So she is not surprised when they enter a room with walls of bright lime green. In the corner, a daybed is covered with a flower-print spread. But the most striking item in the room is a red chair, a simple kitchen chair that has been painted with a fire-engine red lacquer. The chair shines in the sunlight — the red chair against the lime green against the blue of the ocean through the window — and she wonders, as she has wondered before, in what flight of whimsy the painter chose such startling colors.

— I got a call from Vision, he says at once.

— Vision?

— A start-up airline, British and American, jointly owned. Fast growing, out of Logan. In a few years, I could get an international route.

He smiles, the triumphant and complex smile of a man who has planned a surprise and pulled it off.

She puts a foot forward, about to go to him.

— And if you like this house, we're going to buy it.

The sentence stops her. She puts her hand to her chest.

— You've been here? she asks.

He nods. — With Julia.

— Julia knows about this? Kathryn asks incredulously.

— We wanted to surprise you. The house is a wreck. It needs work. Well, obviously.

— When did you come here with her?

— Two weeks ago. I had a layover in Portsmouth.

Kathryn tries to remember. She sees the days of December as blocks on the pages of a calendar. Each trip seems to blend into the next. She cannot precisely remember any of them.

— Julia knew about this? she asks again.

— They've accepted our offer, Jack says.

— Our offer?

She feels slow and doltish. The surprises are piling up before she can sort them out.

— Wait here, he says.

Shaken, she crosses the room and sits on the red chair. The sun from a side window makes an oblong of bright hot light on the bedspread. She wants to crawl into the light to warm her hands and feet.

How could he? she wonders. About such an important matter? This isn't simply hiding a box in a bureau. There were other people involved. Real estate agents. And Julia. Is Julia capable of keeping such a secret? Perhaps for a surprise, Kathryn answers herself. And Jack is good at secrets.

She shakes her head. She cannot conceive of making an offer on a house without Jack.

When he returns, he has a bottle of champagne and two glasses in his hands. She recognizes the glasses from Julia's cupboard.

— I love it that you're here, he says. — I love seeing you here.

She watches as he pops the cork. She thinks: But this is what Jack does best, isn't it? He makes things happen.

She wants to feel happy. In a minute, when she has digested the news, she thinks she will feel happy.

— You'll commute to Boston? she asks.

— I've timed it. Fifty minutes.

My God, she thinks, he's been here and he's timed it already.

He pours the champagne into the two glasses and hands her one of them. Together, they drink. Her hand is trembling, which she knows he sees. He puts his glass down then and comes toward her. He makes her stand up and turns her so that they are both looking out the window. He speaks quietly into her ear.

— We'll have our own home now, he says. — You'll be on the water. You've always wanted to be. Mattie will go to school here. You'll get a teaching job when you finish your degree. Julia is excited that you — we — will be near her.

Kathryn nods slowly.

He lifts the hair off her neck and runs his tongue along the top of her spine and into her hairline. She shivers with the sensation, as she is meant to do, and sets her champagne upon the windowsill. She leans forward and braces herself against the frame of the window. In the glass, she can see a faint reflection of the two of them.

"I WISH YOU'D EAT SOMETHING."

Across the table, Robert Hart was finishing the last of a bowl of chili.

"I can't," she said. She studied his empty bowl. "But you were hungry."

He nudged the bowl to one side.

It was late, and Kathryn had no clear idea what time it was. Upstairs, Mattie and Julia were still asleep. In front of Kathryn, in addition to the chili, there was a loaf of garlic bread and a salad and a cup of lukewarm tea. Earlier, she had made an effort to dip the bread into the chili and taste it, but her throat had refused to swallow. She had on clean clothes — jeans and a navy sweater, ragg socks, a pair of leather boots. Her hair was still wet. She knew her eyes and nose and mouth were swollen. She thought she had probably cried more on the floor of the bathroom than at any other time during the day. Possibly her life. She felt drained, emptied, simply from the crying.

"I'm sorry," he said.

"For what?" she asked. "For eating?"

He shrugged. "For all of it."

"Your job is unimaginable," she said suddenly. "Why do you do it?"

He seemed startled by the question.

"Do you mind if I smoke?" he asked. "I could go outside, if you'd rather."

Jack had hated smokers, couldn't tolerate being in a room with them.

"It's fifteen degrees out there," she said. "Of course you can smoke in here."

She watched as he turned and reached into his jacket on the back of the chair for a pack of cigarettes.

He sat with his elbows on the table, his hands folded under his chin. The smoke curled in front of his face.

He gestured with his cigarette.

"AA," he said.

She nodded.

"Why do I do it?" he asked, clearing his throat nervously. "For the money, I suppose."

"I don't believe you," she said.

"Truthfully?"

"Truthfully."

"I suppose I'm drawn to moments of intensity," he said. "In the range of human experience."

She was silent. Aware for the first time that there was music in the background. Art Tatum. While she had been in the shower, Robert must have put on a CD.

"That's fair," she said.

"I like watching people mend," he added.

"Do they? Mend?" she asked.

"Given enough time, the women usually do. Unfortunately . . ." He stopped. "I'm sorry," he said.

"I'm sick of people saying they're sorry. Really, I am."

"Children don't heal as well," he said slowly. "They say that children are resilient, but they're not. They change . . . they mutate with disaster and make accommodations. I hardly ever see grief-stricken men because not too many women are pilots. And when I do see men, they're fathers, and they're angry, which is another story."

"I'll bet they're angry," Kathryn said.

She thought of Jack as a father and how insane with rage and grief he'd have been if it had been Mattie on the plane. Jack and Mattie had been close. With Jack, there had seldom been any of the whining or bristling that had sometimes characterized Mattie's exchanges with Kathryn. For Jack, the givens, the parameters, had been different right from the beginning: They weren't as fraught.

Soon after the three of them had moved to Ely, when Mattie was in kindergarten, Jack had "hired" her as his assistant while he worked on the house — painting, scraping, fixing broken windows. He talked to her continuously. He taught her to ski and then took her on father-daughter skiing trips each winter, first to northern New Hampshire and Maine, and then out West, to Colorado. Indoors, the two of them watched the Red Sox or the Celtics or sat for hours together at the computer. Whenever Jack came home from a trip, he went first to Mattie, or she to him, and they seemed to have that rarest of parent-child relationships: They were easy together.

Only once had Jack ever lashed out at Mattie. Kathryn could see even now the fury in Jack's face when he discovered that Mattie had shoved a playmate down the stairs. Mattie and her friend were how old? Four? Five? Jack had grabbed Mattie by the arm, whacked her once hard on the butt, and then nearly dragged her to her room and slammed the door with such ferocity that even Kathryn had been shaken. His actions were so instinctive, so swift, that Kathryn imagined that he had himself been punished that way as a child and that he had, for one brief moment, lost his usual control. Later, she tried to talk to him about the incident, but Jack, whose face still bore a deep, rosy flush, would not discuss it, except to say that he didn't know what had come over him.

"You specialize in this," Kathryn said to Robert.

He glanced over at the counter, searching for something that might function as an ashtray. She took the white saucer from under her teacup and slid it across the pine table. He propped the cigarette on the saucer and began to pick up his dishes.

"Not really," he said.

"Let me do this," she said. "You've done enough."

He hesitated.

"Please," she said. "I'm capable of washing dishes."

He sat down and picked up the cigarette again. She walked to the sink and flipped open the dishwasher. She turned on the water.

"I like to think of myself as forming a cocoon around the family," he said, "insulating them from the outside world."

"Which has so grotesquely intruded," she said.

"Which has so grotesquely intruded."

"Containment," she said. "That's what you do. Containment."

"Tell me about *your* job," he said. "What do you teach?"

"Music and history. And I'm in charge of the band."

"Seriously?"

"Seriously. There are only seventy-two students in the high school."

"You like teaching?" he asked.

She thought a minute.

"I do," she said. "Yes, I like it a lot. I've had one or two truly outstanding students. Last year, we sent a girl to the New England Conservatory. I like the kids."

"It's a different life being married to a pilot," he said.

She nodded. She thought about the odd hours, about never celebrating a holiday on the day itself. About Jack's wanting breakfast at seven o'clock in the evening, or dinner and a glass of wine at seven in the morning. Theirs had been a life different from that of other families. Jack might be gone for three days, home two, and that schedule would continue for two or three months. And then, the next month, he might have four days off, six days on, and Mattie and Kathryn would adjust to that rhythm. They didn't live by routine, as other families did — they lived in segments. Bits of time when Jack was home, longer bits of time when Jack was gone. And when he was gone, the house would seem to deflate a bit, settle quietly in on itself. And no matter how much attention Kathryn paid to Mattie or how much they enjoyed each other's company, it always seemed to Kathryn that they were suspended — waiting for real life to begin again, for Jack to walk back in the door.

Kathryn wondered, as she sat across from Robert, whether she would feel like that now — suspended in time, waiting for Jack to once again walk in the door.

"How often did he commute?" Robert asked.

"From here? About six times a month."

"Not too bad. It's what? Fifty minutes?"

"Yes. Do you have a suitcase packed in your office?" she asked. "Packed and ready?"

He hesitated.

"A small one," he said.

"You're going to the inn tonight?"

"Yes, but I could sleep here on the sofa if you'd rather."

"No. I'll be fine. I've got Julia and Mattie. Tell me another story," she said.

"How do you mean?"

She put the last dish in the dishwasher and closed it. She dried her hands on a towel, threaded it through the drawer pull.

"About what it's like when you get to the house."

He scratched the back of his neck. He was not tall, but he gave the impression of height, even when sitting down. She imagined him as a runner.

"Kathryn, this is . . ."

"Tell me."

"No."

"It helps."

"No, it doesn't."

"How would you know?" she asked sharply. "Are we all the same, the wives? Do we all react the same?"

She could hear the anger in her voice, an anger that had been there sporadically throughout the day. Bubbles of anger rising to the surface of a liquid and then popping. She sat down again at the table, across from him.

"Of course not," he said.

"What if it isn't true?" she asked. "What if you got the news and told the wife and found out later it wasn't true?"

"That doesn't happen."

"Why not?"

"I spend a fair amount of time standing at the end of driveways with a cell phone in my hand, waiting for absolute confirmation. You may find this hard to believe, but I don't ever want to tell a woman her husband has died if in fact he has not."

"I'm sorry."

"I thought that was banned."

She smiled.

"Do you mind these questions?" she asked.

"I'm concerned about why you're asking them, but no, I don't mind."

"Then let me ask you this: What are you afraid I'll say to the press?"

He loosened his tie, unbuttoned the top button of his shirt.

"A pilot's wife is naturally very distraught. If she says something, and the press is there to hear it, it goes on the record. A new widow, for example, might say that her husband had been complaining about the mechanics recently. Or she might blurt out, *I knew this would happen. He said the airline was cutting corners on crew training.*"

"Well, wouldn't that be OK? If it was true?"

"People say things when they're distraught they wouldn't say later. Things they sometimes don't mean at all. But if it becomes part of the record, there's no backing away from it."

"How old are you?" she asked.

"Thirty-eight."

"Jack was forty-nine."

"I know."

"While you're waiting, you know, for a crash, what do you do?"

"I wouldn't put it exactly like that," he said, shifting in his chair. "I don't wait around for a crash. I have other responsibilities."

"Such as?"

"I study the crash investigations pretty closely. I do a lot of follow-up with the pilots' families. How old is this house?"

"You're changing the subject."

"Yes, I am."

"It was built in the 1860s. As a convent originally. A kind of retreat."

"It's beautiful."

"Thank you. It needs work. It always needs work. It falls down faster than we can repair it."

She heard the *we*.

There was never anything not to love about the house, which seemed constantly to change, depending on the light, the seasons, the color of the water, the temperature of the air. Even its eccentricities Kathryn had come to appreciate: the sloping floors in the bedrooms; the shallow closets that had been designed for nuns' habits; the windows with the old-fashioned storms that had to be painstakingly put up each fall and taken off each spring (Jack discovering that, like snowflakes, no two were precisely alike, so, until he learned to label each window, the task was like that of fitting puzzle pieces together while standing on a ladder), but which when cleaned were beautiful, lovely objects simply in themselves. Indeed, it was sometimes an effort to pull away from the view through those windows when there were chores at hand. Kathryn had often sat in the long front room and allowed herself to daydream. She'd daydreamed particularly about how easy it would be, in such a house, on such a piece of geography, to retreat from the world, to take up an existence that was solitary and contemplative, not unlike the vocation of the house's earliest inhabitants: the Sisters of the Order of Saint Jean de Baptiste de Bienfaisance, twenty nuns ranging in age from nineteen to eighty-two, wedded to Jesus and to poverty. Often, when she was in the front room, she imagined a long wooden refectory table with a bench set along one side so that the sisters could see the ocean while they ate. For though the nuns had taken vows of poverty, they lived within a landscape of breathtaking beauty.

For years, Kathryn tried to find the place where the sisters had kept their chapel. She had searched the lawn and the adjacent orchard, but had never located a foundation. Had the chapel been inside the house, she wondered, in the room they used as a dining room? Did the sisters dismantle a homespun altar before they left, taking with them a statue of the Virgin Mary and a cross? Or did they travel across the large expanse of salt marsh between Fortune's Rocks and the mill town of Ely Falls so that they could attend services at Saint Joseph's Church with the French-Canadian immigrants?

"You've been here eleven years?" Robert asked.

"Yes."

The phone rang then and startled them both. It seemed that it had been twenty minutes, perhaps thirty, since the phone had last rung, the longest break since the first summons in the morning. She watched Robert answer it.

She had been only twenty-three when she and Jack had moved back to the Ely area. Kathryn had worried about resentment from the people of the town. She would have a house on the water and a husband who was a pilot for Vision. She would no longer be living in Ely proper, but rather at Fortune's Rocks, an ephemeral, transient world of summer people who, for all their patronizing of her grandmother's shop and all their inevitably condescending curiosity about the small town with its quirky charm, remained essentially anonymous. Sleek, tanned bodies with seemingly inexhaustible reserves of ready cash. Although Martha, who owned Ingerbretson's, the only grocery store at Fortune's Rocks, could tell more than a few cautionary tales of men in khaki shorts and white T-shirts who charged up enormous sums — for vodka, lobsters, potato sticks, and Martha's homemade chocolate *konfetkakke* — and then vanished into bankruptcy proceedings, their only legacy a For Sale sign stuck in the sand in front of a $400,000 beach house.

But the local reserves of goodwill toward Julia Hull had been deep and had spilled over onto Jack and Kathryn. She thought about the way Jack and she had merged into the life of Ely, had shepherded Mattie through the schools. Jack's job had taken him away from the town, but still he had managed to play tennis in a town league with Hugh Reney, the vice-principal of the middle school, and Arthur Kahler, who ran the Mobil station at the end of the village. Surprisingly, considering how easily Mattie had been conceived, Jack and Kathryn seemed not to be able to have other children. They had told themselves that they were happy enough with Mattie to forgo the extraordinary measures it might take to conceive again.

Kathryn watched Robert at the phone. He turned once quickly and glanced at her, then turned back again.

"No comment," he said.

"I don't think so.

"No comment.

"No comment."

He hung up the phone and stood looking at the cabinet above it. He picked up a pen from the counter and began to flip it back and forth.

"What?" she asked.

He turned.

"Well, we knew this was going to happen," he said.

"What?"

"This will have a shelf life of twenty-four hours max. Then it will be history."

"What?"

He looked at her hard and took a deep breath.

"They're saying pilot error," he said.

She shut her eyes.

"It's just speculation," he said quickly. "They think they've found some flight data that doesn't make sense. But, trust me, they couldn't know for sure."

"Oh."

"Also," he said quietly, "they've found some bodies."

She thought that if she just kept breathing in and out slowly, she would be all right.

"No identification yet," he said.

"How many?"

"Eight."

She tried to imagine. Eight bodies. Whole? In pieces? She wanted to ask but didn't.

"There'll be more," he said. "They're bringing up more."

British? she wondered. Or American? Women or men?

"Who was it? On the phone?"

"Reuters."

She got up from the table and walked through the hallway to the bathroom. For a moment, she was afraid she might be sick. It was a reflexive reaction, she thought, the inability to take it in, the desire to cough it out. She splashed water on her face and dried it. In the mirror, her face was almost unrecognizable.

When she returned to the kitchen, Robert was on the telephone again. He had one arm across his chest, his hand tucked under the other arm. He was speaking quietly, answering Yes and OK, watching her as she walked into the room. "Later," he said and hung up.

There was a long silence.

"How many of them are pilot error?" she asked.

"Seventy percent."

"What error? What happens?"

"It's a series of events leading to the last one, and the last one is usually called pilot error because by that time the pilots are deeply involved."

"I see."

"May I ask you something?"

"Yes."

"Was Jack . . . ?"

He hesitated.

"Was Jack what?" she asked.

"Was Jack agitated or depressed?"

Robert paused.

"You mean recently?" she asked.

"I know it's an awful question," he said. "But you're going to have to answer it sooner or later. If there was something, if there's anything you know or you can remember, it would be better if you and I talked about it first."

She considered the question. Odd, she thought, how intensely you knew a person, or thought you did, when you were in love — soaked, drenched in love — only to discover later that perhaps you didn't know that person quite as well as you had imagined. Or weren't quite as well known as you had hoped to be. In the beginning, a lover drank in every word and gesture and then tried to hold on to that intensity for as long as possible. But inevitably, if two people were together long enough, that intensity had to wane. It was the way people worked, Kathryn thought, with a need to evolve from being sick with love to making a life with someone who was also changing, altering himself, so that the couple could one day raise a child.

Some lovers didn't make it, she knew from her parents' example. Kathryn could not remember a time when there had not been a feeling of want and need and tension between her parents. Although it was her father who was continuously unfaithful and certainly gave Kathryn's mother just cause to be hurt, it was her mother herself, Kathryn was certain, who had destroyed early on whatever slim chance her parents had had of happiness. For it was her mother's fate to be utterly incapable of forgetting that time when she had been twenty-two and had met Bobby Hull, and he had fallen in love with her and had made her feel alive. For one year — a year during which Kathryn's parents had married and then conceived her — Bobby Hull hadn't taken his eyes off his new wife, nor left her side, so that Kathryn's mother felt, for the first time in her life, both deeply loved and extraordinarily beautiful, a drug that turned out to be even more addicting than the bourbon to which Bobby Hull had introduced her when they met. That year, which Kathryn never doubted was the best of her mother's life — and about which Kathryn knew more than she ought to have, since, as a child, she heard about it in great detail every time her parents fought — took on an importance that became almost sacred as time went on. And Kathryn's father, even when he relented and actually tried to please his wife, could not begin to recreate it. The tragedy of her mother's life, Kathryn had always thought, was the gradual withdrawal of Bobby Hull's attentions to her, which began naturally enough, in the way that even two people who are deeply in love are eventually able to carry on with life and go to work and take care of babies, but became, as soon as her mother felt the withdrawal and named it — labeled it, so to speak — a way of being. Kathryn could hear her mother calling from the upstairs bedroom, in an agonized voice, over and over, the single word *Why?* Sometimes (and it made Kathryn wince to remember this), her mother begged Bobby Hull to tell her she was beautiful, which automatically caused Kathryn's father, who could be stubborn, to be stingy with his love, even though he did love his wife very much and might have told her so if she had not asked.

As for her own marriage, Kathryn thought on balance that it had probably been more difficult for her to make the transition from being lovers to being a couple than it had been for Jack. It had come later for her and Jack than she suspected it came for other couples, and in that they had been lucky. Was it when Mattie was eleven? Twelve? Jack had seemed to withdraw ever so slightly from Kathryn. Nothing she could point to or articulate exactly. In every marriage, she had always thought, a couple created its own sexual drama, played out in the bedroom or silently in public or even over the telephone, a drama that was oft repeated with similar dialogue, similar stage directions, similar body parts as props to the imagination. But if one partner then slightly altered his role or tried to eliminate some of his lines, the play didn't track quite as well as it once had. The other actor, not yet aware that the play had changed, sometimes lost his lines or swallowed them or became confused by the different choreography.

And so it had been, she thought, with Jack and her. He had begun to turn to her less often in bed. And then, when he did, it seemed as though an edge was gone. It was just a gradual sliding away, so gradual as to sometimes be almost imperceptible, until one day it occurred to Kathryn that she and Jack hadn't made love in over two weeks. She'd thought at the time that it was his need for sleep that had overwhelmed him; his schedule was difficult, and he often seemed tired. But sometimes she worried that possibly she was responsible for this new pattern, that she had become too passive. And so she had tried for a time to be more imaginative and playful, an effort that wasn't entirely successful.

Kathryn had vowed not to complain. She would not panic. She would not even discuss the matter. But the price for such steadfastness, Kathryn soon realized, was the creation of a subtle gauze all around her, a veil that kept her and Jack just beyond easy reach of each other. And after a while, the gauze began to make her anxious.

And then there had been the fight. The one truly terrible fight of their marriage.

But she wouldn't think about that now.

"There wasn't anything," she said to Robert. "I think I'll go up to bed."

Robert nodded, agreeing with the idea.

"It was a good marriage," Kathryn said.

She ran her palm over the table.

"It was good," she repeated.

But actually she thought that any marriage was like radio reception: It came and went. Occasionally, it — the marriage, Jack — would be clear to her. At other times, there would be interference, a staticky sound between them. At those times, it would be as though she couldn't quite hear Jack, as though his messages to her were drifting in the wrong direction through the stratosphere.

"Do we need to notify any other of his family?" Robert asked.

Kathryn shook her head.

"He was an only child. His mother died when he was nine," she said. "And his father died when he was in college."

She wondered if Robert Hart already knew this.

"Jack never talked about his childhood," she said. "Actually, I don't know much about his childhood at all. I always had the impression it wasn't a very happy one." Jack's childhood had been one of those subjects Kathryn had thought there was all the time in the world to talk to him about.

"Seriously," Robert said. "I'd be happy to stay here."

"No, you should go. I have Julia here if I need someone. What does your ex-wife do?"

"She works for Senator Hanson. From Virginia."

"When you asked me about Jack," Kathryn said, "about his being depressed?"

"Yes."

"Well, there was one time I would say he was not depressed, exactly, but definitely unhappy."

"Tell me about it," Robert said.

"It was about his job," she said. "This was about five years ago. He became bored with the airline. Nearly, for a short time, terribly bored. He began to fantasize about quitting, giving it up for another job — aerobatics, he said. In a Russian-built YAK 27, I remember. Or opening his own operation. You know, a flying school, charter business, sell a few airplanes."

"I used to think about that, too," Robert said. "I think every pilot probably does at one time or another."

"The company had grown too fast, Jack said. It had become too impersonal, and he hardly knew any of the crew he flew with. A lot of the pilots were British and lived in London. Also, he missed the hands-on flying he'd known earlier. He wanted to be able to feel the plane again. For a while, we got brochures for strange-looking stunt planes in the mail, and he even went so far as to ask me one morning if I'd be willing to go with him to Boulder, where there was a woman who was selling her school.

And of course I had to say yes, because he'd once done it for me, and I remember being worried about how unhappy he was and thinking perhaps he really did need a change. Although I was relieved when the subject finally drifted off the screen. After that, there wasn't any more talk of leaving the airline."

"This was five years ago?"

"About. I'm no good with time. I know that getting the Boston-Heathrow route helped," she said. "I guess I was just so glad the crisis was over, I didn't dare raise the subject again by asking about it. I wish I had now."

"After that, he didn't seem depressed anymore?" Robert asked.

"No. Not really."

She thought that it would be impossible to say with any certainty what accommodations Jack had made inside himself. He had seemed to put his discontent into the same place he had put his childhood — a sealed vault.

"You look tired," she said to Robert.

"I am."

"You probably should go now," she said.

He was silent. He didn't move.

"What does she look like?" she asked. "Your wife, I mean. Ex-wife."

"She's your age. Tall. Short dark hair. Very pretty."

"I trusted him not to die," Kathryn said. "I feel like I've been cheated. Does that sound terrible? After all, he died, and I didn't. He may have suffered. I know he suffered, if only for seconds."

"You're suffering now."

"It's not the same."

"You *have* been cheated," he said. "Both you and your daughter."

At the mention of her daughter, Kathryn's throat tightened. She put her hands in front of her face, as if to tell him not to say anything else.

"You have to let this happen to you," he said quietly. "It has its own momentum."

"It's like a train rolling over me," she said. "A train that doesn't stop."

"I want to help you, but there isn't a lot I can do except watch," Robert said. "Grief is messy. There's nothing good about it."

She put her head down on the table and shut her eyes.

"We have to have a funeral, don't we?" she asked.

"We can talk about that tomorrow."

"But what if there's no body?"

"What religion are you?" he asked.

"I'm nothing. I used to be Methodist. Julia is a Methodist."

"What was Jack?"

"Catholic. But he was nothing, too. We didn't belong to a church. We weren't married in a church."

She felt Robert's fingers touch the top of her hair. Lightly. Quickly.

"I'm going now," he said.

When Robert was gone, Kathryn sat for a minute by herself and then got up and walked through the downstairs rooms of the house, turning out lights. She wondered what precisely was meant by pilot error. A left turn when a right was called for? A miscalculation of fuel? Directions not followed? A switch accidentally flipped? In what other job could a man make a mistake and kill 103 other people? A train engineer? A bus driver? Someone who worked with chemicals, with nuclear waste?

It couldn't be pilot error, she said to herself. For Mattie's sake, it couldn't.

She stood for a long time at the top of the stairs, then turned down the hallway.

It was cold in the bedroom. The door had been shut all day. She let her eyes adjust to the dark. The bed was unmade, just as she had left it at 3:24 in the morning.

She circled the bed and looked at it, the way an animal might do — wary and considering. She pulled back the comforter and top sheet and studied the fitted sheet in the moonlight. It was cream-colored, flannel for the winter. How many times had Jack and she made love on that bed? she wondered. In sixteen years of marriage? She touched the sheet with her fingers. It felt worn and smooth. Soft. Tentatively, she sat on the edge of the bed, seeing if she could stand that. She no longer trusted herself, could no longer say with any certainty how her body would react to any piece of news. But as she sat there, she felt nothing. Perhaps, during the long day, she had finally become numb, she thought. The senses could only bear so much.

"Pilot error," she said aloud, testing herself.

But it couldn't be pilot error, she thought quickly. Would not, in the end, be pilot error.

She lay down on the bed, fully clothed. This would be her bed now, she was thinking. Her bed alone. All that room for only herself.

She glanced over at the bedside clock: 9:27.

Carefully — monitoring herself for seismic shifts — she reached down and pulled the top sheet over her. She imagined she could smell Jack in the flannel. It was possible — she hadn't washed the sheets since he left on Tuesday. But she couldn't trust her senses, didn't know what was real or imagined. She looked over at Jack's shirt flung over the chair. Kathryn had gotten into the habit, early in the marriage, of not bothering to tidy the house until just before Jack got home from a trip. Now, she knew, she would not want to remove the shirt from the chair. It might be days before she could touch it, could risk bringing it to her face, risk catching his smell in the weave of the cloth. And when all of the traces of Jack had been cleaned and put away, what would she be left with then?

She rolled onto her side, looking at the room in the moonlight. Through the small opening in the window, she could hear the water rolling.

She had a vivid image of Jack in the water, bumping along the sand at the bottom of the ocean.

She brought the flannel up over her mouth and nose and breathed slowly through it, thinking that might help to stop the panic. She thought of crawling into Mattie's room and lying down on the floor next to Mattie and Julia. Had she really imagined she could spend this first night alone in the marriage bed?

She got up quickly from the bed and walked into the bathroom, where Robert had left the bottle of Valium. She took one tablet, then another just in case. She thought about taking a third. She sat on the edge of the bathtub until she began to feel swimmy.

She thought perhaps that she would lie down on the daybed in the spare room. But when she passed the door to Jack's office, she saw that the light had been left on. She opened the door.

The office was over bright and colorless — white, metallic, plastic, gray. It was a room she seldom entered, an unappealing space with no curtains on the windows and metal file cabinets lining the walls. A masculine room.

She supposed it had its own order — an order known only to

Jack. On the massive metal desk there were two computers, a keyboard, a fax, two phones, a scanner, coffee cups, dusty models of planes, a mug with red juice in it (Mattie's, she guessed), and a blue clay pencil holder that Mattie had made for Jack when she was in second grade.

She looked at the fax machine with its blinking light.

She walked to the desk and sat down. Robert had been here earlier, using the phone and the fax. Kathryn opened the left-hand drawer. Inside were Jack's logbooks, heavy, dark ones with vinyl bindings and smaller ones that fit into a shirt pocket. She saw a small flashlight, an ivory letter opener he had brought back years ago from Africa, handbooks for airplane types he no longer flew, a book on weather radar. A training video on wind shear. Epaulets from Santa Fe. Coasters that looked like flight instruments.

She closed the drawer and opened up the long middle drawer. She fingered a set of keys that she thought might be left over from the apartment in Santa Fe. She picked up a pair of old tortoiseshell reading glasses that Jack had run over with the Caravan. He insisted they still worked. There were boxes of paper clips, pens, pencils, elastic bands, thumbtacks, two batteries, a spark plug. She lifted a packet of Post-it notes and saw a sewing kit underneath from Marriott Hotels. She smiled at the sewing kit and kissed it.

She opened a larger file drawer on the right. It was intended for legal-size files, she saw, but in it was a stack of papers about a foot high. She took the pile out and put it on her lap. It was a random set of papers and had no order that she could see. There was a birthday card from Mattie, memos from the airline, a local phone book, a series of health insurance forms, a rough draft of a paper Mattie had written for school, a catalog of books about

flying, a homemade valentine Kathryn had given him a year
ago. She looked at the front of the card. *Valentine, I love what you
do for my mind . . .* , the front of the card read. She opened it.
. . . And the things you do for my body. She closed her eyes.

After a time, she propped the papers she had already looked
through against her chest and continued to riffle through the
rest. She discovered several of Jack's bank statements clipped
together. She and Jack had had separate accounts. She paid for
the clothes for Mattie and herself, for food and other household
items. Jack paid for everything else. Any money Jack saved, he
had said, was going toward their retirement.

She was beginning to have trouble keeping her eyes open.
She made an attempt to square the remaining papers in her lap
and to set them back into the drawer. In the drawer, slightly
stuck in the seam, was an unopened envelope, junk mail, yet
another invitation to apply for a Visa card. Bay Bank, 9.9 percent.
This was old, she thought.

She picked up the envelope and was about to toss it into the
wastebasket when she saw writing on the back. Jack's writing.
Another remember list: *Call Ely Falls Pharmacy, Call Alex, Bank
deposit, March expenses, Call Larry Johnson re taxes, Call Finn re Caravan.* Finn, she remembered, was the Dodge-Plymouth dealer in
Ely Falls. They had bought the Caravan four years ago and hadn't,
to her knowledge, had any dealings with Tommy Finn since.

She turned the envelope around. At the other end of the
blank side of the envelope was a note, also in Jack's writing.
Muire 3:30, it read.

Who was Muire? Kathryn wondered. Randall Muir from the
bank? Had Jack been negotiating a loan?

Kathryn looked again at the front of the envelope. She
checked the postmark. Definitely four years ago, she saw.

She put the stack of papers back into the drawer and shoved the drawer closed with her foot.

She was now longing to lie down. She left Jack's office and walked into the spare room, her retreat. She lay back against the flowered spread, and within seconds she fell asleep.

She was wakened by voices — a shouting voice, nearly hysterical, and another voice, calmer, as though trying to make itself heard over the commotion.

Kathryn got up and opened the door, and the voices increased in volume. Mattie and Julia, she could hear, were downstairs in the front room.

They were kneeling on the floor when Kathryn got there, Julia in a flannel nightgown, Mattie in a T-shirt and boxer shorts. Around them was a grotesque garden of wrapping paper — balls and crumpled clusters of red, gold, plaid, blue, and silver interspersed with what seemed to be thousands of yards of colored ribbon.

Julia looked up from the doorway.

"She woke up and came downstairs," Julia explained. "She was trying to wrap her presents."

Mattie lowered herself to the floor and lay on the carpet in a fetal curl.

Kathryn lay down next to her daughter.

"I can't stand it, Mom," Mattie said. "Everywhere I look, he's there. He's in every room, in every chair, in the windows, in the wallpaper. I literally can't stand it, Mom."

"You were trying to wrap his present?" Kathryn asked, smoothing her daughter's hair out of her face.

Mattie nodded and began to cry.

"I'm going to take her to my place," Julia said.

"What time is it?"

"Just after midnight. I'll take her home and put her to bed," Julia said.

"I'll come, too," Kathryn said.

"No," Julia said. "You're exhausted. You stay here and go back to bed. Mattie will be fine with me. She needs a change of scene, a neutral zone, a neutral bedroom."

And Kathryn thought how appropriate that image was, for she had the distinct sense they were involved in a war, that they were all in danger of becoming battle casualties.

While Julia packed an overnight bag for Mattie, Kathryn lay down beside her daughter and rubbed her back. From time to time, Mattie shuddered convulsively. Kathryn sang a song she had made up when Mattie was a baby: *M is for Matigan* . . . , the song began.

After Julia and Mattie had left, Kathryn climbed back up to her bedroom. This time, feeling braver, she crawled between the flannel sheets.

She did not dream.

In the morning, she heard a dog barking.

There was something discordantly familiar about the dog barking.

And then she braced herself, the way she might do if she were stopped at a light and happened to look up in the rear-view mirror to see that the driver behind her was going too fast.

Robert's hair was wet and freshly combed. She could see the comb lines near the widow's peak. He had on a different shirt, a blue that was almost a denim, with a dark red tie. Second-day shirt, she thought idly.

A coffee cup was on the counter. He had his hands in the pockets of his trousers, and he was pacing.

She looked up at the clock: 6:40. Why was he there so early? she wondered.

When he saw her at the bottom of the stairs, he took his hands out of his pockets and walked toward her.

He put his hands on her shoulders.

"What?" she asked, alarmed.

"Do you know what the CVR is?" he asked.

"Yes," she said. "The cockpit voice recorder."

"Well, they've found it."

"And?"

He hesitated. Just a beat.

"They're saying suicide," he said.

HE WALKS WITH HIS ARM AROUND HER TOWARD
the planes, which seem too small, only toys that children might
climb in and over and about. The heat, deep and roasting, radi-
ates from the pavement. This is a masculine world, she thinks,
with its odd bits of machinery, its briefing room, its tower. All
around her there is metal, brilliant or dull in the sun's glare.

He seems solicitous, but he walks briskly. The plane is pretty,
with red and white markings. She takes his hand as she steps
onto the wing, then crawls through the tiny opening into the
cockpit, the size of which is immediately alarming. How could
something as monumental as flight take place in such an unpre-
possessing space? Flight, which has always seemed to Kathryn to
be improbable, now seems clearly impossible, and she tells herself, as she has sometimes done when in a car with a bad driver
or on a ride at a carnival, that this will be over soon and all she
has to do is survive.

Jack hoists himself up on his side. He has on sunglasses with
iridescent blue lenses. He tells her to buckle up and hands her

headphones, which he explains will make it easier for them to talk to each other over the noise of the engine.

They bump along the pitted tarmac. The plane feels loose and wobbly. She wants to tell him to stop, that she has changed her mind. The plane gathers speed, the bouncing stops, and they are up.

Her heart fills her chest. Jack turns to her, his smile full of confidence and amusement, a smile that says, This will be fun, so just relax.

Before her is a vast expanse of blue. What happened to the ground? She has an image of a plane reaching a terrible height, tipping slightly, and then falling, as nature would demand it do. Beside her, Jack gestures toward the window.

— Take a look, he says.

They are over the coast, so high up the surf looks stationary. The ocean ripples back to a darker blue. Just inland from the coast, she can see dark fir trees, what seems like an entire country of fir trees. She spots a boat and its wake, a power plant up the coast. The dark stain of Portsmouth. The glistening bits of rock that are the Isles of Shoals. She looks for Ely, thinks she sees it, follows a road from town to Julia's house.

He banks for a turn, and her hands jerk out to save herself. She wants to tell him to be careful, which immediately strikes her as inane. Of course he will be careful. Won't he?

As if in answer, he angles the plane steeply up, an angle so sharp she thinks he must be testing the very laws of physics. She is certain they will fall from the sky. She calls out his name, but he is intent upon his instruments and doesn't answer.

Gravity pins her against the back of her seat. They climb into a long, high loop, and for a second, at its apex, they are motionless, upside down, a speck suspended over the Atlantic. The plane dives then into a run out the other side of the loop. She screams and grabs for whatever she can reach. Jack glances over at her once quickly and puts the plane nearly vertical to the ground. She watches Jack at the controls, his calm movements, the concentration on his face. It amazes her that a man can make a plane do tricks — tricks with gravity, with physics, with fate.

And then the world is silent. As if surprised itself, the plane begins to fall. Not like a stone, but rather like a leaf, fluttering a bit and then dipping to the right. Heartsick, she glances at Jack. The plane begins then to spin crazily, its nose pointed toward the ground. She arches her back, unable even to scream.

When he pulls out of the spin, they are not a hundred feet from the water. She can see whitecaps, the twitching of a slightly agitated sea. Astonishing herself, she begins to cry.

— Are you OK? he asks quickly, seeing the tears. He puts his hand on her thigh. He shakes his head. — I never should have done that, he says. — I'm so sorry. I thought you would enjoy it.

She turns to look at him. She covers his hand with her own and takes a deep shuddering breath.

— That was thrilling, she says. And she means it.

IT WAS FRIGID IN THE CAR. KATHRYN WAS BARELY ABLE to hold onto the steering wheel, having left the house in a rush and forgotten her gloves. How cold was it out? she wondered. Fifteen? Twenty? Below a certain point, she thought, it didn't seem to matter much. She felt the strain in her shoulders as she hunched forward, trying not to touch anything — not even the seat back — until the heat kicked in.

In the wake of Robert's news — which he insisted Kathryn must absolutely refuse to credit — she had wanted only to be with Mattie. As Kathryn stood at the bottom of the stairs, looking at Robert's face, the desire for her daughter had overwhelmed her, filling her up as quickly as water rushing into a jar. Still in the clothes she had slept in, she had brushed past Robert and nearly simultaneously slipped her arms into her parka, stepped into her boots, and unhooked the keys by the back door. In the Caravan, she had rattled down the long drive, sped past several men who were running toward the gate, and for almost a mile had had the speedometer at nearly sixty. And then she'd skidded badly in a turn and come to rest on a sandy shoulder on the road from Fortune's Rocks into Ely. She put her forehead silently against the steering wheel.

It couldn't be suicide, Kathryn thought. Suicide was absolutely impossible. It was unimaginable. Unthinkable. Out of the question.

How long she sat there, she didn't know, perhaps ten minutes. And then she started out again, this time at a slower pace and with an odd sort of calm — a calm born of exhaustion, possibly, or simply a disguised numbness — descending upon her. She would get to Mattie, she told herself, and it wouldn't be true what was being said about Jack.

The sun broke the horizon line, turning snowy lawns pink and criss-crossing them with the long blue shadows of trees and cars. The town was still, though occasionally Kathryn could see exhaust rising in billows from cars left running in driveways so that the owners could defrost the windshields and bear to sit on the upholstery. Along the eaves of some of the houses were strings of colored lights, and she saw numerous Christmas trees in front windows. She passed a blue-shingled cape with an outline of gaudy colored bulbs at the picture window. *The auto-parts-store-look*, Jack had once commented as they'd driven by.

Once commented. Had commented. Won't ever comment again. The envelope of time, she thought, was starting in earnest to swallow her. But she wondered if she hadn't already adjusted, however slightly, to the concept of Jack's absence. The thought of his death, coming randomly on the tail of another thought — a memory of him, an image — didn't rock her quite as violently as it had done the day before. How quickly the mind accommodated itself, she thought, even in such tiny increments. Perhaps it was that after a series of shocks, the body acclimated itself, like being inoculated — each subsequent shock delivering less impact. Or possibly this momentarily benumbed state was only a lull — a cease-fire. How would she know? There had never been a rehearsal for any of this.

She drove through the center of Ely, the light just beginning to flood the storefronts now, the earth having made its incremental journey eastward, just enough to show the town of Ely to the sun. She passed the hardware store and Beekman's, a five-and-ten-cent store that had survived the mall on Route 24, although its shelves were often dusty and thinly stocked. She passed an empty building that had once been a yarn and fabric shop that sold mill ends when the Ely Falls mill had been in business. She passed the Bobbin, the only place in town where one could get a drink or a sandwich. The Bobbin was open, three cars parked outside. She glanced at the dashboard clock: 7:05. In ten minutes, Janet Riley, a reading specialist for the middle school, and Jimmy Hirsch, an agent for MetLife, would be there having a bagel with cream cheese and an egg sandwich respectively. It was true, Kathryn thought, that you could set your watch by the habits of certain townspeople, and then you could check your watch regularly throughout the day by other villagers and their absolute insistence on routine.

Kathryn, for one, understood routine, which in Julia's house had been a necessary hedge against chaos. And, of course, Jack had understood routine — particularly in a job that required a man to become a machine that would behave in precisely a certain way each time a particular set of circumstances came into play. Oddly, though, he was impatient with routine once out of the plane. He preferred to think of possibilities and be ready for them. Of the two of them, he was always the more likely to say, Let's go into Portsmouth for lunch. Or, Let's take Mattie out of school and go skiing.

Kathryn passed the high school, which lay just at the edge of the town center. She'd been working there now for seven years, having finished her degree when she moved back to Ely. It was an ancient brick building with large windows, a building that had already been old when Julia had gone to school there. There were fewer students in the school now than there had been in Julia's day, when the mills were thriving.

For a few blocks, there were white houses with black shutters in small lots, many of them bordered with white fences — mostly Capes and Victorians, but some early colonials — that lent Ely what charm it had. But once beyond this inner ring, the neighborhood began to thin out, brief patches of woods or salt marsh separating one house from another, and continued to elongate, like a pull of taffy, until the end of that particular road, three miles farther along, where the stone house was.

She made the familiar turn and followed the street up the hill. No lights were on yet, and she guessed that Mattie and Julia were still in bed. She got out of the car and stood a minute in the stillness. There was always a moment in a morning, between the silence of the night before and the noise of the day to come, when it seemed to Kathryn that time stopped for a beat, when all the world was motionless, expectant. The ground around the car was dusted with a powdery snow that had fallen three days earlier and had not yet melted. On the rocks, the snow had frozen into a thin lace.

Julia's house stood on a hill, which sometimes made chores such as bringing in groceries difficult, but the house gave a magnificent view westward if one was in the mood for it. The house was old, mid-nineteenth century. It had once been an outbuilding for a farm a mile away. On one side, the house was bordered by the narrow road; on the other, by a stone wall. Beyond the stone wall was an orderly field of crooked apple trees that by the end of summer would already be bearing dusty, rose-colored fruit.

She shut the car door, walked up the front path, and let herself in. Julia had never locked her door, not when Kathryn was growing up and not even now, when others did. In the kitchen, Kathryn once again smelled the unique scent of Julia's house — a mix of orange sponge cake and onions. Kathryn took off her parka and laid it over a chair in the living room.

The house was cramped, but stood three stories tall. When Kathryn's parents died, Julia had encouraged Kathryn to take over their bedroom on the top floor. After some hesitation, Kathryn had put her books there and a desk that looked out through the single window. On the middle floor were two tiny bedrooms, one of which was Julia's, and on the ground floor of the house were the living room and kitchen. In the living room was Julia's furniture from her marriage — a faded brown velvet sofa, two soft chairs that needed reupholstering, a rug, a side table, and the grand piano that took up nearly all the remaining space.

Holding onto the banister, Kathryn climbed the narrow stairway to her old room, now her daughter's when Mattie slept over, which was often. Kathryn walked to the window and drew the drapes a crack so that she could see her in the bed. Mattie slept, as she nearly always did, huddled into herself, her stuffed tiger having fallen onto the floor. Kathryn could hardly see her daughter's face — it was bent into the covers — but it was enough to see her hair spread out behind her, to see the shape of her delicate body beneath the blankets.

Quietly, Kathryn moved to a chair opposite the bed so that she could keep watch over Mattie. Kathryn didn't want to wake her just yet, was not ready for the way the knowledge of the day before would hit Mattie afresh, just as it had hit her earlier in the morning. But when it did happen, Kathryn wanted to be there.

Mattie lifted her head off the pillow, turned, and rolled over.

The sun was fully up now, the light threading itself around the curtains and making a slit of bright color along the left side of the double bed. It was the same mahogany bed Kathryn's parents had slept in, and she sometimes wondered if couples had made love more often in the old days than they did now, simply because the beds had been narrower. Mattie stirred dreamily, as though snuggling in for another hour or so. Kathryn got up from her chair, picked up the stuffed tiger, and placed it near Mattie's head. For a moment, Kathryn could feel her daughter's warm breath on her fingers. Then, perhaps sensing her mother's presence, Mattie stiffened. Impulsively, Kathryn lay down beside her, folding her arms around her. She held her daughter tightly, heard a quick snort of breath.

"I'm right here," Kathryn said.

Mattie was silent. Kathryn relaxed her grip and began to smooth the top of her daughter's hair. It was thick with an unbrushed curl, the way it always was first thing in the morning. Mattie had inherited the curl from Jack, the color of her hair from Kathryn. From her father, Mattie had also inherited the two-color blue eyes, which until recently had pleased her no end. She thought that bearing a mark different from others made her special in some way. But with the onset of serious middle adolescence, when any characteristic that deviated even slightly from her friends' was cause for severe anguish, she had begun wearing a single contact lens to even out the hues. Of course, she didn't wear it to bed.

There was a movement of the sheet, as though someone were tugging at it. Gently, Kathryn lowered the covers from

Mattie's face. Her daughter's mouth was stuffed with cloth, the white sheet bunched between her teeth.

"Mattie, please. You'll choke."

Mattie's jaws clamped down more tightly on the cloth.

Kathryn pulled gently at the material, but Mattie would not ease up. Kathryn could hear her daughter breathing hard through her nose. There were tiny tears at Mattie's lids, ready to pop and spill if she blinked. She looked at Kathryn with a mixture of pleading and anger. Kathryn could see the muscles of her daughter's face tighten and loosen.

Slowly, Kathryn began once more to pull at the sheet. Mattie suddenly opened her mouth and yanked the sheet out herself.

"This sucks," she said when she could breathe.

Mattie was in the shower. Julia, who was wearing a short red-plaid bathrobe over a nightgown that predated the Carter administration, was at the stove. It was Julia's belief that being tired of an article of clothing wasn't a good enough reason to buy a new one. Another unwritten rule was that if you hadn't worn a certain dress within a year, you should give it away.

She looked tired, and her skin was chalky. Kathryn was surprised to see — or perhaps only to notice for the first time — a thickening at the top of Julia's spine that caused her head and shoulders to bend just slightly forward.

"Robert's still at the inn?" Julia asked, her back a soft barrel of red plaid.

"No," Kathryn said quickly, not wanting to think about Robert and what he had said or hadn't said. "He stayed at the inn last night, but he's at the house now."

She put her mug of coffee on the wooden table, which had an

oilcloth cover stretched tight against it, folded and fastened underneath with thumbtacks. Over the years, the colors of the oilcloths had changed — from red to blue to green — but not the clean, tight surface, the feel of the wavy threads beneath her fingers.

Julia set a plate of scrambled eggs and toast before Kathryn.

"I can't," Kathryn said.

"Eat them. You need it."

"My stomach . . ."

"You're no good to Mattie, Kathryn, if you don't keep your strength up. You're suffering, I can see that, but you're a parent to that girl, and that's your job, whether you like it or not."

There was a long silence.

"Excuse me?" Kathryn said.

Julia sat down. "I'm sorry," she said. "My nerves are shot."

"There's something you need to know," Kathryn said quickly.

Julia looked at Kathryn.

"There's a rumor. It's wild. It's awful."

"What?"

"Do you know what a CVR is?"

Julia's head swiveled abruptly toward the doorway. Mattie was standing at the threshold, as if not sure what to do next, as if she had forgotten how to be. Her hair had soaked the shoulders of a blue sweatshirt that was cropped just short of her waistline. With it, she had on jeans (size two, slim) that she wore low over her Adidas, the hem frayed just so. Her feet naturally turned inward, which gave her, from the waist down, a childlike stance that contrasted startlingly at times with her cool upper-body posture. She put the tips of her fingers into the top slits of her front pockets and drew her shoulders up. Her eyes were reddened from crying. She tossed her head so that all of her hair fell momentarily to one side. Her upper lip trembled. Nervously, she reached up and folded her hair into a quick knot, and then let it go again.

"Hey, what's up?" Mattie asked bravely, looking at the floor.

Kathryn had to turn away. She didn't want Mattie to see the tears that had sprung to her eyes.

"Mattie," she said when she could speak. "Come sit here by me and have some eggs and toast. You hardly ate anything yesterday."

"I'm not hungry."

Mattie pulled out a chair — the chair, as it happened, farthest from her mother's — and sat gingerly at its edge, her shoulders slightly hunched, her hands folded in her lap, her feet making a V pattern on the floor.

"Please, Mattie," she said.

"*Mom*, I'm not hungry, OK? Back off."

Julia looked about to speak to Mattie, but Kathryn caught her eye and shook her head.

"Whatever," Kathryn said in as offhand a voice as she could muster.

"Well, maybe toast," Mattie conceded.

Julia fixed Mattie a plate of toast and a cup of tea. Mattie tore minute pieces of the toast crust off — pieces only as big as white-bread communion offerings — and chewed each slowly and unenthusiastically until she had made the toast crustless, at which point she set it down.

"Am I going to go to school?" Mattie asked.

"Not till after vacation," Kathryn said.

Mattie's face was pale, drawn, the skin gone a grainy white, as though she were operating on only half power. Between her eyes and at the edges of her nostrils were tiny little pimples on bits of reddened skin. She sat hunched over the now unframed toast, pondering the unappetizing cold square on the plate.

"Let's go for a walk," Kathryn said.

Mattie shrugged. The one-shoulder shrug — more dismissive than the two-shoulder shrug.

On the kitchen door, up behind Mattie, was a quilted Christmas tree that had been bought at a church Christmas fair years ago and was taken out of its box in the attic each year in early December. Julia didn't put a lot of decorations up, but she was resolutely faithful: Whatever had been out the year before came out again.

Christmas. A subject Kathryn didn't want to think about hovered at the edges of her brain, like a dull headache.

She stood up.

"Put your jacket on," she said to Mattie.

The cold cleared her head, made her body want to move faster. Beyond the stone house, the road became a dirt path and wound up Ely Mountain. It was a modest slope, a graceful landscape of dark pines, abandoned apple orchards, and fields of blueberry bushes. In the late 1980s, a developer had thought to build a set of luxury condos near the summit, and had even cleared a portion of the land and dug a foundation. But the man's timing had been disastrous, and he'd had to declare bankruptcy six months into a recession that had blanketed and nearly smothered all of New Hampshire. Low scrub now filled the vacant lot, but the abandoned foundation, with its first layer of flooring, gave a stunning view of Ely and Ely Falls to the west, and indeed of the entire valley.

Mattie wasn't wearing a hat. She walked with her fists pushed hard into the pockets of her shiny black quilted jacket, which was unzipped. Kathryn had long ago given up telling Mattie to zip up her jacket or put on a hat. Sometimes, when Kathryn walked out of the high school after work, she would be amazed to see the girls standing at the curb in forty-degree weather with only unbuttoned flannel shirts over their T-shirts.

"Mom, there's Christmas," Mattie said.

"I know."

"What are we going to do?"

"What do you want to do?"

"Not do it. I don't know. Do it, I guess. I don't know."

"Why don't we just wait a few days and see."

"Oh, Mom!"

Mattie stopped short, dug the heels of her hands into her eyes and began to shake uncontrollably. Kathryn put her arms around Mattie, but she wrenched herself away from her mother.

"Oh, God. Mom. Last night when I got out his present . . ."

Mattie was crying hard now. Kathryn sensed that her daughter was too raw, too flayed to be touched again, a hair's breadth from spiraling herself into a frenzy.

Kathryn shut her eyes and waited. She counted slowly to herself, the way she did when she barked her shin on the open dishwasher or shut a window on a finger. One, two, three, four. One, two, three, four. When Kathryn heard the crying subside a bit, she opened her eyes. She nudged her daughter forward, like a sheepdog might a sheep or a cow. Mattie was too dazed to resist.

Kathryn handed Mattie a Kleenex and waited for the girl to blow her nose.

"I got him a CD," Mattie said. "Stone Temple Pilots. He said he wanted it."

The leaves and frozen snow made a complicated matting at the sides of the dirt path. The ground was hard with ruts.

"Mom, let's not do it at home, OK? I don't think I could stand it if we did it at home."

"We'll do Christmas at Julia's," Kathryn said.

"Are we going to have a funeral?"

Kathryn tried to keep pace with Mattie, who was walking fast, her questions like puffs of steam escaping from her mouth. Kathryn thought that Mattie had probably been asking herself these questions all night and now finally had the courage to voice them.

But Kathryn didn't know how to answer the last question. If you didn't have a body, could you have a funeral, or was it called a memorial service? And if you had a memorial service, was it best to have it right away, or wait a bit? And what happened if you had a memorial service and then, a week later, the body was found?

"I don't know," Kathryn said truthfully. "I need to talk to . . ."

She almost said Robert, but caught herself in time.

"Julia," Kathryn said.

Although, surprisingly, it was Robert Kathryn wanted to ask.

"Do I have to go?" Mattie asked.

Kathryn thought a minute.

"Yes, you should," she said. "It's hard, I know; it's awful, Mattie, but they say it's better to experience the funeral of a loved one than not. It's a kind of closure. You're old enough to do that now. If you were younger, I'd say no."

"I don't want to close anything, Mom. I can't do that. I have to keep it open as long as I can."

Kathryn knew precisely what her daughter meant. Yet Kathryn also felt she should do for Mattie what Julia had done for her. When were you supposed to stop being a rational parent, Kathryn wondered, and admit to being just as bewildered as your child?

"He's not coming back, Mattie."

Mattie took her hands out of her pockets, folded her arms across her chest, and made her hands into fists.

"How do you know that, Mom? How can you be so absolutely sure?"

"Robert Hart said there were no survivors. That no one could have survived the explosion."

"What's he know?"

It wasn't a question.

They walked in silence for a distance. Mattie began swinging her arms hard, increasing her speed. Kathryn tried for a minute to keep up with her and then realized she wasn't supposed to. That was the point.

Kathryn watched Mattie walk faster and faster until the girl broke into a run and turned a corner so that she could no longer be seen.

Kathryn had no idea how they would all survive Christmas, only seven days away. An accident had occurred that had thrown their universe off kilter, so that they were spinning in a foreign orbit now — one adjacent to, but different from, that of others around them.

Kathryn found Mattie sitting on the cement wall of the low foundation, breathing hard, the way she did after a field hockey game. She looked up at her mother.

"I'm sorry, Mom."

Kathryn gazed out at the view. That, at least, was still the same. Behind them, to the east, was the Atlantic. If they were to walk farther up the hill to its actual summit, they would be able to see the ocean. Almost certainly smell it.

"Let's declare a moratorium on apologies for a while, OK?" Kathryn said.

"We'll be all right, won't we, Mom?"

Kathryn sat down beside her daughter, put her arm around her. Mattie laid her head on Kathryn's shoulder.

"Eventually," Kathryn said.

Mattie toed the snow. "I know this is hard for you, too, Mom. You really loved him, didn't you?"

"Yes, I did."

"Once I saw this documentary? On penguins? Do you know about them?"

"Not much," Kathryn said.

Mattie sat up. Her face was suddenly animated and flushed. Kathryn slid her arm from her daughter's shoulder.

"Well, what they do is, the male picks out one female from all the others, and sometimes there are hundreds; I don't know how he can tell the difference, they all look just alike. And then when he's picked her out, he goes and finds five smooth stones and, one by one, lays them at her feet. And if she likes him, she'll accept the stones, and they'll be mates for life."

"That's sweet," Kathryn said.

"And later, after the documentary, we went to the aquarium, when we went to Boston with our class. And the penguins — oh, Mom, it was so great — these penguins were, like, mating? And the male, he just covered the female, like he was a blanket lying on her, and then he quivered a bit and flopped down beside her, and they both looked exhausted, but kind of like happy? They nuzzled each other's face and neck, like they were in love. And this guy beside me, Dennis Rollins, what a jerk, you don't know him, kept making all these weird jokes. That part sucked."

Kathryn stroked her daughter's hair. This seemed a giddiness very close to tears.

"You know, Mom, I've done it."

Kathryn's hand stopped in its path down the graceful curve of Mattie's head.

"Are we talking about what I think we're talking about?" Kathryn asked quietly.

"Are you mad?"

"Mad?"

Kathryn shook her head, dazed. She slowly closed her mouth.

She didn't know which she was more surprised by — Mattie's admission or the ease with which she had made it.

"When?" Kathryn asked.

"Last year."

"Last year?"

Kathryn was stunned. This had happened a year ago, and she hadn't known?

"Remember Tommy?" Mattie asked.

Kathryn blinked. Tommy Arsenault, as she recalled, was a cute, brown-haired boy with a sullen attitude.

"You were only fourteen," Kathryn said incredulously.

"Barely fourteen," Mattie said, as if it were a badge of honor to have had sex so young, nearly thirteen.

"But why?" Kathryn asked, already knowing the question was ridiculous.

"You're upset, I can tell."

"No. No. I'm not upset. I'm just . . . I'm just surprised, I guess."

"I just wanted to try it," Mattie said.

Kathryn felt light-headed. The view was bothering her. She

shut her eyes. Mattie had gotten her period late, just last December, and to Kathryn's knowledge, she had had only three of them since. She may not even have been sexually mature when it happened.

"Once?" Kathryn asked, unable to suppress a note of hope.

Mattie hesitated, as though frequency were a subject too intimate to discuss with one's mother.

"No, a few times."

Kathryn was silent.

"It's fine, Mom. I'm fine about it. I didn't love him or anything. But I wanted to find out what it was like, and I did."

"Did it hurt?"

"At first. But then I liked it."

"And you were careful?"

"Of course, Mom. What do you think, I'm going to take chances?"

As if the sex itself weren't chance enough.

"I don't know what to think."

Mattie tied her hair into a knot at the nape of her neck.

"What about Jason?" Kathryn asked, referring to her current boyfriend. Of all of Mattie's friends, Jason, a tall blond boy who was addicted to basketball, was the only one who had been brave enough to call yesterday to see if Mattie was all right.

"No, we don't. He's kind of religious? He says he can't. Which is fine with me. I'm not putting any pressure on him or anything."

"Good," Kathryn managed to say.

For all of Mattie's girlhood, Kathryn had imagined this moment, had hoped, as mothers do, that her daughter would discover sex in combination with love. What dialogue had she written in her mind for the event? Certainly not this.

Mattie gave her a hug.

"Poor Mom," she said.

Her tone was mocking but affectionate.

"Did you know," Kathryn asked, "that in the 1700s in Norway, any woman who was discovered to have had premarital sex was beheaded, her head put on a pike, and her body buried at the site of the beheading?"

Mattie looked at her mother the way Kathryn imagined she might do if Kathryn had just had a stroke.

"Mom?"

"Just a bit of historical detail," Kathryn said. "I'm glad you told me."

"I wanted to before, but I thought . . ."

Mattie bit her lip hard.

"Well, I thought you'd be upset, and I know you'd probably have to tell Daddy."

Her voice quavered at the mention of her father.

"You're sure you're not mad?" Mattie asked again.

"Mad? No. Mad has nothing to do with it. It's just that . . . it's an important part of life, Mattie. It does mean something. It is special. I do believe this."

Kathryn could hear the platitudes. Was sex special? Did it mean something? Or was it just a natural act, performed billions of times a day all over the world in a dizzying number of ways, some of them monstrous? She didn't know what she thought on the subject, and she wondered how often it was that parents were trapped into pronouncing sentiments they did not actually believe.

"I know that now," Mattie said. "I just had to get it out of the way."

She took Kathryn's hand. Mattie's fingers were freezing.

"Just think about the penguins," Kathryn said lamely.

Mattie laughed.

"Mom, you're weird."

"We knew that."

They stood up.

"Mattie, listen."

Kathryn turned to her daughter. She wanted to tell Mattie about the rumors now, about the terrible stories Mattie would almost certainly hear. But when Kathryn pulled Mattie's face up to her own and saw the hurt that lingered there, she couldn't do it. Robert had said that Kathryn must absolutely refuse to credit the rumors. So why bother Mattie with them? she rationalized. Even so, she felt a small twinge of parental guilt, the same sort of twinge she felt whenever she backed away from a difficult task.

"I love you, Mattie," Kathryn said. "You have no idea how much I love you."

"Oh, Mom, the worst part . . ."

"What?" Kathryn asked, pulling away from her daughter and bracing for another revelation.

"That morning, before Daddy left? He came into my room and asked me if I wanted to go to a Celtics game with him on Friday when he got back. And I was in a bad mood, and I wanted to see what Jason was doing on Friday first, and so I said couldn't we just wait and see? And I think . . . Oh, I know he was. He was hurt, Mom. You could see it on his face."

Mattie's mouth began to contort. She looked considerably younger when she cried, Kathryn thought. Still a child.

How could Kathryn explain to her that such rebuffs happened all the time? Parents got hurt and swallowed it and watched their children leave them, incrementally at first, and then with head-spinning rapidity.

"He understood," Kathryn said, lying. "He did. Really. He told me before he left."

"He did?"

"He made a joke about how he was second-string now, but really, he was fine about it. When he jokes about something, it means he's OK."

"Really?"

"Yes, really."

Kathryn nodded her head vigorously, willing her daughter to believe her.

Mattie sniffed. Wiped her upper lip with the back of her hand.

"You have another Kleenex?" she asked.

Kathryn gave her one.

"I've cried so much," Mattie said. "I think my head is going to blow up."

"I know the feeling," Kathryn said.

Julia was sitting at the table when they returned. She had made hot chocolate for them both, which seemed to please Mattie. As Kathryn gingerly sipped the hot liquid, she noticed that the bottom lids of Julia's eyes were reddened, and she was suddenly frightened at the thought of her grandmother crying all alone in her kitchen.

"Robert called," Julia said.

Kathryn looked up, and Julia nodded.

"I'll call him from your bedroom," Kathryn said.

Julia's room was, oddly, the smallest bedroom in the house. She had always maintained that she didn't need much space. There was only her own single body in the bed, and she had always lived by the philosophy that less is more. But it was not without charm, a kind of feminine charm that Kathryn associated with women of that generation. Long pleated chintz drapes, an upholstered chair in a peach silk stripe, a pink chenille bedspread, and an item Kathryn hardly ever saw anymore — a dressing table with a skirt. Kathryn had often tried to imagine Julia at that table as a young woman, fixing her long dark hair, perhaps with thoughts of her husband and of the evening to come.

The phone was on the dressing table. A voice Kathryn did not recognize answered on the first ring.

"May I speak to Robert Hart?" she asked.

"Who's calling?"

"Kathryn Lyons."

"Just a minute," the voice said.

She could hear other voices in the background, male voices. She pictured her kitchen filled with men in suits.

"Kathryn."

"What is it?"

"Are you all right?"

"I'm OK."

"I told your grandmother."

"I thought you might have."

"I'm coming to get you."

"That's ridiculous. I have a car."

"Leave it there."

"Why? What's happening?"

"I need directions."

"Robert."

"There are people here who want to ask you some questions. I think you and I should talk first. Also, you don't want them at Julia's house. Not with your daughter there."

"Robert, you're scaring me."

"It's OK. I'll be right here with you."

Kathryn gave him the directions.

"Robert, what questions?"

There was a short silence at the other end of the line. It seemed to her that the silence was absolute, that all the voices in her distant kitchen were suddenly quiet.

"I'll be there in five minutes," he said.

Mattie was blowing on her hot chocolate when Kathryn walked back into the kitchen.

"I have to go," Kathryn said. "There are some people at the house I need to talk to. From the airline."

"OK," Mattie said.

"I'll call you," Kathryn said, bending to kiss her daughter.

Kathryn stood, in her parka, at the bottom of the drive. She had her hands in her pockets, her collar up. A bright, hard, dry cold without wind had settled in for the day. Normally, this was her favorite kind of weather.

She saw the car in the distance, a gray shape moving rapidly along the road from town. Robert pulled up quickly, leaned over, and opened the door.

She sat facing him with her back pressed against the door handle. In the harsh sunlight, she could see the smallest details of Robert's face: the faintly bluish outline where a beard might have grown if he hadn't shaved, the white ghost of skin below his sideburns where the hair was cut shorter than an old tan line, the under-shadow of his jaw. He put the car in park and turned toward her, laying his arm, like a bridge, between the two front seats.

"What?" she asked.

"There are two investigators from the Safety Board who want to talk to you."

"In my house?"

"Yes."

"Do I have to answer their questions?"

He looked away, toward the stone house, and then back again. He scratched his upper lip with his thumbnail.

"Yes," he said carefully. "If you're well enough. You could always be not well enough, I suppose."

She nodded slowly.

"I can't protect you from the crash investigation itself. Or from legal proceedings."

"Legal proceedings?"

"In the event . . ."

"I thought this was just a wild rumor."

"It is. At the moment."

"Why? What do you know? What is on the tape?"

He tapped the bottom of the steering wheel with the fingers of his free hand. A steady rhythm, thinking.

"A British technician with the British equivalent of our Safety Board who was in the room when the tape was first played called a woman he's involved with who works at a BBC affiliate in Birmingham. He apparently made statements about the tape. I don't know for certain what his motivation was in revealing this, or hers, but we can speculate. CNN is reporting what the BBC has reported. So at best, this is fourth hand."

"But it might be true."

"It might be true."

Kathryn shifted in her seat, swinging her knee up so that she was not so twisted in the waist. She crossed her arms over her chest.

Robert removed a sheet of shiny white paper from his shirt pocket. He handed her the fax.

"This is exactly how the bulletin was read over CNN," he said.

The fax was hard to read. The square letters, some with wavery stems, swam before her. She tried to focus on a sentence, to begin from the top.

CNN has just learned that a source close to the investigation of Vision Flight 384 is reporting that the CVR — that's the cockpit voice recorder — may, and we stress may, reveal an altercation between Captain Jack Lyons, an eleven-year veteran with Vision, and British flight engineer Trevor Sullivan just moments before the explosion of the T-900. According to as yet unconfirmed statements, a malfunctioning headset caused Sullivan to reach into Captain Jack Lyons's flight bag fifty-eight minutes into the flight. The object that Sullivan then pulled out of the flight bag may, and again we stress may, have been the source of the explosion that ripped apart the T-900, sending one hundred and four passengers and crew to their deaths. In addition, the alleged source reports that the transcript of the last several seconds of Vision Flight 384 may indicate that a scuffle of some kind took place between Captain Lyons and Flight Engineer Sullivan, and that several expletives were uttered by Sullivan.

Daniel Gorzyk, a spokesperson for the Safety Board, was heated earlier today in his denial of these allegations, which he called maliciously false and irresponsible. This report, we repeat, comes from an as yet unnamed source who claims to have been present when the tape from the CVR was played. The CVR, as we

noted earlier, was located last night in the waters off Malin Head,
in the Republic of Ireland. . . .

Kathryn shut her eyes and leaned her head back against
the seat.

"What does it mean?" she asked.

Robert looked briefly at the ceiling of the car.

"First of all, we don't even know if it's true. The Safety Board
has already issued a strenuous reprimand. The source who
leaked the quotes has apparently been fired. They won't say his
name, and he hasn't come forward. And second of all, even if it
is true, it doesn't necessarily prove anything. Or even mean anything. Necessarily."

"But it does," Kathryn said. "Something happened."

"Something happened," Robert said.

"Oh, my God," she said.

SHE STARES AT THE COUNTER, AT THE GREASY pots and glasses and the caked roasting pan, at the sickening pile of rotting vegetables in the sink, at the dishwasher, which is full of clean dishes and will have to be unloaded before she can even begin to clear the counter. Upstairs, she can hear the muted tap, tap, tapping of the keyboard and then the stuttered start of an online connection.

She looks down at her wool skirt, her black tights, her sensible pumps. This afternoon, she had band practice after school and was late getting home. The three of them ate dinner in near silence — not so much from strain, she thought, as from exhaustion. Then Jack went up to his office, Mattie to her room to practice her clarinet. Kathryn was left in the kitchen.

She climbs the stairs to Jack's office and stands silently with her glass of wine, leaning against the doorjamb. She has no articulate dialogue, just truncated thoughts, unfinished sentences. Phrases of frustration.

Perhaps she has had too much to drink.

Jack looks up at her with a vaguely puzzled expression on his face. He has on a flannel shirt and jeans. He's put on weight recently, about ten pounds. He has a tendency to beefiness when he isn't careful.

— What's happening? she asks.

— What?

— I mean, you come home from a five-day trip. I've hardly seen you. You don't say a word during dinner. You hardly speak to Mattie. And then, bingo, you vanish, leaving me with all the dishes.

He seems surprised by these accusations, as, in truth, is she. He blinks. He turns his head to something that has caught his attention on the screen.

— Even now, you can't pay attention to what I'm saying. What is so goddamn interesting on the computer, anyway?

He takes his hands off the keyboard and rests his elbows on the arms of the chair.

— What is this all about? he asks.

— You, she says. — And me.

— And?

— We're not, she says. — We're just *not*. She takes a sip of wine.

— You're not there, she says. — You used to be so . . . I don't know . . . romantic. You used to compliment me all the time. I can't remember the last time you told me I was beautiful.

Her lip quivers, and she looks away. She hears her mother's voice then, wailing from the upstairs bedroom of Julia's house, and she feels sick inside. Her mother's pleading voice, begging her husband to tell her she is beautiful. Has this bit of awful dialogue been lying in wait for her? Kathryn wonders. A kind of grotesque legacy?

She shudders. But she can't leave it alone. For months now, Jack has been distant, as though not altogether there, as though constantly preoccupied. Preoccupation can be tolerated, Kathryn thinks, if it is finite.

— My God, she says, her voice rising a notch. — We haven't been out to dinner in months. All you ever do is come up here and work on the computer. Or play on the computer. Whatever you do.

He leans back in the chair.

What possible answer can any man give to the accusation that he hasn't recently told his wife that she is beautiful? she thinks to herself. That he has simply forgotten? That in fact he thinks it all the time, but just doesn't say it? That he thinks she is desperately beautiful right that very minute?

That's the problem with a fight, Kathryn decides. Even when you know the words you are saying are the worst possible utterances, there is always a point of no return. Of no backing off, no retreating. She is already there, and in a flash Jack reaches it.

— Fuck you, he says quietly, and he stands.

Kathryn flinches. She is immediately aware, as she was not before (not when it was her own righteous anger), that Mattie is just down the hall.

— Keep your voice down, Kathryn says.

Jack puts his hands on his hips. His face grows red, as it sometimes does when he is angry, which isn't often. They don't have a history of fighting.

— Fuck you, he says again. This time in a louder, though still controlled voice. — I work five days in a row without a letup. I come home to get a good night's sleep. I come up here to fool around a little on the computer to relax. And before I can even blink, you're up here complaining.

— You came home to get a good night's sleep? she asks incredulously.

— You know what I mean.

— This didn't just happen tonight, she says. — It's been happening for months now.

— Months?

— Yes.

— What exactly has been happening for months?

— You're not here. You're more interested in the computer than you are in me.

— Fuck you, he says, brushing past her toward the stairs. She hears him descend the steps as though running. She hears the refrigerator door being opened, followed by the sound of a beer can being popped.

When she gets to the kitchen, he is drinking the beer in one swallow. He sets the can down on the counter with a hard clink and stares out the kitchen window.

She examines his profile, his face, which she loves, the aggressive thrust of his neck, which alarms her. She wants to give in, to go to him and say she is sorry, to put her arms around him and tell him she loves him. But before she can move, she thinks again about the sensation of being abandoned, for that is what she means to describe, and so repentance quickly gives way to grievance. Why should she back off?

— You never talk to me anymore, she says. — I feel like I don't know you anymore.

His jaw moves slightly more forward, and he clenches his teeth. He tosses the beer can into the sink, where it clatters against all the dirty dishes.

— You want me to go? he asks, looking at her.

— Go?

— Yeah, you want to end it or what?

— No, I don't want to end it, she says, taken aback. — What are you talking about? You're crazy.

— I'm crazy?

— Yes, you're crazy. All I said was that you're getting too wrapped up in the computer, and you . . .

— I'm crazy? he repeats, this time in a louder voice.

When he brushes past her to go up the stairs, she tries to grab his arm, but he shakes her off. In the kitchen, she stands as still as a stone as she hears his angry tread on the steps, hears his office door slam, hears the muffled thudding of objects being roughly moved around on his desk, hears the snap of wires.

He's leaving her and taking the computer with him?

And then, horrified, she watches as the computer monitor comes crashing down the stairs.

The monitor gouges the plaster wall at the foot of the steps. Bits of gray plastic and smoked glass from the shattered screen fly into the air and litter the stairs and the kitchen floor. It is a spectacular smash, loud and theatrical.

Kathryn utters a low moan, knowing that it has all gone too far and that she has caused it, has goaded him.

And then she thinks of Mattie.

By the time Kathryn has made her way over the smashed monitor and gotten to the top of the stairs, Mattie is coming down the hallway in her pajamas.

— What happened? Mattie asks, although Kathryn can see that she knows. Has heard everything.

Jack looks stricken with the instant remorse that follows an insanely childish act in front of one's children.

— Mattie, Kathryn says. — Daddy dropped his computer down the stairs. It's a mess. But everything is OK.

Mattie gives them both the *look*, the one that, even though she is eleven years old, is always dead on and never misses. But Kathryn can see on her daughter's face that superior surveillance is competing ferociously with sheer horror.

Jack turns to Mattie and enfolds his daughter in his arms. That alone says everything, Kathryn thinks. There is no pretending now that this didn't happen. It is just perhaps better not to say it aloud.

And then Jack reaches out his arm and draws Kathryn into the fold, so that the three of them stand in the hallway, swaying and crying and saying I'm sorry and kissing each other and hugging again and then standing back and laughing slightly through the tears and runny noses, with Mattie offering, helpfully, to get the Kleenex.

That night, Kathryn and Jack make love as they have not done in months — with a ragged edge, as though playing out the rest of the scene with open mouths and small bites, locked thighs and pinned wrists. And the voracious momentum of that night changes, for a time, the tenor of their marriage, so that they look more often into each other's eyes as they pass in the hallway, trying mutely to say something meaningful, and kiss each other with more enthusiasm whenever they meet, in the house or outside by the cars or even, several times, in public, which pleases Kathryn. But after a while, that too passes, and she and Jack go back to normal, as they have been before, which is to say that they, like all the other couples Kathryn has ever known, live in a state of gentle decline, of being infinitesimally, but not agonizingly, less than they were the day before.

Which means, on the whole, she thinks, that it is a good marriage.

SHE HAD NEVER SEEN ANYTHING LIKE IT BEFORE—
not even on television or in movies, where a spectacle, she now
understood, lost its immediacy, its garish color, its menace.
Along the beach road, even before she and Robert had reached
the drive, there were parked cars and fat vans with their far
wheels stuck into the sandy shoulders. Kathryn saw call letters on the vans, WBZ and WNBC and CNN, a man running
with a camera and a complicated brace on his shoulder.
People were beginning to look at the car, to peer at the passengers inside. Robert sat hunched over the steering wheel,
as though at any minute they might be assaulted. Kathryn
resisted the urge to turn her head away or to bring her hands to
her face.

"Remind me why we did this?" she asked, her voice tight, her
lips barely moving.

The reporters and cameramen were five deep by the wooden
gate with its wire fencing. Jack and she had not chosen the gate;
it had simply been left over from the convent days. Indeed,

Kathryn thought it surprising the gate even worked: Jack and she had never had any reason to fasten it.

"We're sending someone over to your grandmother's," Robert said.

"Julia won't like that."

"I'm afraid Julia doesn't really have a choice at this point," Robert said. "And in the end, she may be grateful."

He gestured toward the crowd outside the car.

"They'll be all over her lawn before she can blink."

"I don't want them anywhere near Mattie," Kathryn said.

"Julia looked pretty formidable to me," Robert countered. "I'm not sure I'd want to try to get past her."

A man banged hard against the passenger door window, and Kathryn flinched. Robert moved the car forward, trying to get as close to the gate as he could. He peered through the windshield, looking for a policeman, and almost immediately, the car was engulfed, men and women shouting through the glass.

"Mrs. Lyons, have you heard the tape?"

"Is that her? Wally, is that her?"

"Move, get her face."

"Can you comment, Mrs. Lyons? Do you think it was suicide?"

"Who's the guy with her? Jerry, is he from the airline?"

"Mrs. Lyons, how do you explain . . . ?"

To Kathryn, the voices sounded like dogs barking. Mouths appeared magnified and watery, the colors around her heightening and then subduing themselves. She wondered briefly if she was fainting. How could she possibly be the focus of so much attention, she who had lived the most ordinary of lives under the most ordinary of circumstances?

"Jesus Christ," Robert said when a camera lens banged sharply against his window. "That guy just broke his camera."

Sitting taller to see beyond the crowd, Kathryn spotted Burt Sears, a long, spindly man, stooped with years, pacing behind the gate. He had only the top half of his uniform on, as if he hadn't been able to find the rest of it in his hurry to get out of the house. Kathryn waved through the windshield, trying to catch his attention, but Burt seemed shocky, his eyes unfocused, as helpless on his side of the gate as they were on theirs. He moved his hands in a slow, unconfident circle, as though he were directing traffic and weren't particularly good at it.

"It's Burt," she said. "He's on the other side of the gate. He's retired, but he's been called back for this."

"You drive," Robert said. "Lock the door after me. What's his last name?"

"Sears."

With one fluid motion, so swift it was over before it had registered, Robert stepped out of the car and slammed the door. Kathryn slid awkwardly over the gearshift into the driver's seat and locked the door. She watched Robert put his hands into the pockets of his topcoat and shoulder his way through the reporters and cameramen. He yelled *Burt Sears* so loudly that everyone stopped for a moment to look at the man separating the crowd. Kathryn began to move the car forward into the vacuum Robert created as he walked.

What would happen, she wondered, if the wall of people in front of her simply refused to part?

She watched Robert unfasten the gate. Everywhere she glanced there were cameras, women in suits, men in brightly colored windbreakers, and still she inched forward, urged toward the gate by Robert's insistent hand. She worried for a moment that the crowd might simply go with her, move with her to the house like a cortege — a grotesque cortege with the widow trapped inside the car, a beetle under glass. But an unwritten law, one she hadn't known about and didn't quite understand, halted the crowd behind the gate when it easily might have overwhelmed Burt and Robert. Once inside the gate, she stopped.

"Go," Robert said, slipping into the passenger seat.

With shaking hands, she put the car in drive and began to inch forward.

"No, I mean *move*," Robert said brusquely.

She had thought, when she first saw the throng in front of the gate, that her house would be a refuge if only Robert and she could reach it. But she quickly realized that that would not be the case. Four cars she hadn't seen before were parked in the driveway, one haphazardly, with its door still open, a bell dinging from inside. Four cars meant at least that many strangers.

She turned off the engine.

"You don't have to do this now," he said.

"But I'll have to do it sometime," she said.

"Possibly."

"Shouldn't I have a lawyer?"

"The union's taking care of it." He put his hand on her shoulder. "Just don't give these guys any answers you're not absolutely sure of."

"I'm not sure of anything," she said.

They were in her kitchen and in the front room, men in black uniforms and dark suits, Rita from yesterday in pale gray. A large man with oval wire-rimmed glasses and excessively gelled hair

came forward to greet Kathryn first. His collar, she noticed, cut
into his neck, and his face was flushed. He waddled somewhat,
in the way of heavy men, leading with his stomach.

"Mrs. Lyons," he said, holding out a hand. "Dick Somers."

She let him take her hand. His grip was tentative and damp.
The phone rang, and she was glad Robert didn't leave her to
answer it.

"From?" Kathryn asked.

"I'm an investigator with the Safety Board. Let me say how
very sorry I am, we all are, for your terrible loss."

Kathryn could hear a low, steady male voice on a television in
another room.

"Thank you," she said.

"I know this is a difficult time for you and your daughter," he
added.

Her face must have registered wariness at the word *daughter,*
for she saw him make a quick scan of her features.

"But I do have to ask you some questions," he said.

There were Styrofoam coffee cups on the kitchen counter,
and two bright pink Dunkin' Donuts boxes on the table. Kathryn
had a sudden and powerful craving for a donut, a plain donut
dipped in hot coffee, disintegrating from the coffee as she
brought it to her mouth. She remembered she hadn't eaten anything for more than thirty-six hours.

"My colleague, Henry Boyd," Somers said, introducing a
younger man with a blond mustache.

She shook the colleague's hand.

Four other men came forward to be introduced now, men in
Vision uniforms, with their caps tucked under their arms, the
uniform, with its gold buttons and braid, its familiarity, causing
Kathryn to catch her breath. They were from the airline, from

the chief pilot's office, they said, and Kathryn thought how strange these greetings were, these niceties, these condolences, these cautious condolences, when all about them there was the palpable strain of waiting.

A man with iron-filing hair stepped more forward than the rest.

"Mrs. Lyons, I'm Chief Pilot Bill Tierney," he said. "We talked on the phone briefly yesterday."

"Yes," she said.

"Let me once again express for myself and for the entire airline how deeply sorry we are for the loss of your husband, for your personal loss. He was an excellent pilot, one of our best."

"Thank you," she said.

The words *how deeply sorry* seemed to float on the air in the kitchen. She wondered why all the expressions of sympathy sounded so tired, so very much the same. Was there no other language with which to express one's sorrow? Or was the formality the point? She thought about how many times the chief pilot must have imagined himself saying these very words to the widow of one of his pilots, perhaps even practiced saying the words aloud. The newish airline had never had a fatal crash before.

"What can you tell me about the tape?" she asked the chief pilot.

Tierney pursed his lips and shook his head.

"No information about the tape has been officially released," said Somers, stepping forward.

"I understand that," Kathryn said, turning to the investigator. "But you *know* something, don't you? You *know* what's on the tape."

"No, I'm afraid I don't," he said.

But behind the wire-rimmed glasses, the investigator's glance was skittish and evasive.

Kathryn stood in the center of her kitchen, in her boots and jeans and jacket, the subject of intense scrutiny. She felt vaguely embarrassed, as if she had committed a grievous social error.

"One of you left your car door open," she said, gesturing toward the driveway.

"Why don't we go sit in your living room?" Somers suggested.

Feeling unfamiliar with her own house, Kathryn walked into the front room and squinted at the six oblongs of diffuse light from the windows. There was only one seat left, an oversized wing chair facing the windows, Jack's chair, not hers, and she felt dwarfed by the chair's upholstered appendages. The television, she noticed now, had been turned off.

Somers appeared to be in charge. He stood while the others sat.

"I'm just going to ask you one or two questions," he said, putting his hands into his trouser pockets. "This won't take a minute. Can you tell us anything about how your husband was behaving just prior to his departure for the airport on Sunday?"

Kathryn saw that no one had a tape recorder out or was writing anything down. Somers seemed almost excessively casual. This couldn't be official, then, could it?

"There's not a lot to tell," she said. "It was routine. Jack took a shower around four in the afternoon, got dressed in his uniform, came downstairs, and shined his shoes."

"And where were you?"

"I joined him in the kitchen. To say good-bye."

The word *good-bye* triggered a quick jolt of sadness, and she bit her lip. She tried to remember Sunday, the last day Jack had been home. Occasionally, she had fragments, dream bits, like the fluttering glints of silver in the dark. It seemed to her that it had been an ordinary day, nothing special about it. She could see Jack's foot on the pulled-out drawer, the old green-checked rag in his hands as she passed through the kitchen on the way to the laundry room. The length of his arms, lengthened even more by the weight of his bags as he walked to the car in the driveway. He'd said something over his shoulder. She'd had the rag in her hand. *Don't forget to call Alfred*, he'd said. *And tell him Friday.*

He'd shined his shoes. He'd left the house. He would be home, he said, on Tuesday. She was freezing in the doorway, slightly annoyed he hadn't done it himself. Called Alfred.

"To your knowledge, did Jack call anyone that day?" Somers asked. "Talk to anyone?"

"I have no idea," she said.

She wondered: Could Jack have talked to someone that day? Of course he could have. He could have talked to twenty people for all she knew.

Robert had his arms crossed over his chest. He seemed to be studying the coffee table with great interest. On the table were art books, a stone plate Jack and she had brought back from Kenya, an enameled box from Spain.

"Mrs. Lyons," Somers continued. "Did your husband seem agitated or depressed that day or the night before?"

"No," she said. "Nothing out of the ordinary. The shower was leaking, I remember, and he was a bit annoyed at that, since we'd only recently had it repaired. I remember he said to call Alfred."

"Alfred is?"

"Alfred Zacharian. The plumber."

"And when did he ask you to call Alfred?"

"Twice, actually. Once upstairs about ten minutes before he left. And again as he was walking to the car."

"Did Jack have a drink prior to his departing for the airport?"

"Don't answer that," Robert said, sitting forward on the sofa.

Kathryn crossed her legs and thought about the wine Jack and she had had with dinner on Saturday night and had continued to have after dinner, and she quickly calculated the number of hours between his last drink and his flight. At least eighteen. That was all right then. What was the phrase? Twelve hours from bottle to throttle?

"It's all right," she said to Robert. "Nothing," she said to Somers.

"Nothing at all?"

"Nothing at all."

"Did you pack his suitcase?" he asked.

"No, I never do."

"Or his flight bag?"

"No. Absolutely not. I virtually never looked in there."

"Do you usually unpack his suitcase?"

"No. That's Jack's responsibility. He takes care of his own bags."

She heard the words, *takes care of*. Present tense.

She looked around at the men in the room, all of whom were examining her intently. She wondered if the airline would want to question her, too. Perhaps she ought to have a lawyer with her right now, she thought. But if that were true, wouldn't Robert have said so?

"Did your husband have any close friends in the U.K.?" Somers asked. "Did he regularly talk to someone there?"

"The U.K.?"

"England."

"I know what U.K. means," she said. "I just don't understand the relevance of the question. He knew a lot of people in the U.K. He flew with them."

"Have you noticed any unusual withdrawals from or deposits into any of your bank accounts?" Somers asked.

She wondered where they were going with this, what any of it meant. She felt herself to be on shifting ground, as though at any moment she might step unthinkingly into a crevice.

"I don't understand," she began.

"In the last several weeks, or at any time, have you noticed any unusual withdrawals from or deposits into your bank accounts?"

"No."

"In the last several weeks did you notice any unusual behavior in your husband?"

She had to answer this one, for Jack's sake. She wanted to answer it.

"No," she said.

"Nothing out of the ordinary?"

"Nothing."

Rita, from the airline, stepped into the room, and the men looked up at her. Beneath her suit, she had on a jewel-necked silk blouse. Kathryn couldn't remember the last time she herself had worn a suit. At school, she almost always wore pants and a sweater, sometimes a jacket, occasionally jeans and boots when the weather was bad.

"Mrs. Lyons?" Rita said. "Your daughter is on the phone. She says she has to talk to you right now."

Alarmed, Kathryn spun out of the chair and followed Rita into the kitchen. She glanced at the clock over the sink: 9:14.

"Mattie," she said, picking the phone up from the counter.

"Mom?"

"What is it? Is everything OK?"

"Mom, I called Taylor. Just to talk to someone. And she was acting funny?"

Mattie's voice was tight and high, a tone Kathryn knew from previous experience indicated strenuous control over imminent hysteria. Kathryn shut her eyes and pressed her forehead to the cabinet.

"And so I asked her what it was," Mattie said, "and Taylor said it's in the news about its being suicide?"

Kathryn could picture Mattie's face at the other end of the line, the eyes uncertain and wide and panicky. Kathryn could imagine how the news would have bruised Mattie, how her daughter must have hated hearing about the rumor from Taylor. How Taylor, being a normal teenage girl, would have been slightly puffed up to be the one to break the news to Mattie. How Taylor would then feel compelled to call all of their mutual friends with a detailed description of Mattie's reaction.

"Oh, Mattie," Kathryn said. "It's just a rumor. The news media, they get an idea and they go with it before they've even checked it out. It's awful. It's irresponsible. And it isn't true. It absolutely isn't true. I'm here with the airline safety board, and they would know, and they're denying the rumor very strongly."

There was a silence.

"But, Mom," Mattie said. "What if it is true?"

"It's not true."

"How would you know?"

Kathryn heard the note of anger in her daughter's voice. Unmistakable. Why hadn't she told Mattie the truth that morning during their walk?

"I just know," Kathryn said.

There was another silence.

"It's probably true," Mattie said.

"Mattie, you *knew* your father."

"Maybe."

"What does that mean?"

"Maybe I didn't know him," Mattie said. "Maybe he was unhappy."

"If your father was unhappy, I'd have known."

"But how do you ever know that you know a person?" she asked.

The query momentarily stopped the volley of questions and answers between them, allowing a wave of uncertainty to rise up in front of Kathryn. But she knew that Mattie didn't want uncertainty now, however much she might have been challenging her mother. Kathryn was sure of this.

"You feel it," Kathryn said with more bravado than conviction.

"Do you feel that you know me?" Mattie asked.

"Pretty well," Kathryn said.

And then Kathryn realized that she had fallen into a trap. Mattie was good at this, always had been.

"Well, you *don't*," Mattie said with a mixture of satisfaction and dread. "Half the time you have no idea what I'm thinking."

"OK," Kathryn said, backing off, conceding. "But that's different."

"No, it's not."

Kathryn brought the heel of her hand to her forehead, massaged it.

"Mom, if it's true, does that mean that Daddy murdered all those people? Would it be murder?"

"Where did you hear the word?" Kathryn asked quickly, as if Mattie were a child who had just uttered an obscenity she'd learned at school or from a friend. Yet the word *was* profane, Kathryn thought. It was appalling. More appalling for coming from the mouth of her fifteen-year-old daughter.

"I didn't hear it anywhere, Mom. But I can think, can't I?"

"Look, Mattie. Just hang on. I'll be right there."

"No, Mom. Don't come here. I don't want you to come. I don't want you to come here and try to tell me a lot of lies to make things better. Because I don't want lies right now. It can't be made better, and I don't want to pretend. I just want to be left alone."

How did a fifteen-year-old girl come by such unflinching honesty? Kathryn wondered. The truth was more than most adults could tolerate. Perhaps the young were better at reality, she decided, having had less time to dissemble, create fictions.

Kathryn stifled the impulse to raise her voice, to simply overpower her daughter's fears and doubts, but she knew from experience not to press Mattie now.

"Mom, there are men here," Mattie said. "Strange men. All over the place."

"I know, Mattie. They're security men to keep the press and public away from the house."

"You think strangers would want to get in?"

Kathryn didn't want to frighten her daughter any more than was necessary.

"No, I don't," Kathryn said. "But the press can be a nuisance. Look, just sit tight. I'll be there in just a little while."

"Fine," Mattie said tonelessly.

Kathryn stood a minute at the counter with the phone in her hand, regretting the severed connection. She considered calling Mattie back immediately, trying to calm her down, but Kathryn knew that such an effort would be futile. Dealing with a fifteen-year-old, she had learned, sometimes required appeasement. Kathryn hung up the phone and walked to the threshold of the front room. She leaned against the door frame. She crossed her arms over her chest and studied the assembly of investigators and pilots.

There was a question on Robert's face.

"Everything all right, Mrs. Lyons?" Somers from the Safety Board asked.

"Just fine," Kathryn answered. "Just fine. That's apart from the fact that my daughter is struggling to absorb the idea that her father may have committed suicide and taken a hundred and three people with him."

"Mrs. Lyons . . ."

"May I be permitted to ask you a question, Mr. Somers?"

Kathryn heard the anger in her voice, a good mimic of her daughter's. Perhaps anger was contagious, Kathryn thought.

"Yes, of course," the investigator said warily.

"What other scenarios besides suicide have you imagined, given the material that is theoretically on the CVR?"

Somers looked discomfited. "I'm not at liberty to discuss that just now, Mrs. Lyons."

Kathryn uncrossed her arms, folded her hands in front of her.

"Oh, really?" she asked quietly.

She looked down at her feet, then up at the faces in her living room. They were backlit, haloed by the light from the windows.

"Then I guess I'm not at liberty *just now* to answer your questions," she said.

Robert stood up.

"This interview is over," she said.

———

Walking blindly across the lawn, her head down against the wind, she made wispy footprints in the frost gauze of the grass. Within minutes, she was at the seawall, the granite boulders slick with sea spit. She hopped onto a stone the size of a bathtub, felt herself slipping, then sensed that the only way to stay upright was to keep moving, alighting briefly on each rock and then springing to the next. In this way, she reached the "flat rock," so dubbed by Mattie when she was five and first able to negotiate the rocky sea border. Thereafter, the flat rock became a favored picnic spot for the two of them on sunny days. Kathryn jumped off the edge of the rock onto a five-foot square of sandy beach nestled among the boulders — an outdoor room, a partial shelter from the wind, a hiding place. She turned her back to the house and sat down on the wet sand. She slid her arms out of their sleeves and hugged her chest inside her zippered parka.

"Shit," she said to her feet.

She let the white noise of the water fill her head, pushing away the voices and faces from the house, faces with thin veils of sympathy over features marked by intense ambition, faces with solemn mouths below keen eyes. Kathryn listened to the soft click of pebbles tumbling in the receding waves. In the pebbles, there was a memory, flirting with her, teasing her. She shut her eyes and tried to concentrate, then gave it up, and in the moment of giving up, found it. A memory of her father and her sitting on pebbles in their bathing suits and letting the sea rush beneath them and wobble the small stones under their thighs and calves. It was summer, a hot day, and she was perhaps nine or ten years old. They were at Fortune's Rocks, she remembered, and the pebbles tickled her skin. But why were she and her father at the beach without her mother or Julia? Perhaps

Kathryn remembered this moment because it was such a rare occurrence, her father and her alone together. He was laughing, she recalled, laughing with genuine, unalloyed pleasure, as a child might do, as he so seldom did. And she thought she would join him in this laughter and just let herself go, but she was so overcome by the sight of her father happy — happy in her presence — that she felt more reverent than uninhibited and, as a result, became confused. And when he turned to ask her what was wrong, she had the distinct sense that she had disappointed him. And so she had laughed then, too, too loudly, too earnestly, hoping he'd forget the disappointment, but the moment was over, and already he was staring out to sea. She remembered the way her laughter had sounded hollow and contrived, and the way her father had turned away from her, already lost in his own reveries, so much so that Kathryn had had to call to him to get his attention.

Kathryn drew curlicues in the wet sand. It was one of the things she and Jack had had in common, she thought: They were orphans. Not true orphans, precisely, and not for their entire childhoods, but as good as, both of them abandoned when they were too young to know what was happening to them. In Jack's case, his being orphaned had happened in a more conventional way. His mother had died when he was nine, and his father, who had never been an emotionally demonstrative man, apparently withdrew so far into himself when his wife died that Jack had always had the distinct feeling that he was on his own. In Kathryn's case, her parents had been physically present but emotionally absent, and had not even been able to provide the simple rudiments of a child's care. For nearly all of her childhood, Kathryn and her parents had lived with Julia in her narrow stone house three miles southwest of town. It was Julia who supported her parents, who had both been laid off from work when the Ely Falls mills had begun to close. Julia, whose husband had died when Kathryn was only three, did this with the proceeds from her antiques shop. This unusual arrangement did little to improve the relationship between Kathryn's mother and Julia, and gave Julia a position of control within the household that even Kathryn's father sometimes found hard to take. But when Kathryn was a girl, she did not think that her family was unusual in any respect. In her class at school, which numbered thirty-two in first grade and dwindled each year until there were only eighteen at graduation, nearly all of the children seemed to live at the margins. Kathryn had friends who lived in trailers, or who had no central heat in the winter, or whose houses would remain dark and shuttered the entire day so that their fathers or uncles could sleep. Kathryn's parents fought often and drank every day, and even this was not unusual. What was unusual was that they didn't behave like adults.

For years, it had been only Julia who had fed and dressed Kathryn, taught her to read and to play the piano, and saw her off each day to school. In the afternoons, Kathryn would help Julia at the shop or would be sent outside to play. Together, they watched the soap opera of her parents' lives unfold — perhaps not always from a distance, but from a safe place inside Julia's tall and oddly shaped house. For nearly all of Kathryn's childhood, Julia and she had been cast into the curious role of parents to the parents.

When Kathryn went away to college and was sitting in her dormitory in Boston, she was sometimes certain she would not ever be able to go back to Ely, that she did not ever again want to witness the endlessly repeatable drunken scenes between her parents. But on an unseasonably warm January afternoon during Kathryn's freshman year, her parents fell into the runoff from Ely Falls, which inexplicably they seemed to have been trying to cross, and drowned. Kathryn discovered, to her surprise, that grief overwhelmed her — as if children had died — and that when the time came to return to Boston after the double funeral, she could not leave Ely or Julia.

Julia had been at least as good as two parents, Kathryn thought now, and in that she had been lucky.

She was startled by a footfall on a rock above and behind her. Robert's hair was standing out from his head, and he was squinting.

"I was hoping you would bolt," he said, hopping down into the protected space.

She put her arms back into the sleeves of her jacket and tried to hold her hair in the wind so that she could see his face.

He leaned against a rock and brushed his hair back in place. He took a lighter and a pack of cigarettes out of his coat pocket. He turned away from the wind, but even in the shelter of the rocks, he was having trouble with his lighter. Finally, the cigarette caught, and he inhaled deeply, snapping the lighter shut. He slipped it back into his pocket, and immediately the wind blew embers off the end of the cigarette and threatened to put it out.

Was Robert Hart telling the truth? she wondered. Was he glad she'd bolted? "Have they gone?" she asked.

"No."

"And?"

"They'll be all right. They have to do this. I don't think they really expected you to say anything."

She rested her elbows on her upraised knees, clutched her hair into a ponytail.

"We do need to have a funeral," she said.

He nodded.

"Mattie and I need to honor Jack," she said. "Mattie needs to honor her father."

And she thought suddenly that this was true. Jack should be honored.

"It wasn't suicide," she said. "I'm sure of that."

A gull screeched down at them, and together they looked up at the bird that was circling overhead.

"When I was small," she said, "I used to think I wanted to come back in my next life as a gull. Until Julia told me how filthy they are."

"The rats of the sea," Robert said, stubbing out the cigarette on the sand with his foot. He slipped his hands into his pockets and seemed to hunch even more deeply into his coat. He was cold, she could see that. The skin around the eyes had gone papery and white.

She removed a strand of hair from her mouth.

"People in Ely," she said, "they say never live on the water. It's too depressing in the winter. But I've never been depressed."

"I envy you," he said.

"Well, I've been depressed, but not because of the ocean."

She saw now in the strong light that his eyes were hazel, not brown.

"But it's hell on windows," she added, looking in the direction of the house. "The salt spray."

He crouched down near the sand, where it was warmer.

"When Mattie was little, I worried about being so close to the ocean. I had to watch her all the time."

Kathryn gazed at the water, contemplating the danger there.

"Two summers ago," she said, "a girl drowned not far from here. A five-year-old girl. She was on a boat with her parents and got washed overboard. Her name was Wilhelmina. I remember thinking that was such an old-fashioned name to give a girl."

He nodded.

"When it happened, all I could think was how treacherous the ocean is, how quickly it can snatch a person. It happens so fast, doesn't it? One minute your life is normal, the next it isn't."

"You of all people should know that."

She dug the heels of her boots into the sand.

"You're thinking it could have been worse," Kathryn said. "Aren't you?"

"Yes."

"It might have been Mattie on the plane."

"Yes."

"That would have been unbearable. Literally unbearable."

He brushed his hands together to get rid of the wet sand.

"You could go away, you know," he said. "You and Mattie."

"Go away?"

"To the Bahamas. To Bermuda. For a couple of weeks, until this dies down."

Kathryn tried to imagine being in Bermuda right now with Mattie, then shook her head.

"I couldn't do that," Kathryn said. "They'd take it as true about Jack. They'd see us as running away. And besides, Mattie wouldn't go. I don't think she would."

"Some of the relatives have gone to Ireland," he said.

"And what? Stay in a motel with a hundred other families who are out of their minds? Or go to the crash site and wait for the divers to bring up body parts? No, I don't think so."

She felt around in the pockets of her parka. A used Kleenex. Coins. An outdated credit card. A couple of dollar bills. A tube of Lifesavers.

"You want one?" she asked, holding the Lifesavers forward.

"Thanks," he said.

Tired of crouching, he sat on the sand and leaned back against a rock.

He'll ruin his coat, she thought.

"It's beautiful here," he said. "Beautiful part of the world."

"It is."

She stretched her legs out in front of her. The sand, though wet, was oddly warm.

"Until this goes away, the media is going to be relentless," he said. "I'm sorry for that."

"It's not your fault."

"Even I've never seen anything like that scene at the gate."

"It was frightening."

"You must be pretty used to a quiet life here."

"A quiet, *ordinary* life," she said.

He had his elbows hooked around his knees, his hands clasped in front of him.

"What was your life like before this?" he asked. "What was your routine?"

"It was different each day. Which one do you want?"

"Oh, I don't know. Thursdays."

"Thursdays." She thought a minute. "On Thursdays, Mattie had field hockey or lacrosse games. I did Band at noon. It was pizza day in the cafeteria. We had roast chicken for supper. We watched *Seinfeld* and *ER*."

"And Jack?"

"When Jack was there, he was there. He did it all. The games.

The roast chickens. *Seinfeld.* What about you? What do you do when you're not working for the union?"

"I'm an instructor," he said. "I give flying lessons in my spare time at an airport in Virginia. It's just a pasture, really, with a couple of old Cessnas. It's a lot of fun, except when they won't come down."

"What won't come down?"

"The students on their first solo flights."

She laughed.

They sat in an easy silence, leaning against the rocks. The lulling noise of the sea was momentarily peaceful.

"Maybe I should start to think about the details of the funeral," she said after a time.

"Have you had any thoughts about where you want to do it?"

"I suppose it'll have to be Saint Joseph's in Ely Falls," she said. "That's the closest Catholic church."

She paused.

"They'll certainly be surprised to see me," she said.

"Christ," Robert said.

Confused by this response, she felt Robert tugging at her sleeve, making her stand up. She turned to see what Robert had seen. A young man with a ponytail was aiming a camera as big as a television at them. Kathryn could see herself and Robert reflected in the enormous lens.

She heard the soft, professional *click, click, click* of a man at work.

They were in the kitchen when she returned, Somers rolling a fax in his hand, Rita with the telephone cradled under her chin. Without taking off her jacket, Kathryn announced that she had a short statement to make. Somers looked up from the fax.

"My husband, Jack, never gave me or anyone else any indication of instability, drug use, abuse of alcohol, depression, or physical illness," she said.

She watched Somers fold the fax into squares.

"As far as I know," she continued, "he was healthy, both physically and mentally. We were happily married. We were a happy, normal family living within a small community. I will not answer any other questions without a lawyer present, and nothing is to be removed from this house without proper legal documents. As you all know, my daughter is staying with my grandmother here in town. Neither of them is to be interviewed or contacted in any way. That's all."

"Mrs. Lyons," said Somers. "Have you been in touch with Jack's mother?"

"His mother is dead," Kathryn said quickly.

And, then, in the silence that ensued, she knew that something was wrong. Perhaps there was the most minute lifting of an eyebrow, the barest suggestion of a smile on Somers's face. Or possibly it was only later that she imagined these signals. The silence was so complete that even with nine people in the room, all she could hear was the hum of the refrigerator.

"I don't think that's the case," said Somers softly, placing the shiny, folded square into a breast pocket.

The floor seemed to dip and waver like a ride at an amusement park.

Somers pulled a torn piece of notebook paper from another pocket.

"*Matigan Rice,*" he read. "*Forest Park Nursing Home, 47 Adams Street, Wesley, Minnesota.*"

The ride picked up speed and dropped fifty feet. Kathryn felt light-headed, dizzy.

"Seventy-two years old, born October 22, 1924," he read. *"Married three times. Divorced three times. First marriage to John Francis Lyons. One child, a son, John Fitzwilliam Lyons, born April 18, 1947, Faulkner Hospital, Boston."*

Kathryn's mouth went dry, and she licked her top lip. Perhaps there was something she hadn't understood correctly.

"Jack's mother is alive?" she asked.

"Yes."

"Jack always said . . ."

She stopped herself. She thought about what Jack had always said. His mother had died when he was nine. Of cancer. Kathryn glanced quickly at Robert, and she could see from the expression on his face that he, too, was taken aback. She thought about the arrogance, the smug certainty, with which she had made her statement just seconds earlier.

"Apparently," Somers said.

The investigator was enjoying this, Kathryn thought.

"How did you discover her?" she asked.

"She's listed in his military records."

"And Jack's father?"

"Deceased."

She sat on the nearest chair and shut her eyes. She felt vaguely drunk, the room swirling unpleasantly behind her eyelids.

All this time, she thought, and she had never known. All this time, Mattie had had a grandmother. A grandmother for whom she had been named.

But why? she asked herself.

Jack, why? she silently asked her husband.

THEY WALK ALONG THE BEACH IN THE FOG.
Mattie, in a Red Sox jacket, runs ahead to look for crabs. The
beach is flat and shallow, curved like a shell, the sand the color of
weathered wood with a calligraphy of seaweed written along its
crust. Behind the seawall are the summer houses, empty now.
Too late, Kathryn realizes she should have told Mattie, only five,
to take off her shoes.

Jack's shoulders are hunched against the cold. He wears his
leather jacket always, even on the coldest of days, unwilling to
invest in a parka, or perhaps too vain, she has never been exactly
sure. Her own flannel shirt hangs below her jacket, and she has
a woolen scarf doubled around her neck.

— What's wrong? she asks.

— Nothing, he says. — I'm fine.

— You seem subdued.

— I'm OK.

He walks with his hands in his pockets, staring straight
ahead. His mouth is set in a hard line. She wonders what has
happened to upset him.

— Did I do something? she asks.

— No, he says.

— Mattie has a soccer game tomorrow, she says.

— Good, he says.

— Can you be there? she asks.

— No, I have a trip.

There is a pause.

— You know, she says. — Once in a while you could bid a schedule that gave you more free time, more time to be at home.

He is silent.

— Mattie misses you.

— Look, he says. — Don't make it worse for me than it already is.

From the corner of her eye, she can see Mattie twirling in circles on the beach. Kathryn feels distracted, pulled toward the man beside her by a gravity that seems unnatural. She wonders if he's feeling well. Perhaps he is simply tired. She has heard the stories, the statistics: Most airline pilots die before they reach retirement age, which is sixty. It's the stress, the strain of the unusual schedules. The wear and tear on the body.

She moves toward him, tucks her hands around his stiffened arm. Still he stares straight ahead.

— Jack, tell me. What is it?

— Drop it, will you?

Stung, she lets his arm go and walks away.

— It's the weather, he says, catching up to her. — I don't know.

Apologetic now. Mollifying.

— What about the weather? she asks coldly, unwilling to be so easily mollified.

— The gray. The fog. I hate it.

— I don't think anyone likes it much, she says evenly.

— Kathryn, you don't understand.

He removes his hands from his pockets and hikes his collar against the cold. He seems to slip further into his leather jacket.

— Today is my mother's birthday, he says quietly. — Or would have been.

— Oh, Jack, she says, going to him. — You should have said.

— You're lucky, he says. — You're lucky to have Julia. You say you didn't have parents, but you did.

Is this a note of jealousy that she hears?

— Yes, I am lucky to have Julia, she agrees.

Jack's face is pinched and red. His eyes are watering from the cold.

— Was it very bad when your mother died? she asks.

— I don't like to talk about it.

— I know you don't, she says gently. — But sometimes talking about it can make it better.

— I doubt it.

— Was she sick a long time?

He hesitates. — Not too long. It was quick.

— What was it?

— I told you. Cancer.

— No, I know, she says. — I mean what kind?

He sighs slightly. — Breast, he says. — In those days, they didn't have the kinds of treatments . . .

She puts her hand on his arm.

— It's a terrible age to be left without a mother, she says.

Just four years older than Mattie, she thinks suddenly, and the realization makes her go cold all over. It is agonizing to think of Mattie left without a mother.

— She was Irish, you once said.

— She was born there. She had a beautiful voice, a beautiful accent.

— You had your dad.

Jack makes a short, derisive sound. — *Dad* isn't exactly the correct word. My father was an asshole.

The word, which Jack seldom uses, shocks her.

She unzips his jacket, snakes her arms inside.

— Jack, she says.

He softens slightly and pulls her head toward him. She smells leather mixed with sea air.

— I don't know what it is, he says. — Sometimes I'm afraid. Sometimes I think I have no center on gray days. No beliefs.

— You have me, she says quickly.

— This is true.

— You have Mattie, she says.

— I know, I know. Of course.

— Aren't we enough? she asks.

— Where *is* Mattie? he asks, suddenly pulling away.

Kathryn whips around and scans the beach. Jack spots her first, a brief flash of red among the gray. Kathryn, inexplicably paralyzed, watches Jack race across the sand and wade with high steps into the waves. She waits an endless minute and then sees Jack snatch Mattie like a small dog from the surf. He holds his daughter facedown by the waist, and she thinks for a moment that he will shake Mattie dry like a dog as well. But then she hears a familiar cry. Jack kneels on the beach, whips off his leather jacket, and enfolds the small body. When Kathryn reaches the two of them, he is wiping seawater from his daughter's face with the tail of his shirt.

Mattie looks stunned.

— The wave knocked her down, Jack says breathlessly.
— And the undertow was taking her out.

Kathryn picks Mattie up, cradles her in her arms.

— Let's go, Jack says quickly. — In a minute, she'll be freezing.

They begin to walk fast back to the house. Mattie coughs and wheezes from the seawater. Kathryn murmurs soothing words. Mattie's face is bright pink from the cold.

Jack holds Mattie's hand as if attached to his daughter by an umbilical cord. His pants are soaked, his shirt untucked. Kathryn thinks that he, too, must be freezing. The thought of what might have happened to Mattie had he not seen her in time weakens her arms, her knees.

She stops abruptly on the beach, and, in a natural movement, Jack encircles her and Mattie with his arms.

— Aren't we enough? she asks again.

Jack bends his head and kisses Kathryn on her forehead.

— Enough of what? Mattie asks.

two

SOMETIMES IT WAS AS THOUGH SHE HAD LIVED THREE, four years in eleven days. At other times it seemed just minutes ago that Robert Hart stood at her door and uttered the two words — *Mrs. Lyons?* — that had changed her life. She could not remember time looping in on itself in such a manner before, except perhaps for those two or three sublime days when she had first met Jack Lyons and fallen in love, and life had been measured out in minutes rather than in hours.

She lay on the daybed in the spare room, her arms outstretched, her head slightly raised on a pillow so that she could see past the red lacquered chair and out to sea. It was sunny when she'd driven to the house, but now the sky was beginning to cloud over, just swirls of cloud, milk drops in a water glass. She pulled a butterfly clip from the back of her head and tossed it to the floor, where it skidded along the polished wooden boards and came to rest against the baseboard. She had meant that morning to reenter the house and begin the long process of cleaning up and clearing away all traces of the past eleven days so that Mattie and she might move back from Julia's and begin their lives again. The gesture had been an admirable one, Kathryn thought, but her courage had thinned and dissipated when she'd walked into the kitchen and seen the pile of news-papers with their front-page photographs of Jack and her and Mattie, one edition of which had fallen onto the floor, making small tents on the tiles. There were rock-hard bagels in a waxed-paper bag on the table and a half dozen opened cans of Diet Coke on the counter, although someone had thoughtfully taken the trash out of its bin, so the house didn't smell as awful as Kathryn had feared it might. Climbing the stairs, she had opened the door to Jack's office and gazed at the pulled drawers and scattered papers on the floor, the strange nakedness of the desk without its computer equipment. She had known that the FBI would come with search warrants and documents, but she hadn't known precisely when. She had not been back to the house since the memorial service, two days before Christmas. Nor had Robert, who had returned to Washington immediately after the service. Shutting the door to Jack's office, Kathryn had walked the length of the hallway, entered the spare room, and lay down on the bed.

She was thinking that she'd been foolish to come back so soon, but she could not ignore her house forever. The clearing up had to be done. Julia, Kathryn knew, would have come in her place, but Kathryn could not allow that. Julia was exhausted, near to collapse herself, not only from the memorial service and the caring for Kathryn and Mattie, but also from her own finely honed sense of obligation: Julia had been determined to fill the Christmas rush orders from the shop. Privately, Kathryn had thought this misguided effort might kill her grandmother, but Kathryn could not dissuade Julia from her sense of duty. And so the two of them, with Mattie helping sporadically, had spent several long nights boxing and packing and wrapping and ticking off names and addresses from a list. And in its own way, Kathryn thought, the work had been mildly therapeutic. Julia and she had slept when they literally could no longer see, and thus they had avoided the insomnia that might have been their fate.

This morning, however, Kathryn had insisted that Julia stay in bed, and, not too surprisingly, Julia had finally acquiesced. Mattie, too, was sleeping late and might remain in bed until the early afternoon, as she had been doing for days. Actually, Kathryn wished her daughter would sleep for months in a peaceful coma and then awaken to a consciousness dulled by time, so that she would not be hit again and again with the pain that was always absurdly and cuttingly fresh. It was why Mattie slept so long, Kathryn thought, to postpone that awful moment of *knowing*.

Kathryn wished she herself could manage a coma. Instead, she felt herself to be inside a private weather system, one in which she was continuously tossed and buffeted by bits of news and information, sometimes chilled by thoughts of what lay immediately ahead, thawed by the kindness of others (Julia and Robert and strangers), frequently drenched by memories that seemed to have no regard for circumstance or place, and then subjected to the nearly intolerable heat of reporters, photographers, and curious onlookers. It was a weather system with no logic, she had decided, no pattern, no progression, no form. Sometimes she was unable to sleep or eat or, most oddly, to read even a single article through to the end. And not because the subject matter was Jack or the explosion, but because she couldn't summon the necessary concentration. At other times, when speaking to Julia or Mattie, she couldn't get to the end of a sentence without forgetting what the beginning had been, nor could she remember, from moment to moment, what task it was that she had been engaged in. Occasionally she found herself with the telephone to her ear, a number ringing, and no idea who it was she had called or why. Her mind felt crowded, as though there were a critical fact teasing her at the periphery of her brain, a detail she ought to be thinking about, a memory she ought to be seizing, a solution to a problem that seemed just beyond her grasp.

Worse, however, were the moments of relative calm that suddenly gave way to anger, all the more confusing because she could not always attach the anger to the appropriate person or event. It seemed composed of bits, tiny stone chips of an ugly mosaic: irritation at Jack, as though he were standing next to her, for something as trivial as the fact that he had neglected to tell her the name of their insurance agent (which she realized she could easily get, and did get, for herself by calling the company), or for the infinitely more innocent yet utterly infuriating fact that he had left her for good. Or anger at Arthur Kahler, with whom Jack had played tennis for years, for treating Kathryn as though she were vaguely toxic when he'd met her one day at Ingerbretson's. Even the sight of a tourist couple touching in front of Julia's shop (this other couple intact when Jack and she were not) caused such a rage inside Kathryn that she could not speak to them when they entered the store.

Kathryn knew that there were more appropriate and more obvious targets for her anger, but, inexplicably, she most often found herself mute or helpless in the face of them: the media, the airline, the agencies with their acronyms, and the hecklers — disturbed and frightening hecklers on the telephone, in the streets, at the memorial service, and even once, mind-numbingly, on the television, when a woman, asked for a man-on-the-street comment about the crash investigation, turned to the camera and accused Kathryn of hiding critical information about the explosion.

Shortly after her interview with the Safety Board investigator, Robert had suggested they go for a drive. They left the house and walked toward the car. He held the door for her, and only after it had closed did it occur to her to ask where they were going.

"Saint Joseph's Church," he said quickly.

"Why?" she asked.

"I think it's time for you to talk to a priest."

They drove through Ely and then across the road that traversed the salt marsh and led into Ely Falls, past abandoned mills and storefronts with signs that hadn't been updated since the 1960s. Robert parked in front of the rectory, a dark brick edifice that needed scouring, a building Kathryn had never entered. As a girl, she had often taken the bus into Ely Falls with her friends on Saturday afternoons and gone with them to confession at Saint Joseph's. Sitting alone on a darkened pew, she had been entranced by the seemingly moist stone walls, the intricately carved wooden cubicles with their maroon drapes behind which her friends confessed their sins (what they'd been, Kathryn could not now imagine), the captivatingly lurid paintings of the Stations of the Cross (which her best friend, Patty Regan, had once tried without success to explain to Kathryn), and the tawdry red glass globes that held the flickering candles that Patty would pay for and then light on her way out. Kathryn's own childhood church, Saint Matthew's Methodist on High

Street in Ely, had been almost aggressively sterile by comparison, a brown-shingled church, trimmed in yellow wood, with long multipaned windows through which the sun bountifully shone on Sunday mornings, as though the architect had been specifically commissioned to include the light and air of Protestantism in his design. Julia had taken Kathryn to Sunday school, though not much past the fifth grade, the age at which stories from the Bible no longer mesmerized her as they once had. And after that time, Kathryn had not been to church much at all, except at Christmas and Easter with Julia. Sometimes, Kathryn had felt a small twinge of parental guilt at not sending Mattie to Sunday school, not allowing her daughter the opportunity to learn about Christianity and then decide its validity for herself, as Kathryn had been allowed to do. Kathryn guessed that Mattie hardly ever thought about God, although in this she knew she could be wrong.

In the early years of their marriage, Jack had been aggressively scornful of the Catholic Church. He had attended the School of the Holy Name in Chelsea, with the worst that such parochial schools had to offer, including corporal punishment. It was hard for Kathryn to imagine schooling much worse than her own, which had been so spectacularly dull that when Kathryn thought about her years at Ely Elementary, the first image that came to mind was that of dust in the corridors. Lately, however, Jack's vehemence against the church had seemed to subside, and she wondered if he'd changed his mind. As he never talked about it, she couldn't say.

They got out of the car and knocked on a large wooden door. A tall man with dark, wiry hair answered the bell.

"There's been a terrible death," Robert said at once.

The priest nodded calmly and gazed from Robert to Kathryn.

"This is Kathryn Lyons," Robert said. "Her husband died yesterday in a plane crash."

It seemed to Kathryn that the color left the priest's face for just a moment and then returned.

"I'm Father Paul LeFevre," he said to both of them, extending his hand. "Please come in."

They followed the priest into a large room with leaded glass casement windows and seemingly thousands of books. Father Paul gestured for them to take seats around a small black fireplace grate. He looked to be in his late forties, and he seemed unusually muscular and fit under his dark shirt. She wondered idly as she sat there what priests did to keep in shape, if they were allowed to go to the gym and lift weights.

"I want to honor my husband," Kathryn said when Father Paul had seated himself. He held a pad of paper and a pen in his lap.

Kathryn searched for more explicit words but couldn't find them. Father Paul nodded slowly and appeared to understand. Indeed, Kathryn had the distinct impression, throughout the interview, that the Catholic priest knew a great deal more about her needs and her immediate future than she herself did.

"I'm not a Catholic," she explained. "But my husband was. He was raised a Catholic and educated in Catholic schools. I'm sorry to say that he hadn't gone to church in quite a long time."

There was a pause as the priest took this in. Kathryn wondered why she had felt it necessary to apologize for Jack.

"And what about yourself?" Father Paul asked.

"I was raised a Methodist, but I haven't been to church much either."

No, she thought, she and Jack hadn't gone to church on Sunday mornings. Sunday mornings, when Jack had been home, had been for waking in the bed with the burr of sleep upon them both, for the languid ease with which they'd reached for each other — without a word between them, without the day between them, trailing dreams instead of responsibilities — and then afterward, for lying in the crook of Jack's arm while he slept.

"Are there other family members to inform?" the priest asked.

Kathryn hesitated and glanced at Robert.

"No," she said, uncomfortably aware that she was lying to a priest in a Catholic rectory.

"Tell me about your husband," the priest said softly.

"He died yesterday when his plane exploded," she said. "He was the pilot."

Father Paul nodded. "I read about it in the paper," he said softly.

Kathryn thought about how to describe Jack.

"He was a good man," she said. "Hardworking. Loving. He had a special relationship with his daughter. . . ."

Kathryn pressed her lips together, and tears instantly filled her eyes. Robert reached over and put his hand on hers. The priest waited patiently for her to compose herself.

"He was an only child," Kathryn said haltingly. "His mother died when he was nine, and his father died when he was in college. He grew up in Boston and went to Holy Cross. He fought in Vietnam. I met him later, when he was a cargo pilot. Now he works for . . ."

She stopped herself, shook her head.

"He liked to fish and to fool around on the computer," she said when she could go on. "He played tennis. He spent a lot of time with Mattie, our daughter."

These were the facts, she thought, but the real Jack, the Jack she knew and loved, wasn't in them.

"He liked risk," she said suddenly, surprising the priest. "He didn't like rainy days. He blotted his pizza to get the oil off. His favorite movie was *Witness*. I've seen him cry at the end of sad movies. He couldn't tolerate traffic jams. He'd get off the highway and go fifty miles out of his way just to avoid one. He wasn't a particularly good dresser. He wore a uniform for work and never gave much thought to clothes. He had a leather jacket that he loved. He could be very tender and loving . . ."

She looked away.

"And what about you?" the priest asked. "How are you?"

"Me?" Kathryn asked. "I feel like I've been beaten up."

The priest nodded knowingly. Like a therapist might, she thought.

"And your marriage?" the priest asked. "What was your marriage like?"

Kathryn glanced at Robert.

"It was a good marriage," she said. "We were close. I would say that we were in love for a long time, longer than most couples. Well, I don't how you can ever tell about other people. It's just something you guess at."

"And then what happened?" the priest asked.

"And then?" she repeated. "And then we just loved each other. We passed out of being in love to just loving."

"Just loving is all that God asks of you," said the priest.

Not once in her entire marriage, Kathryn thought, had she considered what God wanted.

"We'd been married sixteen years," she said.

The priest crossed his legs. "Captain Lyons has been returned?"

"Returned?" she asked, at first bewildered.

"The body," the priest said.

"There isn't a body," Kathryn said quickly. "My husband's body hasn't been found yet."

"Then I assume you're speaking of a memorial service."

Kathryn looked to Robert for help. "I guess so," she said.

"Well," Father Paul said, "we can do one of two things. We can hold a memorial service for Captain Lyons, in which case I'd advise you to do so before Christmas so that the holiday might become part of the healing process rather than of the tragedy for both you and your daughter."

Kathryn contemplated this idea, about which she did not feel hopeful.

"Or," the priest added, "we could wait until your husband has been located."

"No," Kathryn said vehemently. "For my daughter's sake, for my sake, for Jack's sake, we need to honor Jack now. They're crucifying him in the papers and on television."

She heard the word *crucifying* and felt embarrassed for having used it with a priest. But wasn't that in fact what was happening? she thought. They were crucifying Jack's honor, his memory.

"They're saying that he committed suicide, that he murdered a hundred and three people," Kathryn said. "If Mattie and I don't honor Jack, I don't know who will."

The priest studied her.

"Honor him," she added, though she could not explain herself further.

"And I . . ."

She cleared her throat and tried to sit up straighter.

"I doubt very much there will be a body," she said.

———

That night, pacing sleeplessly in Julia's kitchen long after Julia and Mattie had gone to bed, Kathryn began to wonder if she shouldn't, after all, tell Father Paul that there was a living relative — Jack's mother. And wasn't it wrong of Kathryn not to inform the woman herself that her son had died? she wondered. She suspected that it was, but the thought of Jack's mother alive, the image of an elderly woman who looked like Jack sitting in a nursing home, caused for Kathryn an unpleasant noise in the air, like the irritating and insistent whine of a mosquito that she wished would go away. It wasn't simply the discovery that Jack had lied to her that troubled Kathryn; it was the continued existence of the woman herself, a woman Kathryn did not know quite what to do with. Impulsively, Kathryn reached for the telephone on the wall and called information.

When she had the correct number, she dialed the nursing home.

"Forest Park," a young woman answered.

"Oh, hello," Kathryn said nervously. "I'd like to speak to Matigan Rice."

"Wow, that's amazing," said the woman, who was eating, Kathryn thought, or chewing gum.

"This is Mrs. Rice's third call today," the woman added, "and she hasn't gotten a call in, oh, six months, anyway."

The woman made a sucking sound, as if draining a drink with a straw.

"And in any event," the woman continued, "Mrs. Rice can't come to the phone. She isn't well enough to leave her room, and in addition to all her other problems, she can't hear very good, either, so a phone call is really out of the question."

"How is she?" Kathryn asked.

"About the same."

"Oh," Kathryn said. She hesitated. "I was just trying to remember . . ." she added, "when it was exactly that Mrs. Rice entered the nursing home."

There was a silence at the other end.

"Are you a relative?" the young woman asked warily.

Kathryn pondered the question. Was she a relative? Jack, for reasons of his own, had chosen not to acknowledge that his mother was alive, and so, for all intents and purposes, she hadn't been — certainly not to Kathryn or to Mattie. And Kathryn wasn't at all sure to what end Matigan Rice should be resurrected. Was it shame that had made Jack lie about his mother? Had he and his mother had an irreparable falling-out?

"No, I'm not a relative," Kathryn said. "There's going to be a memorial service for her son, and I wanted her to be informed."

"Her son died?"

"Yes."

"What was his name?"

"Jack. Jack Lyons."

"OK."

"He was killed in a plane crash," Kathryn added.

"Really? You mean that Vision crash?"

"Yes."

"Oh, my God, wasn't that awful? What kind of a man would commit suicide and take all those innocent people with him?"

Kathryn was silent.

"Well, this is the first I've heard of Mrs. Rice's son being on the plane," the woman said. "You want me to try to tell her? I can't promise you she'll understand. . . ."

"Yes," said Kathryn coolly. "I think you should try to tell her."

"Maybe I'd better talk to my supervisor first. Well, listen, thanks for telling us, and I hope you didn't have any relatives yourself on that flight."

"I did, as a matter of fact."

"Oh, my gosh, I'm so sorry."

"My husband was the pilot," Kathryn said.

In the days that followed her meeting with the priest, Father Paul and Kathryn spoke often, and twice the priest drove to Julia's house to visit. At the first meeting at the rectory, Robert had stressed the need for security, and Father Paul had seemed not to think this was beyond his ken, although in this, as it happened, he was overconfident. Repeatedly, Kathryn herself could get little farther than the word *honor*, though Father Paul did not demand much beyond that, and for that she was grateful. When she thought about Father Paul now, it was with a shudder of relief, for if it had not been for his firm hand, the memorial service would have been a fiasco beyond all proportions.

As it was, she and Julia and Mattie had had to go to the church an hour ahead of time to insure that they would have clear passage through the streets, which later would become so clogged that nothing — not even an ambulance — could get through. Mattie wore a long gray silk skirt with a cropped black jacket, and shook violently when Father Paul said that her father had now made a safe landing. Julia and Kathryn had worn suits and had held hands. Or rather, Julia had held Kathryn's hand, and Kathryn had held Mattie's, and this passing on of strength, this willing of strength from one to the other to the other had helped Kathryn, and she thought Mattie and Julia as well, survive the service. But afterward, when Kathryn stood up from the pew and turned to face the back of the church and saw the rows upon rows of pilots in dark suits, pilots from many airlines, most of whom had never met Jack, and then the rows of students from her classes, some of whom had already graduated and had come back for this event, she faltered, and then stumbled, and it was Mattie, in a sudden reversal of roles, who held her up, supported her. Mattie and Kathryn and Julia had then walked the length of that long aisle, and Kathryn thought now that it had been, possibly, the longest walk of her life. For as she walked, she had the distinct sense that when she reached the door of the church and slipped inside the black car that was waiting for her outside, her life with Jack truly would have ended.

The next day, in the newspapers, there was a photograph of Kathryn emerging from Saint Joseph's, and she was surprised not only by the repetition of her image on the front page of several papers in the stand outside Ingerbretson's, but also by the image itself: Grief transformed a face, she saw, carved hollows and etched lines and loosened muscles, so that the face was almost unrecognizable. In the picture, clutching her daughter's arm for support, Kathryn looked dazed and stricken and years older than she was.

She winced now to think of that picture, and of others, the most unfortunate being that of her and Robert in the shelter at the beach, Robert pulling at her sleeve, both of them looking momentarily cowed and cornered. It was, she thought, a particularly painful picture because in actuality Robert had been incensed by the photographer's shameless opportunism, and even now she could hear Robert shouting at the man as he climbed up the rocks and chased the photographer across the lawn. And then Robert's anger and the chase had so filled Kathryn with righteous confidence that she had been moved to make her pronouncement when she'd entered the house — the pronouncement that had so quickly disintegrated when Somers had told her of Jack's mother.

After that day at Ingerbretson's, Kathryn had stopped looking at newspapers or watching television. A visit to Julia's that
was meant to last only the night following the memorial service
extended through Christmas and beyond. Kathryn, like Mattie,
could not reenter her own house, and she could not reasonably
ask Mattie to return with her to their home until it had been
cleared of any artifacts that might send Mattie spinning out the
door. Only once, at Julia's, had the television inadvertently been
left on, so that before Kathryn had quite realized what was
happening, she found herself looking at an animated rendition
of the events following the explosion in the cockpit of Vision
Flight 384. According to the sequence, the cockpit broke away
from the body of the plane, which itself disintegrated into
smaller fragments during a second explosion. The animation
showed the trajectory of the various parts as they fell into the
ocean. According to the reporter, the descent would have taken
approximately ninety seconds. Kathryn could not move her eyes
away from the screen. She followed the arc of the small animated cockpit to the water, where it made a little cartoon splash
and sank.

The cloud layer, its milky swirls gradually thickening, dimmed
the light in the window of the spare room. Kathryn sat up in
the daybed, determined to begin the cleaning now. She heard
footsteps in the hallway and swung her legs over the side of the
bed. It would be Julia, she thought, coming to help after all. But
when Kathryn glanced up, she saw that it was not Julia, but
Robert Hart who was standing in the doorway.

"I went to your grandmother's," he said straight away, "and
she said you were here."

He had his hands in the pockets of his sport coat, an indistinct smooth color, taupe, maybe. He looked different in jeans. His hair was windblown, as though he had just combed it with his fingers.

"I'm not here officially," he said. "I have a few days off. I wanted to see how you were doing." He stepped into the room.

She wondered if he had knocked on the back door, and if he had, why she hadn't heard him.

"I'm glad to see you," she said, surprising herself.

And it was true. She could feel a weight — not all of the weight, but something small and gelatinous — slide off her shoulders.

"How's Mattie?" he asked, crossing the room and sitting down on the red lacquered chair.

It would make an interesting photograph, Kathryn thought suddenly, the man on the red lacquered chair against the lime green paint. An attractive man. An arresting face. The widow's peak and the dust-colored hair, combined with the way he sat slouched with his hands in his pockets, made him look vaguely British, like a character in a World War II movie. Someone who would have been in ciphers, she thought.

"Terrible," Kathryn said, feeling relieved to have someone to talk with about Mattie. Julia's fatigue had been such that Kathryn had not wanted to burden her grandmother too much with her private worries. Julia's were harrowing enough, more than any seventy-eight-year-old woman should have to bear.

"Mattie's a mess," Kathryn said simply to Robert. "She's jumpy. She's nervous. She can't concentrate on anything. Sometimes she tries to watch television, but that's not safe anymore. Even if it isn't a news bulletin, there's always something that reminds her of her father. Last night, she went over to Taylor's house to be with some of their friends, and she came back inconsolable. A friend of Taylor's father who was at the house asked Mattie if there would be a trial, and Mattie apparently just dissolved. Taylor's dad had to drive her home."

Robert, Kathryn noticed, was studying her intently.

"I don't know," she said. "I'm worried, Robert. Really worried. Mattie's brittle. She's fragile. She doesn't eat. Sometimes she breaks into hysterical laughter. She doesn't seem to have the appropriate reaction to anything anymore. Although I'd like to know what is appropriate. I told Mattie that life doesn't just disintegrate, that we can't break all the rules, and Mattie said, quite rightly, that all the rules had already been broken."

He crossed his legs the way men do, an ankle resting on a knee.

"How was Christmas?" he asked.

"Sad," she said. "Pathetic. Every minute was pathetic. The worst was how hard Mattie was trying. As if she owed it to Julia and me. As if she owed it somehow to her father. I wish now we had canceled the whole thing. How was yours?"

"Sad," he said. "Pathetic."

Kathryn smiled.

"What are you doing in here?" he asked, looking around the room as though something in it might provide a clue.

"I'm trying to avoid having to clean the house. I've always used this room as a kind of retreat. I hide in here. What are you doing here? is a better question."

"I have a few days off," he said.

"And?"

He uncrossed his legs and put his hands in the pockets of his trousers.

"Jack didn't spend his last night in the crew apartment," he said.

In the room, the air went thick and heavy.

"Where was he?" Kathryn asked quietly.

How quickly a person could ask a question she didn't want the answer to, Kathryn thought, and not for the first time. As though one part of the psyche dared the other to survive.

"We don't know," Robert said. "As you know, he was the only American on the crew. When the plane landed, Martin and Sullivan got in their cars and drove home. We do know that Jack went to the apartment, however briefly, because he made two phone calls, one to you and one to a restaurant for a reservation for that night. But according to the maid, no one slept there Monday night. Apparently, the Safety Board has known for some time. It will be on the news today. At noon."

Kathryn lay back on the bed and stared up at the ceiling. She hadn't been home when Jack had called, and he'd left a message on the machine. *Hi, hon,* he'd said. *I'm here. I'm going downstairs to get something to eat. Did you call Alfred? Talk to you soon.*

"I didn't want you to be taken by surprise," he said. "I didn't want you to be alone."

"Mattie . . . ," she said.

"I've told Julia," he said. He got up, crossed the room, and sat at the bottom of the daybed, at its edge, barely sitting at all. His shirt was a darkish cotton, possibly gray, although Kathryn wondered if it, too, could be called taupe.

Her mind felt pushed, compressed. If Jack hadn't slept in the crew apartment, where had he been? She shut her eyes, not wanting to think about it. If anyone had asked her, she would have said that she was certain her husband had never been unfaithful. It wasn't like Jack, she wanted to tell Robert. That wasn't him at all.

"This will end," Robert said.

"It wasn't suicide." She felt compelled to say this at least. She felt it absolutely.

He reached over and put his hand on hers. Instinctively, she started to pull her hand away, but he held on to it.

She didn't want to ask, she didn't, but she had to, and she could see that he was waiting for the question. She sat up slowly, withdrawing her hand, and this time Robert let it go.

"The reservation was for how many?" she asked as casually as she could.

"For two."

She pressed her lips together. It didn't mean anything necessarily, she thought. It could easily have been for Jack and a member of his crew, couldn't it? She saw Robert's gaze flicker to the window and back. Which member of the crew? she wondered.

"How did you keep in touch with Jack when he was away?" Robert asked.

"He called me," she said. "It was easier that way, because my schedule was always the same. He'd call me as soon as he got to the crew apartment. If I had to reach him, I would leave a message on his voice mail. We had arranged it that way because I could never be sure when he was trying to get some sleep."

She thought about that arrangement. Had it been her idea or Jack's? They had done it for so many years, she could no longer remember when it had begun. And it had always seemed a logical system, too practical to question. Odd, she thought, how a fact, seen one way, was one thing. And then, seen from a different angle, was something else entirely. Or perhaps not so odd.

"Obviously, we can't ask the crew," she said.

"No."

She thought about the question Mattie had asked her on the day she'd learned of the suicide rumor: How do you ever know that you know a person?

Kathryn stood up and walked over to the window. She had on an old sweatshirt and a pair of jeans with shot knees that she had been wearing for days. Even her socks weren't clean. She hadn't thought she would see anyone today. With grief, she thought, appearance was the first thing to go. Or was it dignity?

"I can't cry anymore," she said. "That part is over."

"Kathryn . . ."

"It's unprecedented," she said. "It's absolutely unprecedented. No pilot has ever been accused of committing suicide in an airliner."

"Actually," said Robert, "it's not unprecedented. There is one case."

Kathryn turned from the window.

"In Morocco. A Royal Air Maroc airliner crashed near Agadir in August of 1994. The Moroccan government, basing its opinion on the CVR tapes, said the crash was caused by the captain's suicidal act. Apparently, the man deliberately disengaged the autopilot and pointed the aircraft at the ground. The plane began to break up before impact. Forty-four people died."

"My God," she said.

She put her hands over her eyes. It was impossible not to see, if only for an instant, the horror of the copilot as he watched his captain kill himself, the terrified bewilderment of the passengers in the cabin as they felt the sudden descent.

"When will they release the tape?" she asked. "Jack's tape."

Robert shook his head. "I doubt very much that they ever will," he said. "They don't have to. The transcripts are exempt from the Freedom of Information Act. When tapes have been released, either what's on them isn't sensitive or else they've been heavily censored."

"So I won't ever have to listen to it."

"I doubt it."

"But then . . . how will we ever know what happened?"

"Thirty separate agencies in three countries are working on this crash," Robert said. "Believe me, the union hates the accusation of suicide more than anyone — even the hint of suicide. Every congressman in Washington is calling for stricter psychological testing of pilots, which from the union's point of view is a nightmare. The sooner the case gets resolved, the better."

Kathryn rubbed her arms, trying to get the circulation going. "It's all political, isn't it?" she said.

"Usually."

"It's why you're here."

He was silent as he sat on the bed. He smoothed the bedspread with his palms. "No," he said. "Not at the moment."

"So you're here as . . . ?"

"I'm here," he said, looking up at her. "I'm just here."

She nodded her head slowly. She wanted to smile. She wanted to tell Robert Hart how glad she was that he was there, how very hard it was to go through all of this alone, to not have with her the one person she needed, who was Jack.

"Is that a good shirt?" she asked quickly.

"Not particularly," he said.

"You feel like doing some chores?"

RAIN FALLS IN HEAVY SHEETS OUTSIDE THE MAS-sive paned windows of the auditorium. The room is old and sloping, built in the 1920s and not yet renovated. The walls are wood paneled, etched here and there with declarations of love and students' initials. Heavy maroon drapes that never seem to work exactly right hang to either side of the stage. Only the seats, mercilessly poked at and ripped open over the years with pens and pocket knives, have been replaced. Now the audience sits on seats removed from the Ely Falls Cinema when that building was demolished to make way for a bank.

The auditorium slowly fills with parents as the band struggles courageously with "Pomp and Circumstance." Conducting in the pit just below the stage, Kathryn manages to coax from the twenty-three high school musicians a barely passable rendition of the graduation processional. Susan Ingalls, on the clarinet, is wildly off-key, and Spence Closson, on the bass drum, seems particularly nervous tonight, hesitating just a fraction on each measure.

Overtime, Kathryn thinks to herself. In any other job, this would be called overtime.

Fortunately, this is not graduation itself, just Awards Night. Kathryn has five seniors in the band, two of whom might win academic prizes. It's one of the few advantages of a small school, she thinks. Awards Night is usually short.

With her baton still in her hand, she sits on a chair next to Jimmy DeMartino, tuba. She debates the merits of taking Susan Ingalls backstage and trying to tune her clarinet. The principal begins his address, which will be followed by talks from the vice-principal and the valedictorian of the senior class. Kathryn tries to pay attention, but her mind is more fixed on the grades she must do tonight when she gets home. The last several weeks of the school year are always harried and emotional. Every day for the past five days, she's conducted band practice during lunch so that the seniors — all twenty-eight of them — can practice marching to "Pomp and Circumstance" for graduation. Not once this week has the song, even badly played, failed to produce tears. But by graduation night, Kathryn knows, all the tears will be used up, the wistful heartache of leaving school will be well played out, and the seniors will be thinking only of the all-night party ahead. Every year it is the same.

The speeches over, the principal begins to announce the awards. Kathryn looks at her watch. A half hour at the outside, she calculates. Then the band will play "Trumpet Voluntary," everyone will go home, and she can start computing grades for her sophomore history class. Mattie has a math final tomorrow.

She hears applause, the hush of anticipation as a name is read, another round of applause, sometimes a whistle from the crowd. Seniors from the front row of the auditorium mount the stage and return with ribbon-tied scrolls in their hands, occasionally a trophy. Beside her, Jimmy DeMartino receives an award for out-standing academic achievement in physics. She holds his tuba for him while he is on stage.

After thirty minutes have passed, Kathryn listens for the lull in the proceedings that will signal that the evening is coming to a close. In preparation, she stands and walks toward the conduc-tor's box, making small motions with her hand to remind the musicians to pick up their instruments. She changes the music on the stand, waits with her hands folded in front of her to begin.

But she is mistaken. The principal is not done. There is one more award to be given.

Kathryn hears the words *highest possible score* and *sophomore*. A name is called. A girl stands and hands Kathryn her clarinet. In a white T-shirt, a skimpy black skirt, and work boots, the girl ascends the stage. The audience, in a mixture of admiration for the achievement and relief that the assembly is over, breaks into applause. Kathryn tucks Mattie's clarinet under her arm and claps as hard as any of them.

Jack should be here, Kathryn thinks.

Afterward, in the band room, Kathryn smothers Mattie in a hug.

— I'm so proud, she says.

— Mom, Mattie says breathlessly, breaking away, — can I call Dad and tell him? I really want to.

Kathryn thinks a moment. Jack is in London and will be sleeping in preparation for another trip, but she knows he wouldn't mind being woken for this.

— Sure, Kathryn says to Mattie. — Why not? We'll use the phone in the principal's office.

Using her calling card number, she dials the crew apartment, but there is no answer. She hangs up and tries again. Through the window, she can see the wind sending gusts of rain down the street. Kathryn tries a third time, thinking that the repetition of calls alone will signal to Jack that she's trying to reach him. It's one-thirty in the morning in London. Where is he?

— We'll call from home, she tells Mattie with a smile.

But at home, when she dials the London number, there is still no answer. Kathryn calls three times, twice while Mattie isn't looking. She leaves a message on the voice mail. Feeling the enthusiasm and pride of the evening beginning to dissipate, Kathryn abandons the effort to reach Jack, and to celebrate Mattie's achievement, makes up a batch of brownies. Mattie, too excited to study for her math test, sits at the kitchen table while her mother mixes the batter. For the first time ever, they discuss colleges, and Kathryn thinks of schools she might not have considered before. She looks at her daughter in a slightly new way.

When Mattie goes to bed, Kathryn's forced good cheer begins to wane. She stays up late, calculating grades. She calls the London number at midnight, five in the morning in London, and is frustrated to listen to the phone ringing in the crew apartment with no one to pick it up. In an hour, Jack will have to leave for the airport for his flight to Amsterdam and Nairobi. She begins to worry then that something serious may have happened to him. For a while, she vacillates between anger and concern, until she falls asleep on the couch with her grade book and calculator on her lap.

He calls at quarter to one. Quarter to six, his time. His voice wakes her with punctuated bursts.

— Kathryn, what is it? What's happened? Are you all right?

— Where were you? she asks groggily, sitting up.

— Here, he says. — I was here. I just checked the voice mail.

— Why didn't you answer the phone?

— I had the ringer turned off. I was exhausted and had to sleep. I think I might be coming down with a flu.

She hears the congestion in his voice. Airliners are notorious breeding grounds for colds.

— It's a good thing it wasn't an emergency, she says, allowing a note of pique to seep into her voice.

— Look, I'm really sorry. But I was so tired, I thought it was more important to sleep. So what is it? he asks. — What's the news?

— I can't tell you. Mattie wants to tell you herself.

— It's nothing bad?

— No, no. It's great.

— Give me a hint.

— No, I can't. I promised.

— I don't suppose you want to wake her up now?

— No, she has a final in the morning.

— I'll call her from the air, he says. — I'll time it so I call when she wakes up.

Kathryn rubs her eyes. There is a small silence over the phone. She would like to see her husband's face right now. She would like to crawl into the bed in the crew apartment with him. She has never seen the crew apartment. Sterile, he has described it. Like a suite of hotel rooms.

— So, she says.

— Kathryn, I really am sorry. I'll get the airline to get a system that bypasses the voice mail if it's an emergency. I'll get a beeper.

She sighs into the phone. — Jack, do you still love me?

For a moment he is silent.

— Why do you ask?

— I don't know, she says. — I guess I haven't heard you say it in a while.

— Of course I love you, he says. He clears his throat. — I really love you. Now go to sleep. I'll call at seven.

But he doesn't hang up, and neither does she.

— Kathryn?

— I'm here.

— What's wrong?

She doesn't know precisely what is wrong. She has only a vague feeling of vulnerability, a heightened sense of having been left alone for too many days. Perhaps it is only being exhausted herself.

— I'm cool, she says, borrowing Mattie's expression of the moment.

— You're cool, Jack says.

— Yeah, whatever.

She can almost see her husband smiling.

— Later, he says, and hangs up.

— Later, she says, holding the lifeless telephone in her hand.

THEY MOVED FROM ROOM TO ROOM, DUSTING, VACU-
uming, washing tiles, hauling trash, making beds, putting laundry into hampers. Robert worked at these tasks like a man, she
noticed: sloppy with the beds, good in the kitchen, washing the
floor there as though he were punishing it. With Robert in her
bedroom and in Mattie's, potentially dangerous objects were
defused: A shirt flung over a chair was just a shirt that Robert
tossed onto the floor with a bundle of other laundry. Bed linens
were bed linens, in need of washing like everything else. He
picked up discarded papers in Jack's office and, without examining them, as Kathryn would have had to do, put them all into a
drawer and closed it. In Mattie's room, Kathryn felt Robert's
scrutiny, sensing that he was afraid it would be in that room she
would falter, but she surprised him and herself by being particularly speedy and efficient. Even more stoically, she had helped
Robert take the Christmas tree down, both of them dragging
the dried-out tree through the kitchen and out the back hallway,
the tree shedding its needles on the floorboards and the tiles. By

the time they were finished with the cleaning, the milky swirls in the sky had given way to low, lead-stained clots.

"It's supposed to snow," he said, spraying out the inside of the kitchen sink with the hose.

She opened the cupboard beneath the sink and put away the bathroom cleaner, the Pine Sol, the Comet. She rinsed her hands in the spray from the hose and dried them on a dish towel.

"I'm hungry," she said, feeling the mild satisfaction that always came from having a clean house. Like having had a bath.

"Good," he said, turning. "I've got lobsters in the car."

She raised an eyebrow.

"From Ingerbretson's," he explained. "I picked them up on my way here. I couldn't resist."

"I might not have liked lobster," she said.

"I saw the picks and crackers in the silverware drawer."

"Observant," she said.

"Occasionally."

But standing there, she suddenly had the sense that Robert Hart was always observant. Always watching.

Robert cooked the lobsters while Kathryn set the table in the front room. A dry snow shower had begun, and swirls of snow-flakes fell silently against the glass of the windows. Kathryn opened the fridge and took out two bottles of beer. She had opened one and was about to open the other when she remembered that Robert didn't drink. She tried to put the two bottles back into the fridge without Robert's noticing.

"Please," Robert said from the stove. "Drink the beer. It doesn't bother me. In fact, it would bother me more if you didn't."

Kathryn looked at the clock: 12:20. Time out of time. Once again, the envelope began to open. It was a Friday. Normally, she would be at school, fifth period. Normally, she would not be drinking a beer. Although it *was* Christmas vacation, she thought; she was theoretically not due back until the second of January. She had given no thought to how she would manage in the classroom. An image of students moving in a hallway rose to the surface, but she banished it.

At five minutes before noon, Robert had turned off all the ringers on the telephones. There was nothing so urgent it couldn't wait an hour or two, he had said, and she had agreed.

In that spirit, she had covered the table near the windows in the front room with a red flowered cloth, the gaiety of the cloth incongruous against the somber sky outside. Robert put on music: B.B. King. Kathryn wished she had flowers. But what exactly was she celebrating? she wondered, feeling vaguely guilty. Having survived the last eleven days? Having cleaned the house? She set utensils, bowls for the shells, bread, melted butter, and a thick roll of paper towel on the table. Robert walked into the front room from the kitchen bearing wet, slippery plates of lobsters. There were water spots on the front of his shirt.

"I'm famished," he said, setting the plates down and sitting across from her.

She examined the lobster in front of her. And it was then that the swift, sharp shock of memory once again assailed her. She looked up quickly and then out the window. She brought a hand to her mouth.

"What is it?" Robert asked.

She shook her head quickly, side to side. She held herself still, locked in an image, not daring to move either forward or back-

ward for fear of the crevices. She breathed in deeply, let her
breath out, laid her arms on the table.

"I've just had a memory," she said.

"What is it?"

"Jack and me."

"Here?"

She nodded.

"Doing this?"

It was like this, she wanted to say, but not like this. It was
early summer, and the screens were on. Mattie was at a friend's
house, and it was later in the day, nearer four o'clock or five. The
light was unique, she remembered, shimmery and green like sea
glass. They had had champagne. What were they celebrating?
She couldn't remember. Possibly nothing, possibly themselves.
She had wanted to make love, she remembered, and so had he,
but neither of them would sacrifice a hot boiled lobster, and so
they had waited with a kind of delicious tension between them.
She had sucked the legs of her lobster with exaggerated kisses,
and Jack had laughed and said she was a tease, which she
enjoyed. Being a tease. She seldom did that.

"I'm sorry," Robert said. "I should have known. I'll take these
into the kitchen."

"No," she said quickly, stopping his hand as he reached for
her plate. "No, you couldn't have known. And anyway, my life is
filled with these. Hundreds of little memories that catch me off
guard. They're like mines in a field, waiting to detonate. Hon-
estly, I'd like to have a lobotomy."

He moved his hand from under hers and laid it over her fingers. He held her hand in the way a man might hold the hand of
a woman friend, waiting for a small crisis to blow over. His hand
felt warm, because Kathryn's had suddenly gone cold. All her

memories did this to her; they made the blood leave her hands and feet. Like fear did.

"You've been good to me," she said.

Time passed. How much? She could no longer gauge seconds, minutes. She closed her eyes. The beer had made her slightly sleepy. She wanted to turn her hand over, to have him touch her palm. To slide his hand along her palm and up her wrist. She imagined she could feel the warmth of his hand traveling along the underside of her arm, past the elbow.

Her fingers under Robert's went slack, and she felt the tension drain from her body. It was erotic, but not, that loosening, that giving up. Her eyes seemed to have unfocused themselves, and she couldn't see Robert or anything else properly, only a sense of light from the windows. That light, diffuse and dimmed, created an aura of languid ease. And she thought that she ought to feel disturbed for thinking of Robert and herself in that way, but a kind of leniency seemed to have descended upon them with the haze, and she felt merely vague and drifting. So much so that when Robert, perhaps in an effort to bring her back, tightened the pressure on her hand, she felt jolted into the present moment.

"You're like a kind of priest," she said.

He laughed. "No, I'm not."

"I think that's how I've come to see you."

"Father Robert," he said, smiling.

And then she thought: Who was to know if this man's hand traveled up the inside of her arm? Who was to care? Weren't all of the rules now broken? Hadn't Mattie said so?

The silence of the steady snowfall enclosed them. She could see that he was struggling to understand precisely where she was and why, but she couldn't help him, because she herself didn't know. The front room was always slightly too cold in winter, she thought, and she shivered once in spite of the steam she could hear rushing into the radiators. Outside, the sky was becoming so dark it might have been mistaken for dusk.

He withdrew his hand, leaving hers uncovered. She felt exposed.

She drank another bottle of beer. Between them, they ate all of the bread and the lobsters. In the middle of the meal, Robert got up and changed the CD. From B.B. King to Brahms.

"You have wonderful music," he said when he returned.

"You're interested in music?"

"Yes."

"What kind?"

"Piano, especially. Was the music Jack's or yours?" he asked, sitting down.

She cocked her head, not certain she understood what he meant.

"Usually the CDs and the sound system are the passion of either the husband or the wife, but not both," he explained. "At least in my experience."

She thought about this.

"Mine," she said. "Jack was tone-deaf. But he liked rock and roll. And some of Mattie's music — for the beat, I think. What about you?"

"Mine, too," he said. "Although my ex-wife kept the sound system and most of the CDs. One of my sons has inherited an ear. He plays the saxophone at school. The other one seems to have no interest."

"Mattie plays the clarinet. I tried to get her to play the piano," Kathryn said, "but it was torture."

Kathryn thought about all of the hours she had spent with Mattie at the piano, Mattie clearly not wanting to be there, exaggerating her nearly pathological reluctance by having obsessively to scratch her back where she couldn't quite reach, or adjust the bench, or take an inordinately long time finding her fingering. It was an effort just to get Mattie to play a song once, never mind actually practice the piece several times. Often, Kathryn had ended up having to leave the room in a barely restrained rage, at which point Mattie would begin to cry. Before the first year was out, Kathryn could see that if she insisted Mattie keep on with the lessons, their relationship would be in tatters.

Now, of course, Mattie was almost never without her music — in her room, in the car, and plugged into headphones as if they delivered oxygen through the ears.

"You play?" Kathryn asked.

"Used to."

She studied him and added a small detail to a portrait that had been forming since the day he'd entered her house. It was what one did with people, Kathryn thought, form portraits, fill in missing brush strokes, wait for form and color to materialize.

He dipped a piece of tail in butter and brought it dripping to his mouth.

"The night before Jack left for his trip," Kathryn said, "he went into Mattie's room and asked her if she wanted to go to a Celtics game with him on Friday night. A friend had given him really good seats. What I want to know is this: Would a man ask his daughter to go with him to a Celtics game if he planned to kill himself before he got back?"

Robert wiped his chin and thought a minute.

"Would a man who had really good seats to a Celtics game kill himself before he got to see the game?"

Her eyes widened.

"I'm sorry," he said quickly. "No. It doesn't make any sense, not in any realm of human nature I've ever heard of."

"And Jack told me to call Alfred," Kathryn said. "He told me to have Alfred come on Friday to fix the leaky shower. If Jack wasn't planning on coming back, he wouldn't have done that. Not in the way he did it, almost as an afterthought as he walked to the car. And he'd have been different with me. He'd have said good-bye differently. I know he would. There'd be one small thing that maybe wouldn't register at the time, but would after the fact. Something."

Robert reached for his water glass and pushed himself slightly away from the table.

"Do you remember," she asked, "when the Safety Board questioned me, they asked me if Jack had any close friends in England?"

"Yes."

She stared at the bowl of discarded shells.

"I've just had a thought," she said. "I'll be right back."

As she climbed the stairs, she tried to recall if she had done that particular wash. She'd worn the jeans for two days and then thrown them in the hamper. But not her own hamper, she remembered, Mattie's hamper. And Kathryn hadn't done any wash at all of Mattie's because Mattie hadn't been there. Any laundry Mattie had needed had been done at Julia's.

She found the jeans at the bottom of the pile of soiled laundry, buried beneath clothes Robert and she had tossed into the hamper just hours ago. She removed the handful of papers and receipts, which were slightly damp from a long-buried towel.

When she returned to the front room, Robert was contemplating the snowfall. He watched her as she pushed her plate away and unfolded the papers.

"Look at this," she said, handing the lottery ticket to Robert. "I found these papers wadded up in the pocket of Jack's jeans on the back of the bathroom door on the day he died. I didn't think much of them at the time and just stuck them in the pocket of my own jeans. But do you see that notation, *M at A's,* and the numbers following it? What does it look like to you?"

Robert studied the number, and she could see from the flicker of his eyes that he understood what she was thinking.

"A U.K. phone number, you think," he said.

"It's a London exchange, isn't it? The one eight one?"

"I think so."

"Isn't that the right number of digits?"

"I'm not sure."

"Let me see," she said. She put out her hand, and Robert gave her back the ticket, though not without a certain reluctance.

"I'm curious," she said, defending herself. "If it's a phone number, why is it written on this ticket? And this is recent. He must have bought this ticket the day before he left." She looked at the ticket's date. "Yes, he did," she said. "December fourteenth."

This was a perfectly reasonable thing to do, she thought as she walked to the telephone by the sofa. She picked up the receiver and tapped in the numbers. Almost immediately, she could hear a distinctly foreign ring, a sound that always put her in mind of old-fashioned Parisian telephones with spindly black cradles.

A voice answered at the other end, and Kathryn, startled by the voice, unprepared for it, glanced quickly up at Robert. She'd given no thought at all to what she wanted to say. A woman said *hello* again, this time in a slightly irritated voice. Not an old woman, not a girl.

Kathryn searched for a name. She wanted to ask: *Did you ever know a man named Jack Lyons?* but the question suddenly seemed absurd.

"I must have the wrong number," Kathryn said quickly. "Sorry to have bothered you."

"Who is this?" the woman asked, wary now.

Kathryn couldn't bring herself to say her name.

There was the click of a phone hung up in annoyance. Followed by silence.

Her hands shaking badly, Kathryn replaced the receiver and sat down. She felt rattled much in the same way she once had as a girl, in junior high school, when she had called a boy she liked but hadn't been able to say her name.

"Let this go," Robert said quietly from the table.

Kathryn rubbed her hands along the thighs of her jeans to stop their trembling.

"Listen," she said. "Can you find out something for me?"

"What?"

"Could you find out the names of all of the crew Jack has ever flown with?"

"Why?" he asked.

"I might be able to recognize a name if I saw it. Or put a name to a face I've once seen."

"If that's what you want," he said slowly.

"It's hard to know what I want," she said.

While Robert went up to Jack's office to get the crew list, Kathryn spread out all of the other papers from the crumpled wad and scanned them. She noticed particularly the receipt from the post office for a twenty-two-dollar purchase. Perhaps it was not for stamps, she thought, peering at the receipt more closely. She opened up the piece of white-lined paper and looked at the lines of poetry Jack had copied.

Here in the narrow passage and the pitiless north, perpetual
Betrayals, relentless resultless fighting.
A random fury of dirks in the dark: a struggle for survival
Of hungry blind cells of life in the womb.

What did the poem mean? She glanced up at the white-out beyond the windows. Already there was a significant accumulation on the lawn, and she thought she should probably call Julia to make sure she and Mattie were OK. She wondered if Mattie was up yet.

She unfolded the second piece of lined paper — the remember list. *Bergdorf FedEx robe to arrive 20th.*

Odd, she thought, but a FedEx package had not come on the twentieth. She was certain of that.

Rising from the table, she once again pondered the significance of the lines of poetry. They meant little to her now, but perhaps she could find the whole poem and that would suggest an idea to her. She walked over to the bookshelf. It was little more than a tall tier of wooden planks, stretching nearly to the ceiling. Jack had read books about airplanes and biographies about men, sometimes a novel with a clever plot. For her part, Kathryn mostly read fiction written by women, usually contemporary novels, although she had a special fondness for Edith Wharton and Willa Cather. She searched for an old anthology of poetry and found it on the bottom shelf.

She sat on the edge of the sofa. She propped the book on her lap and began to turn the pages. When nothing immediately revealed itself, she decided to start at the beginning with the intention of turning each page until she had found the lines she was looking for. But it quickly became clear to her that she wouldn't have to do that: The early poems were ancient. Using the language in the lines of the poem as a guide, she opened the book about halfway through. There, the verse was by poets who wrote in a syntax similar to the lines she had in her hand. She began methodically to make her way through the pages when Robert called to her from Jack's office.

Outside, the snow was thickening steadily, falling against the windows in swift cascades. The forecasters were predicting six to eight inches, Robert had said. At least Kathryn knew where Mattie was and that she wouldn't be going out in a car.

She put the book down and went up to Jack's office, where Robert was seated at the desk. In his hands, he held the shiny paper of a fax. And she realized suddenly, as she saw him sitting in Jack's chair, that Robert knew what was on the tape — of course he did.

"Tell me about the tape," she said.

"This is a list of all of the people Jack ever flew with at Vision," he said, handing her the fax.

"Thank you," she said, taking the list from him but not looking at it. She could see that he hadn't thought she would ask. "Please," she said. "Tell me what you know."

He crossed his arms and rolled the chair away from the desk, putting a little distance between them. "I haven't heard the tape itself," he said. "None of us has."

"No, I know that."

"I can only tell you what I've been told by a friend of mine who works with me at the union."

"I know."

"You really want to hear this?"

"Yes," she said, although she didn't know, she couldn't be

sure. How could she be sure she wanted to hear it until she'd heard it?

He stood abruptly and walked to the window, his back to Kathryn. He spoke briskly, in a businesslike manner, as though to strip the words of any emotional content.

"The flight is normal until fifty-six minutes into it," he said. "Jack is apparently taken short."

"Taken short?"

"He leaves the cockpit at fifty-six minutes and fourteen seconds into the flight. He doesn't say what's wrong, only that he will be right back. They — the people who have heard the tape — assume he went into the bathroom." He turned to look in her direction, though not quite at her.

She nodded.

"Two minutes later, First Officer Roger Martin announces he's having trouble with his headset. He asks to borrow those of Trevor Sullivan, the engineer. Sullivan hands Martin his own headset and says, *Try these.* Martin tries the engineer's headset, finds Sullivan's works just fine, and says to him, *Well, it's not the plug. My headset must be bad.*"

"Roger Martin's headphones are bad," Kathryn said.

"Yes. So Martin gives Sullivan his headset back, and then Sullivan says, *Here, wait a minute. Maybe Lyons has a spare.* Apparently, Sullivan then unfastens his seat belt and reaches over into Jack's flight bag. You know where the flight bags are stowed?"

"Beside the pilots?"

"On the outside bulkhead beside each pilot. Yes. And Sullivan must then pull out something from Jack's flight bag that he doesn't recognize. Because he says, *What the hell?*"

"It's something he didn't expect."

"It seems that way."

"Not headphones."

"We don't know."

"And then?"

"And then Jack enters the cockpit. Sullivan says, *Lyons, is this a joke?*"

Robert paused. He leaned against the windowsill, half sitting.

"There may have been a scuffle here," Robert said. "I've heard conflicting reports. But if there was, it was quick. Because Sullivan says almost immediately, *What the fuck?*"

"And?"

"And then he says, *Jesus Christ.*"

"Who says *Jesus Christ?*"

"Sullivan."

"And?"

"And that's all."

"No one says anything else?"

"The tape ends."

She tilted her head toward the ceiling, contemplating what the end of the tape meant.

"He had a bomb in his flight bag," she said quietly. "An armed bomb. That's why they think suicide."

Robert stood. He put his hands in his pockets.

"Even one phrase different," Robert said, "and the whole tape could mean something else. Even with the words exactly as I've just said them, the tape doesn't necessarily mean anything. You know that. We've talked about that."

"Do they know for sure Jack was in the cockpit at the time?"

"They can hear the latch of the cockpit door opening and closing. After which Sullivan addresses him specifically."

"What I don't understand," she said, "is how Jack could possibly have something that dangerous in his flight bag."

"Actually," Robert said, "that's the easy part." He turned to look out at the snow. "It's harmless. Absolutely harmless. Everyone does it."

"Does what?"

"A lot of international pilots do it, almost every flight attendant I've ever known," Robert said. "Usually, it's jewelry. Gold and silver, sometimes gems."

She wasn't sure she understood. She thought of the jewelry she had received from Jack over the years: a thin gold bracelet on an anniversary, a gold S-chain for a birthday, diamond-studded earrings once for Christmas.

"A hundred times in and out of an airport, you get to know the security people pretty well," Robert said. "They chat about their families and they wave you through. It's a courtesy. When I was flying, I probably had to show my passport one time in fifty. And customs almost never looked in my flight bag."

Kathryn shook her head. "I had no idea," she said. "Jack never said."

"Some of the pilots, they keep it to themselves. I guess if what you're bringing in is a present, it spoils the gift if the wife knows you smuggled it past customs. I don't know."

"Did you do it?" she asked.

"Always at Christmas," he said. "That would be the question when you met in the lobby to take the van to the airport: What'd you get the wife?"

She put her hands into the pockets of her jeans; she stood with her shoulders hunched.

"Why doesn't Jack say anything on the tape?" Kathryn asked. "If he didn't know it was a bomb, he'd have been just as surprised as Trevor Sullivan. He'd have said something. He'd have said, What are you talking about? He'd have exclaimed or shouted."

"Not necessarily."

"Jack lied about his mother," Kathryn said.

"So?"

"He didn't sleep in the crew apartment," she said.

"It's not enough."

"Someone put a bomb on the plane," she said.

"If it was a bomb, someone put it there. I'll grant you that."

"And Jack must have known about it," she said. "It was his flight bag."

"I won't grant you that."

"The Moroccan pilot committed suicide," she said.

"That was entirely different."

"How do we know it was different?"

"You're just playing devil's advocate," Robert said to her with some heat. "You don't really believe Jack did this." Robert sighed with frustration and turned his back to her.

"You wanted to know about the tape," he said, "and so I told you."

She unfolded the fax that she'd tucked under her arm. There were a great many names, nine or ten pages of names, beginning with Jack's most recent crew and receding in time until 1986, the year he had started with the airline. She looked at the list: Christopher Haverstraw, Paul Kennedy, Michael DiSantis, Richard Goldthwaite . . . Occasionally, a face would appear, a man or woman she and Jack had once had dinner with, or someone she'd met at a party, although most of the names were unknown to her, and half of them lived in England. In that way, she thought, the life of a Vision pilot was an odd one, an almost antisocial profession. Members of a crew Jack flew with might live fifty miles away or across the ocean.

And then, on a list dated 1992, she saw the name she hadn't even realized she'd been looking for, the unusual name that rose right up from the paper and traveled through her bones with a charge.

Muire Boland.

Flight attendant.

Kathryn spoke the name aloud.

Muire Boland.

She was pretty sure it was a woman's name. She wondered if it was French and whether she was pronouncing it correctly. Kathryn reached down in front of her and opened the large drawer of Jack's desk. The junk-mail envelope with the name penciled in a corner wasn't there, but she could see it just as clearly as she could see the typed name on the list she held in her hands. *Muire 3:30,* the hastily scrawled note had read. On an envelope, a solicitation from Bay Bank.

Knowing instinctively that if she hesitated she'd be paralyzed with indecision, Kathryn took the lottery ticket out of her pocket and laid it on Jack's desk. She lifted up the telephone and once again punched in the number written on it. A voice answered, the same voice as before.

"Hello," Kathryn said quickly. "Is Muire there?"

"Who?"

Kathryn repeated the name.

"Oh, you mean *Muire,*" the voice at the other end said, and Kathryn heard the corrected pronunciation: *Meur-ah,* with a bit of a drumroll on the *R.* "No," the woman said.

"Oh, sorry," Kathryn said, feeling a tremendous rush of relief. She wanted only to get off the phone now.

"Muire *was* here," the English voice said, "but she's gone back to her own place. Are you a friend?"

Kathryn couldn't answer her. She sat heavily in the chair.

"Who is this?" the woman in London asked.

Kathryn opened her mouth but couldn't say her name. She pressed the receiver to her chest.

M at A's, the lottery ticket in front of her read. *Muire 3:30,* the junk-mail envelope had read. Two notations, in Jack's hand, written four years apart and connected with a phone call.

Robert took the receiver from her and placed it back on its cradle.

"What made you ask for Muire?" he asked quietly. "You've gone white."

"Just a guess," she said.

Who was the woman called Muire? And what was Jack's connection to her? Might he have spent his last night with this woman? Had Jack been having an affair? The questions pushed against her chest, threatening to suffocate her. She thought about all the jokes people routinely made about airline pilots and flight attendants. She had always dismissed the jokes, as if no real pilot would be so obvious.

"Robert, can you find out anything more about one particular name?" she asked. "Where a person lives?"

"If you're sure that's what you want," he said.

"This is hell," she said.

"Then leave it alone."

She thought about the possibility of leaving this alone.

"Would you be able to?" she asked.

"She wanted to watch TV," Julia was saying. "I had to think of something else instead. Someone once gave me *Witness* for Christmas."

Robert had left the office. Kathryn thought he might be washing dishes.

"Jack did."

"Well, she seems involved. She woke up at two. She's eaten."

"Don't let her watch the TV," Kathryn said. "I'm serious. Cut the cable if you have to."

Kathryn swiveled in the office chair and gazed out at a rising snow line on the outside windowsill. It looked like water in a fish tank. *Muire was here*, a voice had said.

"Robert is with you?" Julia asked.

"Yes."

"He came here, you know."

"I know."

"Then you know about . . ."

"The crew apartment? Yes." Kathryn drew a leg up, wrapped an arm around her knee. Two notations, four years apart, connected by a single initial. Kathryn felt a squeeze of anxiety, one that immediately produced beads of sweat on her forehead.

"Don't lose your faith," Julia said.

"What faith would that be, exactly?"

"You know what I mean."

"I'm trying not to."

"They've revised the forecast," Julia said. "Ten to twelve."

"I'd better come now," Kathryn said, wiping her forehead with her sleeve.

"Don't be silly. Don't go out if you don't have to. Have you got food?"

Just like Julia to think of food.

"I've eaten," Kathryn said. "Can I talk to Mattie?"

There was a silence at the other end of the line.

"You know," Julia said carefully, "Mattie's occupied. She's fine. If you talk to her, she'll just get sad and distant again. She needs to rest for a few days, just watch videos and eat popcorn. It's like a drug, and she needs it for as long as possible. She needs to heal, Kathryn."

"But I'd like to be with her," Kathryn protested.

"Kathryn, you've been with her every minute of every day for ten days. You understand that just by your presence, you're tearing each other apart. You can't bear her grief, and she can't bear to think of how much you're hurting. You don't normally spend time with her like that."

"This isn't normally."

"Well, maybe we could all use a bit of normally right now," Julia said.

Kathryn walked to the window and wiped away the condensation that had formed on the panes. The snow was indeed thick, and the driveway had not been plowed. There must have been eight inches already on the cars.

She sighed. It was always difficult to refute Julia's wisdom, especially as Julia so often turned out to be right.

"Don't leave the house," Julia repeated.

Through the long afternoon, the snow fell steadily, thickening as it did so. From time to time, the wind whistled and howled but then seemed almost immediately to subside, as though the storm were giving up its attempt to become a blizzard. While Robert made calls from Jack's office, Kathryn meandered from one room to another, looking at the walls and out the windows, crossing her arms, uncrossing them, then wandering into a different room and standing in it and staring at the walls or out the windows again. Lately, just standing and thinking had sometimes been all she could manage.

After a time, she found herself in the bathroom. She took off her clothes and turned on the shower, letting the water heat up until it was almost scalding. When she stepped in, she bent the back of her neck to the spray and stood in that attitude for a long time. It was such a pleasurable sensation that she stood there until the hot-water tank had emptied itself and the water turned cool.

When she shut the water off, she could hear music. Not a CD, although it was piano music.

She adjusted the collar of a long gray bathrobe, a brushed cotton that fell to her ankles. An ancient woman stared at her from the mirror, a washed-out face with hollow eyes.

Brushing her hair as she walked, she followed the music down the stairs and into the front room, where Robert was playing the piano.

She knew the piece: Chopin. She lay down on the sofa, folding the robe closed over her lap and legs.

She shut her eyes. *Fantaisie Impromptu* was a lavish piece, unabashedly pretty, with an extravagant number of notes. Robert played it as she seldom heard it, without sentimentality, yet it carried with it the delicious weight of stirred memories and forgotten secrets. When she heard the glissandi, she thought of scattered diamonds.

The piano stood in the corner, sideways to the windows. Robert had rolled his sleeves, and she watched first his hands and then his forearms. There was something about the hush of snow that improved the acoustics in the room, or perhaps it was that there was no competition from any other noise; the piano sounded better than she remembered, even though it had not been tuned in months.

It must have been like this years ago, she thought, listening to Robert play. No television, no radio, no videos, just the space of a long white afternoon in which to make one's own time, one's own sound. And it was safe. She could put her mind elsewhere, not think about the crash or Jack or Mattie. The piano hadn't been something she and Jack had ever shared. It had been Kathryn's alone, a solitary pursuit, though a link to Julia, who was also safe.

"I had no idea," she said when he had finished.

"It's been a while," he said, turning to her.

"You're a romantic," she said, smiling. "A closet romantic. You play wonderfully."

"Thank you."

"Play something else?"

She saw then, in a way she hadn't quite before, that Robert was a man with a past — of course he was. He had an entire life she knew almost nothing about, a life during which he'd mastered the piano, learned to fly, become a drunk, married, had children, divorced his wife, and then had somehow become involved in his extraordinary job.

She recognized the tune: "The Shadow of Your Smile." Changing the mood in an instant.

When he had finished, he scratched the back of his neck and looked out at the snow. "There must be a foot at least out there," he said.

"The driveway's not plowed," she said. "What time is it?"

He looked at his watch. "Three," he said. "I think I'll go for a walk."

"In this?"

"Just to the end of the driveway and back. I need some air."

"I hope you know you don't have to go to the inn tonight. There are plenty of beds in this house. A lot of rooms. You can sleep on the daybed in my spare room," she added. "It's comfortable there. That's what it's for."

"For hiding, you said."

"Yes."

"The information you asked me for is on Jack's desk," he said. She started to speak, but he shook his head.

"Of all people," he said, "this should not have happened to you."

Kathryn dozed on the couch for a few minutes and then somewhat groggily climbed up to the bedroom with the idea of slipping into the bed and taking a long nap. She took the book of poetry with her.

She lay on the bed on her stomach and began to turn the pages, halfheartedly looking for the lines. She read bits of poems by Gerard Manley Hopkins and Wordsworth and Keats. About halfway through the book, the word *betrayals* suddenly caught her eye, and she realized she had found the correct poem. But then almost immediately, before she could even read the lines through, she saw a faint notation along the inner margin.

M!

Written in pencil, lightly, with an exclamation point.

And there. Unmistakably there.

She sat up sharply and looked closely at the poem, reading it through. The poem was called "Antrim" and was written by Robinson Jeffers. It seemed to be about ancient struggles on one small patch of land, presumably Antrim. About blood spilled for many causes, various ambushes and betrayals, the patriotism itself and the bodies sacrificed, all turned now to dust, the dust waiting for a resurrection.

What did it mean?

She let the book fall over the side of the bed and onto the floor. She lay down again and rolled her face into the pillow. She felt as though she had traveled a thousand miles.

When she woke, she glanced instinctively at the clock on her bedside table. It was three-thirty in the morning. She had slept nine hours. What day was it, anyway? The twenty-eighth? The twenty-ninth?

She twisted herself off the bed and half staggered out into the hallway. The door to the spare room was shut. Robert must have returned from his walk and gone in there to sleep, she thought. Or had he had a meal? Watched television? Read a book?

In the kitchen, there were no signs of anyone having cooked a meal. Kathryn made a pot of coffee and poured herself a cup. Through the windows over the sink, she could see it had stopped snowing. She moved to the back door and opened it and was immediately hit with a chilled spray of fine powder that fell from the eave. She blinked and shook her head. Adjusting to the darkness, she saw that the world was shrouded in a thick quilt of white, a candlewick quilt with shallow stitching, so that the trees and shrubs and cars were simply mounded humps. Indeed, there seemed to be so much snow that she wondered if the predictions of twelve inches hadn't been wildly optimistic. She closed the door and leaned against it.

M at A's.

Muire 3:30.

M!

Drawing her robe more tightly around herself, Kathryn quickly climbed the stairs to Jack's office, its dusty emptiness still a surprise. She saw the paper Robert had spoken of on Jack's desk.

Muire Boland, she read, had left the airline in January of 1993. Trained by Vision in London, she had been a flight attendant with the airline for three years. There was an address, a phone number, and a date of birth. Muire Boland was now thirty-one.

Robert had written a note beside the phone number. *Tried this,* it said. *When I called, no one had ever heard of her.* Beneath this information was a list of phone numbers. There were seven M. Bolands listed in the London directory.

Kathryn tried to formulate a question, a reasonable request. Did the person answering the phone know of a Jack Lyons? If so, could Kathryn ask a question or two? Was that such an unusual thing to ask?

Kathryn glanced around at the office, at its metallic blandness, its masculine aesthetic. She would not allow herself to believe that Jack had been having an affair. How could she, when she had seen firsthand what happened when a sensational story was woven around only a few facts, as had happened with the press when the CVR tape was leaked?

She picked up the telephone and dialed the first number. A man answered, and he sounded as though she had woken him. She quickly calculated the time in London — nine-forty in the morning. She asked if Muire was there.

The man coughed into the phone like a heavy smoker.

"Who's it you're wanting?" he asked, as if he hadn't heard the question correctly.

"Muire Boland," she said.

"No Muire Bolands here," the man said confidently.

"Sorry," Kathryn said and hung up the phone.

She crossed out the first number and tried the second. No response. She tried the third number. A man answered in a crisp, businesslike voice.

"Michael Boland here," he said, as if expecting a particular call.

"Sorry," Kathryn said. "Wrong number."

She crossed out the third number. She tried the fourth number. A woman answered the phone. "Hello?" the woman said.

"Hello," Kathryn said. "I'm looking for a Muire Boland."

The silence at the other end of the line was so complete Kathryn could hear the faint echo of someone else's transatlantic conversation.

"Hello?" Kathryn tried again.

The woman hung up. Kathryn sat with the dead receiver to her ear. She picked up the pencil to cross out the fourth number, but then she hesitated.

She called the fifth number instead. Then the sixth. Then the seventh. When she had finished, she looked at her list. On it, she had a man who didn't know a Muire; an unanswered number; a Michael Boland, businessman; a woman who didn't speak; another unanswered number; a message on an answering machine in an almost unintelligible accent saying that Kate and Murray hoped she would leave a number; a teenage girl who didn't know a Muire but said her mother's name was Mary.

She tried the fourth number again.

"Hello?" the same woman said.

"I'm sorry to bother you," Kathryn said quickly, before the other woman could hang up. "But I'm trying to locate a Muire Boland."

Eerily, there was a similar silence to the first. Something was in the background. Music? A dishwasher? And then Kathryn heard a small sound from the back of the woman's throat, like the beginning of a word that might be spoken. Followed by another silence, shorter this time.

"There's no Muire here," the voice said finally.

Kathryn thought there might have been a delay between her thoughts and her voice, because by the time she opened her mouth to speak, the line had gone dead.

When Robert found her in the morning, she was sitting at the table in the front room. The sun had come up, and the snow outside the windows was so blisteringly bright Robert had to squint to look at her. In the glare, she could see every line and pore on his face.

"It's bright in here," he said, turning his head away.

"Sometimes you need sunglasses in this room," she said. "Jack used to wear them."

She watched as Robert tucked in his shirt.

"How'd you sleep?" he asked.

"Fine," she said. "And you?"

"Great."

She could see that he had slept in his clothes. He had probably been too exhausted to get undressed, she thought.

Adjusting to the light, Robert seemed to see her face more clearly.

"What's wrong?" he asked.

Kathryn sat forward in the chair.

"I'm going to London," she said.

He didn't hesitate. He didn't hesitate at all.

"I'm going with you," he said.

THE TABLECLOTHS LIE SPREAD ACROSS THE FIELD, a giant's patchwork quilt. Knots of families sit on the cloths with paper plates or real silverware, iced tea in plastic thermoses. Small children run along the grassy pathways, sometimes through the middle of another family's lunch. Kathryn opens the picnic basket, an old pie basket of Julia's, and takes out grapes and Terra Chips, pita bread and hummus, a wedge of Brie and a small rectangle of something smelly. Stilton, she decides, sniffing the cheese. Not far from her, Jack stands talking with two other fathers. The day is overcast, slightly muggy, and already the blackflies are annoying. Kathryn watches as Jack bends his head and listens to men who are smaller than he is. He has a cup of soda in one hand; the other is in the pocket of his jeans. He laughs and lifts his head, catching Kathryn's eye. Behind the laugh, she can see the slight strain of sociability, the good-natured question in his eyes: When will this be over?

Farther across the field, Kathryn spots Mattie standing in a huddle with a group of friends, her arms crossed and wrapped at her sides as if she were cold, which she is not. It is simply being fifteen and not knowing where to put one's hands. Mattie's face, which is familiar and yet not to Kathryn, seems a work of art in transition, its shape newly elongated, the mouth no longer pouty from braces.

— Good turnout, Barbara McElroy says from an adjacent blanket.

Kathryn takes in the McElroy menu at a glance: fried chicken, supermarket potato salad, coleslaw, Fritos, brownies.

— Better than last year, Kathryn says.

— They'll do the softball game, don't you think?

— If it doesn't rain.

— Mattie's gotten taller, Barbara says, looking in Mattie's direction.

Kathryn nods. — Is Roxanne here? she asks. And then wishes she hadn't, for Roxanne, a slender fifteen-year-old with a lip ring, almost certainly wouldn't be seen at the annual school picnic. Kathryn occasionally speaks to the girl, who is wildly truant and heavily endowed with attitude, in the corridors at school. Barbara will be here then for Will, her seven-year-old, Kathryn decides. Barbara's husband, Louie, a cod fisherman, is often away, gone for long stretches at a time.

Like Jack, Kathryn thinks.

— Your grandmother has a wonderful old pie safe in the window, Joyce Keys calls from the cloth just beyond Barbara's. Kathryn takes in the Keys picnic as well: curried rice salad, cold salmon, Perrier, Martha Ingerbretson's *konfetkakke.* Joyce and her husband, James, are architects with their own firm in Portsmouth. Keys & Keys.

The whole social history of the town just in the picnics, Kathryn thinks.

— I haven't seen it, Kathryn says.

— Jack'll play, won't he? Barbara asks.

— Oh, I think so, Kathryn says.

She watches her husband dip his head to speak to Arthur
Kahler, the owner of the Mobil station, Jack's sometime tennis
partner. It is why his back so often bothers him, she decides; he's
always bending to listen to others. He has on a white polo shirt,
a pair of boat shoes. Another uniform of sorts. He slaps behind
his ear, looks at his hand, flicks a blackfly from his finger. He sees
her watching him.

— I'm starved, he says, coming to her and lowering himself
to the blanket.

— Should I get Mattie?

— No. She'll come by when she's ready.

— You're going to play softball?

— I guess so, he says, pouring himself another soda.

— You always think you'll mind and then you love it, she
teases.

He runs his fingers up and down her back. The touch is unexpected and delicious. She wants to bend her head forward and
close her eyes. He hasn't touched her in days.

— Actually, I could use a nice cold beer right now, he says,
dropping his hand.

— At a school picnic?

— Doesn't seem to bother Kahler.

Kathryn glances in Arthur Kahler's direction and notices
now the large red plastic cup in his hand.

Kathryn hands Jack a half moon of pita bread with hummus
inside.

— Martha said he was going to close the pumps next week.
Put in new ones. We'll have to go to Ely Falls for gas.

Jack nods silently.

— But, of course, you won't be here, Kathryn says, remembering that Jack will be away for two weeks — in London for his twice-annual training session.

— No. I won't.

— You know, I could go with you on this one. School ends next Wednesday. I could fly to London and meet you there. We'd have almost a week together. It'd be fun.

Jack looks away. The invitation hovers over the tablecloth like cigarette smoke on a wet day.

— We could leave Mattie with Julia, Kathryn adds. — Mattie would be thrilled to get rid of us for a week.

— I don't know, he says slowly, turning back to her.

— I haven't been to London in ages, she argues. — And never for any length of time.

He shakes his head. — You'd hate it. These training sessions, they're endless. We spend all day in the simulator. We have classes at night. We eat with the British crews. I'd never see you. We wouldn't be able to do anything.

— I'm pretty good at entertaining myself, she says. And then she wonders suddenly why she needs to argue this proposal at all.

— Then what's the point of going when I'm over there? he asks somewhat dismissively. — You might as well go by yourself.

Stung, she bites the inside of her cheek.

— Listen, he says apologetically, — I'd just be frustrated the whole time, knowing you were back in the hotel, knowing we could be doing London together. These sessions are bad enough. I don't think the extra pressure is a good idea.

She studies his face. A handsome face, a face people turn to look at when they walk by.

— I'll tell you what, he says. — Why don't you come over at the end of the session, and we'll go to Spain. I'll take some time off, and we'll fly to Madrid. No, better yet: I'll meet you there.

He seems more animated now, relieved to have worked out this compromise.

— We'll do Barcelona, too, he says. — Barcelona is great.

— You've been there? she asks.

— No, he says quickly. — I've just heard about it.

She thinks about a trip to Spain with Jack. It would be enjoyable, she knows, but Spain isn't really what she had in mind. Jack will still be away from her for two weeks, away from Mattie for longer. She wanted to go to London.

Over Jack's shoulder, Kathryn can see that Barbara McElroy is watching her intently. Barbara, who knows what it is like to be left for long periods of time.

— Sounds like a date, Kathryn says, forcing a note of cheer.

— Hey, Lyons, a voice calls from above the blanket. Kathryn looks up and squints into the glare of the overcast sky. Sonny Philbrick, a man with a pronounced beer belly under his Patriots T-shirt, kicks Jack playfully in the foot.

— Hey, Sonny, Jack says.

— So how's the airline business? Sonny asks.

— Oh, fine, Jack says. — How's the video business?

— Hangin' in there. So where you off to now?

Kathryn busies herself with the picnic.

Jack draws his feet in from the edge of the tablecloth. He won't stand up, she knows, because he doesn't want to encourage Philbrick. Philbrick's son, who is Mattie's age, is a slight boy with a pretty face — a chess wizard, possibly a prodigy.

— London, Jack says.

— London, huh?

— London, Jack repeats. Kathryn can hear the effort to be

polite in her husband's voice. They both know where this conversation is going. The same place all of Jack's conversations with men like Philbrick go.

— For how long? Philbrick asks, looking straight at Kathryn.

— Two weeks, Jack says.

— Two weeks! Philbrick bends backward in mock surprise. — You over there with those stewardesses for two weeks, man, you better behave yourself.

Philbrick winks slyly at Kathryn. Philbrick would have been the class bully in school, she decides.

— Flight attendants, Jack says.

— Hey, whatever.

— Actually, Jack says slowly and evenly, — I try to screw around as much as I possibly can.

For just a second, Philbrick's face loosens with incomprehension. Then he grins, jabs the air with his paper cup. He laughs too loudly, causing others to look up at him from nearby blankets.

— Lyons, you're something else, you know that?

There is an awkward pause then. Jack doesn't respond.

— Well, see you at the game, Philbrick says. — You're gonna play, right?

Jack nods, turns toward the picnic basket as if looking for something inside. Kathryn watches Philbrick walk away.

— Jesus, Jack says under his breath.

AT THE GATE, THEY STOOD APART FROM THE OTHERS. Beyond the plate-glass windows, large mounds of improbably still-white snow stood guard over the apron. Robert had his overcoat folded twice and set upon a molded plastic seat. He had put his overnight bag on top of the coat (something a woman never would have done, Kathryn thought), and he was reading the *Wall Street Journal*. Kathryn held her coat over her arm and examined the plane in front of her, tethered to the gate by its accordion umbilical. The plane was pretty, she thought, white with bright red markings, the Vision logo written in a snappy script. The T-900 was angled in such a way that she could see into the cockpit, could see men in shirtsleeves, their faces in shadow, their arms moving along the instrument panel as they worked their way through the checklist. She wondered if she had ever met any of the crew before. Had they come to the memorial service?

Her feet hurt, and she wanted to sit down. But to do so would have meant sandwiching herself between two overburdened passengers. In any event, there were only minutes left until they boarded. Kathryn had on her black wool crepe suit, her funeral suit, and she resembled, she thought, more a businesswoman than a schoolteacher. A lawyer, possibly, headed to London for a deposition. She wore her hair in a loose twist, and she had on pearl earrings. She had her leather gloves in one hand and a black chenille scarf around her neck. She thought she looked rather good, under the circumstances, certainly more put together than she had in weeks. But she had lost weight in her face and knew she looked older than she had twelve days ago.

That morning, after she had told Robert about her proposed trip to London, she had driven over to Julia's to tell Mattie of her plans. Mattie had been painfully indifferent to Kathryn's trip. Her only lucid comment, amidst sighs and a muffled groan of exasperation, had been a dismissive *Whatever*.

"I'm only going for two days," Kathryn had said.

"Cool," Mattie had said. "Can I go back to bed now?"

In the kitchen, Julia had tried to explain Mattie's seeming indifference.

"She's fifteen," said Julia, who had been up for hours. She was dressed for her day in a pair of jeans with an elastic waist and a green sweatshirt. "She has to have someone to blame, so she's blaming you. I know it's irrational. You don't remember this, but for a time, right after your parents died, you blamed me."

"I did not," Kathryn said heatedly.

"Yes, you did. You never said it outright, but I knew. And it passed. Like this, too, will pass. Right now, Mattie wants to blame her father. She's furious with him for leaving her, for upsetting her life in such a drastic way. But blaming him is out of the question. She's practically his only defender. Eventually,

Mattie's anger will slide away from you and find its proper target. What you need to do is to make sure the anger doesn't come about full circle so that she begins to blame herself for her father's death."

"Then I should stay," Kathryn said weakly.

But Julia had been adamant that Kathryn should go. Privately, Kathryn understood that Julia wanted to get her out of the house not for her sake, but for Mattie's.

As the widow of a pilot, Kathryn was entitled to fly on a pass wherever Vision went, in the first-class section whenever seats were available. She gestured to Robert to take the window, and she stowed her luggage under the seat in front of her. Immediately she became aware of the stale air inside the plane, with its distinctive artificial smell. The door to the cockpit was open, and Kathryn could see the crew. The size of the cockpit never failed to startle her: Many of them were smaller than the front seats of automobiles. She wondered how it was possible for the scenario suggested by the CVR on Jack's plane to have taken place. There seemed hardly room for three men to sit, let alone move around and have a scuffle.

From her vantage point, she could see only the inner third of the cockpit, bits of each pilot in shirtsleeves. It was impossible, gazing at the tableau — the thickish arms, the confident gestures — not to imagine the man in the left-hand seat as Jack. She pictured the shape of his shoulder, the whiteness of his inner wrist. She had never been a passenger on an airliner Jack was flying.

The captain rose and turned toward the cabin. His eyes found Kathryn's, and she understood that he meant to express his sympathy. He was an older man with a fringe of gray hair and light brown eyes. He seemed almost too kindly to be in charge. He was hopeless with the condolences, and she liked him for his inarticulateness. She thanked him and even managed a slight smile. She said she was doing as well as could be expected under the circumstances, which was all anyone ever wanted to hear. He asked her if she would be traveling on to Malin Head to be with the other family members, and she answered, quickly and perhaps too emphatically, no. He seemed embarrassed for having asked. She turned then and introduced the captain to Robert Hart. The captain studied Robert as if he might be someone he had met before. Then the man excused himself, went back up to the cockpit, and locked the door behind him. For his safety. For their safety.

The flight attendant collected the champagne glasses she'd brought around earlier, and Kathryn saw to her surprise that she had drained hers. She couldn't remember drinking it, though she could taste it in her mouth. She looked at her watch: 8:14 in the evening. It would be 1:14 A.M. in London.

The plane lumbered to the runway. The pilot — the captain with the washed-out eyes? — revved the engines for the takeoff. Her heart stalled for one prolonged beat, then kicked painfully inside her chest. Her vision narrowed to a dot, the way the picture used to do when one turned off the TV. Kathryn held the armrests and closed her eyes. She bit her lower lip. A veil of protective mist dissipated, and she saw all that was possible: Pieces of bulkhead flooring ripped from the cabin; a person, perhaps a child, harnessed into a seat, spinning through the open air; a fire beginning in a cargo hold and spreading into the cabin.

The plane gathered speed with unnatural momentum. The staggeringly heavy mass of the T-900 would refuse to lift. She shut her eyes and began to pray the only prayer she could remember: *Our Father* . . .

She had never before known fear on an airliner. Even on the bumpiest transatlantic flights. Jack had always been relaxed on a plane, as both a pilot and a passenger, and his calm had seemed to seep into Kathryn through a kind of marital osmosis. But that protection was gone now. If she had believed herself safe in an airplane because Jack had, didn't it follow that she could die in a plane if he had? She felt then the shame and revulsion of knowing she was going to be sick. Robert put his hand on her back.

When the plane was airborne, Robert signaled to the flight attendant, who brought ice water and cold towels and a discreet paper bag. Kathryn's body, unable to perceive relief in having made it aloft, rebelled. To her chagrin, she vomited up the champagne. She was amazed at how intensely visceral the fear of one's own death was: She hadn't been this sick even when she'd learned that Jack had died.

As soon as the seat belt sign was turned off, Kathryn rose unsteadily to use the lavatory. A flight attendant handed her a plastic envelope containing a toothbrush, toothpaste, a washcloth, a bar of soap, and a comb, and Kathryn realized such kits were kept on hand expressly for physically distraught passengers. Were they for first-class passengers only, or did everyone get one?

In the tiny lavatory, Kathryn washed her face. Her slip and blouse were soaked with sweat, and she tried to dry the skin of her shoulders and neck with paper towels. The plane lurched, and she banged her head against a cabinet. She brushed her teeth as best she could and thought of all the times she'd felt condescending toward people who were afraid to fly.

When she returned, Robert rose from his seat and took her arm.

"I can't explain," she said, sitting down and gesturing for him to do the same. "I suppose it was fear. I was certain the plane wouldn't get off the ground and that we'd be going so fast, we'd crash."

He gently squeezed her arm.

She pressed her seat back, and Robert aligned his seat with hers. Almost reluctantly, it seemed, he took a magazine from his briefcase.

She fingered her wedding ring.

Over the intercom, the captain spoke with a resonant voice that was meant to be reassuring. Yet flight itself still felt wrong. The difficulty lay with the mind accommodating itself to the notion of the plane, with all its weight, defying gravity, staying aloft. She understood the aerodynamics of flight, could comprehend the laws of physics that made flight possible, but her heart, at the moment, would have none of it. Her heart knew the plane could fall out of the sky.

When she woke, it was dark both inside and outside of the plane. Overhead, a washed-out movie played silently on a screen. They were flying toward morning. When Jack had died, he'd flown into darkness, as if he were outrunning the sun.

Through the windows, she saw clouds. Over where? she wondered. Newfoundland? The Atlantic? Malin Head?

She wondered if the heart stopped from the concussion of the bomb, or if it stopped at the moment of certain knowledge that one would die, or if it stopped in reaction to the horror of falling through the darkness, or if it did not stop until the body hit the water.

What was it like to watch the cockpit split away from the cabin, and then to feel yourself, still harnessed to your seat, falling through the night, knowing that you would hit the water at terminal velocity, as surely Jack would have known if he were conscious? Did he cry out Kathryn's name? Another woman's name? Was it Mattie's name he called in the end? Or had Jack, too, in the last desperate wail of his life, called out for his mother?

She hoped her husband had not had to cry out any name, that he had not had a second to know he would die.

Beside her in the taxi, Robert stretched his legs. The gold buttons on his blazer had set off the airport security alarm. He wore gray trousers, a white shirt, a black-and-gold paisley tie. He looked thinner than he had just yesterday.

She raised a hand to her hair and tried to refasten a wisp. Between them were two overnight bags, both remarkably small. She had packed hastily, without much thought. Her case contained a change of underwear and stockings, a different blouse. They entered London proper and began to pass through pleasant residential areas. The taxi pulled abruptly to a curb.

Through the rain, Kathryn saw a street of white stucco town houses, an immaculate row of almost identical facades. The houses rose four stories tall and were graced with bow-front windows. Delicate wrought-iron fences bordered the sidewalk, and each house bore a lantern hanging from a columned portico. Only the front doors spoke of individuality. Some were thick, wood-paneled doors; some had small glass panes; others were painted dark green. The houses closest to the taxi were identified with discreet numbers on small brass plaques. The house they'd parked in front of read Number 21.

Kathryn sat back on the upholstered seat.

"Not yet," she said.

"Do you want me to go instead?" he asked.

She thought about the offer and smoothed her skirt. Like the steady hum of the engine, the driver seemed unperturbed by the wait.

"What would you do when you got there?" she asked.

He shook his head, as if to say he hadn't given it any thought. Or that he would do what she asked him to.

"What will you do?" he asked.

Kathryn felt light-headed and thought she could no longer predict with any accuracy the actions and reactions of her body. The difficulty with not thinking about the immediate future, she decided, was that it left one unprepared for its reality.

The drive to the hotel was brief, the block on which it stood eerily like the one they had just left. The hotel had taken over seven or eight town houses and had a discreet entrance. The upper floors were ringed with pristine white balustrades.

Robert had booked two adjacent, but not adjoining, rooms. He carried her bag to the door.

"We'll have lunch downstairs in the pub," he said. He checked his watch. "At noon?"

"Sure," she answered.

"You don't have to do this," he said.

Her room was small but perfectly adequate. The walls bore an innocuous wallpaper, brass wall sconces. There was a desk and a bed, a trouser press, an alcove where one could make a cup of coffee or tea.

She showered, changed her underwear and blouse, and

brushed her hair. Looking into the mirror, she put her hands to her face. She could no longer deny that something was waiting for her here in this city.

Sometimes, she thought, courage was simply a matter of putting one foot in front of another and not stopping.

The pub was dark, with wood-paneled alcoves. Irish music played from overhead. Prints of horses, matted in dark green and framed in gold, were hung upon the walls. A half-dozen men sat at the bar drinking large glasses of beer, and pairs of businessmen were seated in the alcoves. She spotted Robert across the room, comfortably slouched against a banquette cushion. He looked contented, perhaps more than contented. He waved to her.

She crossed the room and lay her purse on the banquette.

"I took the liberty of ordering you a drink," he said.

She glanced at the ale. In front of Robert was a glass of mineral water. She slipped in next to him. Her feet brushed his, but it seemed rude to pull away.

"What happened to you?" she asked suddenly, gesturing toward the water. "I mean with the drinking? I'm sorry. Do you mind my asking?"

"No," he said, shaking his head. "My parents were both professors at a college in Toronto. Every evening, they held court for the students — a kind of salon. The tray with the bottles on it was always the focal point of the gathering. The students loved it, of course. I started joining them when I was fifteen. Actually, now that I think of it, my parents probably created a lot of alcoholics."

"You're Canadian?"

"Originally. Not now."

Kathryn studied the man beside her. What did she know about him, except that he had been kind to her? He seemed good at his job, and he was undeniably attractive. She wondered if accompanying her to London was somehow part of his job description.

"We might have come here for no good reason," she said, and could hear the note of hope in her voice. Like finding a suspicious lump in your breast, she thought, and then having the doctor tell you it was nothing, nothing at all. "Robert, I'm sorry," she said. "This is nuts. I know you must think I'm out of my mind. I'm really sorry to have dragged you into it."

"I love London," he said quickly, seemingly unwilling to dismiss their joint venture so quickly. "You need to eat something," he said. "I hate Irish music. Why is it always so lugubrious?"

She smiled. "Have you been here before?" she asked, acquiescing to the change in subject. "To this hotel?"

"I come here fairly often," he said. "We *liaise*, I believe the word is, with our British counterparts."

She studied the menu, laid it down on the polished but slightly sticky veneer of the table.

"You have a beautiful face," he said suddenly.

She blushed. No one had said that to her in a long time. She was embarrassed that she had colored, that he could see it mattered. She picked up the menu again and began to reexamine it. "I can't eat, Robert. I just can't."

"There's something I want to tell you," he began.

She held her hand up. She didn't want him to say anything that would require her to respond.

"I'm sorry," he said, glancing away. "You don't need this."

"I was just thinking about how enjoyable this is," she said quietly.

And she saw, with surprise, that he couldn't hide his disappointment at the tepid offering.

"I'm going to go now," she said.

"I'll go with you."

"No," she said. "I have to do this alone."

He leaned over and kissed her cheek.

"Be careful," he said.

She went out onto the street blindly, moving now with a momentum she didn't dare to question. The taxi dropped her in front of the narrow town house she had seen little more than an hour before. She surveyed the street, studied a small pink lamp in a ground-floor window. She paid the driver and was certain, as she stepped out onto the curb, that she had given the man too many coins.

The rain poured over the edges of her umbrella and soaked the back of her legs, spotting and then running down her stockings. There was a moment, as she stood on the steps in front of the imposing wooden door, when she thought: I don't have to do this. Though she understood in the same moment that it was knowing that she would positively do this that had allowed her the luxury of indecision.

She raised the heavy brass knocker and rapped on the door. She heard footsteps on an inner staircase, the short impatient cry of a child. The door opened abruptly, as though the person behind it were expecting a delivery.

It was a woman — a tall, angular woman with dark hair that fell along her jawline. The woman was thirty, perhaps thirty-five. She held a child on her hip, a child so astonishing that it was all Kathryn could do not to cry out.

Kathryn began to tremble inside her coat. She held the umbrella at an unnatural angle.

The woman with the child looked surprised, and for a moment quizzical. And then she did not seem surprised at all.

"I've been imagining this moment for years," the woman said.

THE FEATURES OF THE WOMAN IMPRESSED THEM-
selves upon Kathryn's consciousness, like acid eating away at a
photographic plate. The brown eyes, the thick, dark lashes. The
narrow jeans, long-legged. The ivory flats, well worn, like slip-
pers. The pink shirt, sleeves rolled. A thousand questions competed for Kathryn's attention. When? For how long? How was it
done? Why?

The baby in the woman's arms was a boy. A boy with blue
eyes. The hues were slightly different, though the difference was
not as pronounced as it had been in his father's eyes.

The envelope of time ripped open, and Kathryn dropped in.

She struggled not to have to lean against the door with the
shock of the woman, of the boy's face.

"Come in."

The invitation broke the long note of silence that had passed
between the two women. Although it was not an invitation at
all, not in the way such offers are normally made, with a smile or
a step backward into a hallway to allow entry. It was, rather, a

statement, simple and without inflection, as though the woman had said instead: Neither of us has a choice now.

And the instinct was, of course, to enter the house, to get in out of the wet. To sit down.

Kathryn lowered the umbrella and collapsed it as she stepped over the doorsill. The woman inside the house held the door with one hand, the baby with the other arm. The baby, perhaps having noted the silence, looked at the stranger with intense curiosity. A child in the hallway had stopped her playing to pay attention.

Kathryn allowed the umbrella to drip onto the polished parquet. In the several seconds the two women stood in the entryway, Kathryn noticed the way the woman's hair swayed along her chin line. Expertly cut, as Kathryn's was not. She touched her own hair and regretted doing so.

It was hot in the hallway, excessively hot and airless. Kathryn could feel the perspiration trickling inside her blouse, which was under her suit coat, which was under her wool coat.

"You're Muire Boland," Kathryn said.

The baby in Muire Boland's arms, despite the different sex, despite the slightly darker hair color, was precisely the baby that Mattie had been at that age — five months old, Kathryn guessed. The realization created dissonance, a screeching in her ears, as though this woman she had never met were holding Kathryn's child.

Jack had had a son.

The dark-haired woman turned and left the hallway for a sitting room, leaving Kathryn to follow. The child in the hallway, a beautiful girl with enlarged pupils and a cupid mouth, picked up a handful of construction blocks, pressed them to her chest, and, eyeing Kathryn the entire time, edged along the wall and entered the sitting room, moving closer to her mother's legs.

The girl looked like her mother, whereas the boy, the son, resembled the father.

Kathryn put down the umbrella in a corner and walked from the entryway to the sitting room. Muire Boland stood with her back to the fireplace, waiting for her, although there had been no invitation to sit down, wouldn't be.

The room had high ceilings and had been painted a lemon yellow. Ornately carved moldings were shiny with glossy white paint. At the front, the curved windows had long gauzy curtains on French rods. Several low chairs of wrought iron, cushioned with oversized white pillows, had been placed around a carved wooden cocktail table, reminding Kathryn of Arab rooms. Over the mantle, behind the woman's head, was a massive gold mirror, which reflected Kathryn's image in the doorway, so that, in essence, Kathryn and Muire Boland stood in the same frame. On the mantle was a photograph in marquetry, a pinkish-gold glass vase, a bronze figure. On either side of the bow window were tall bookcases. A carpet of muted grays and greens lay underfoot. The effect was of light and air, despite the grand architecture of the house, despite the dark of the weather.

Kathryn had to sit. She put a hand on a wooden chair just inside the doorway. She sat heavily, as though her legs had suddenly given out.

She felt old, older than the woman in front of her, who was nearly her own age. It was the baby, Kathryn thought, that somehow testified to the newness of love, certainly to the relative proximity of sex. Or the jeans in contrast to Kathryn's dark suit. Or the way Kathryn found herself sitting, her pocketbook primly in her lap.

Beneath her coat, her right leg spasmed, as though she had just climbed a mountain.

The baby began to fret, uttering small impatient cries. Muire Boland bent to pick up a rubber pacifier from the cocktail table, put the nipple end in her own mouth, sucked it several times, and then put it into the baby's mouth. The boy wore navy corduroy overalls and a striped T-shirt. The dark-haired woman had full, even lips and wore no lipstick.

Moving her eyes away from the woman with the baby, Kathryn caught sight of the photograph on the mantle. When the picture came into focus, she started, nearly rose from her seat. The photograph was of Jack, she could see that even across the room. Unmistakable now from where she sat. Cradling an infant, a newborn. His other hand ruffling the deep curls of another child, the girl who was in the room with them. In the picture, the girl had a solemn face. The trio appeared to be on a beach. Jack was smiling broadly.

Visceral evidence of another life. Although Kathryn had needed no proof.

"You're wearing a ring," Kathryn said almost involuntarily.

Muire fingered the gold band with her thumb.

"You're married?" Kathryn asked, disbelieving.

"I was."

Kathryn was confused for a moment, until she understood the meaning of the past tense.

Muire shifted the baby to her other hip.

"When?" Kathryn asked.

"Four and a half years ago."

The woman hardly moved her mouth when she spoke. The consonants and vowels rolled from her tongue with a distinctive melodic lilt. Irish, then.

"We were married in the Catholic Church," Muire volunteered.

Kathryn felt herself backing away from this information, as if from a blow.

"And you knew . . . ?" she asked.

"About you? Yes, of course."

As though that were understood. That the dark-haired woman had known everything. Whereas Kathryn had not.

Kathryn put down her pocketbook, shook her arms free of her coat. The flat was overheated, and Kathryn was sweating profusely. She could feel the perspiration under her hair, at the back of her neck.

"What's his name?" Kathryn asked, meaning the baby. She was astonished at her own politeness even as she asked the question.

"Dermot," Muire said. "For my brother."

The woman bent her head suddenly, kissed the baby's pate.

"How old is he?" Kathryn asked.

"Five months. Today."

And Kathryn thought at once, as who would not, that Jack might have been there, in that flat, to share the small milestone.

The baby, pacified, appeared now to be falling asleep. Despite the revelations of the last several minutes, despite the unnatural relationship between herself and the baby (despite the very fact of the child's existence at all), Kathryn felt an urge, akin to sexual, to hold the infant to her breast, to that hollow space that wants always to embrace a small child. The resemblance to Mattie at five months was uncanny. It might actually be Mattie. Kathryn closed her eyes.

"Are you all right?" Muire asked from across the room.

Kathryn opened her eyes, wiped her forehead with the sleeve of her jacket.

"I have thought . . . ," Muire began. "I have wondered if you would come. When you called, I was sure that you knew. I was sure when he died it would come out."

"I didn't know," Kathryn said. "Not really. Not until I saw the baby. Just now."

Or had she known? she wondered. Had she known from the moment she'd heard that transatlantic silence?

There were shallow wrinkles about the eyes of the dark-haired woman, the suggestion of parentheses that would one day form at either side of her mouth. The baby woke suddenly and began to wail in an uninhibited, lusty way that had once been familiar to Kathryn. Muire tried to comfort the child, bringing him to her shoulder, patting his back. But nothing seemed to work.

"Let me put him down," Muire said over the cries.

When she left the room, the girl trailed after her, not willing to be left alone with the stranger.

Jack had been married in a Catholic church. The dark-haired woman had known that he was already married.

Kathryn tried to stand, then felt she could not. She crossed her legs in an effort to look not quite so shaken. Not quite so flattened. Slowly, she swiveled her head, trying to take in the entire room. The brass sconces with the electric candles on the walls. The magazines on the cocktail table, an oil painting of a working-class city street. She wondered why it was that she could not feel rage. It was as though she had been cut, the knife having gone so deep that the wound was not yet painful; it produced merely shock. And the shock seemed to be producing civility.

Muire had known, had imagined this day. Kathryn had not.

Along one wall was a cabinet that Kathryn guessed would contain a television and a sound system. She thought suddenly of Pink Panther movies, the ones she and Jack and Mattie had rented, movies guaranteed to reduce Jack and Mattie to helpless giggles. They had prided themselves on being able to quote long passages of dialogue.

Kathryn turned her head at a sound. Muire Boland stood in the doorway, watching her from the side. She stepped into the room, crossed to one of the white chairs, and sat down. Immediately, she opened a wooden box on the cocktail table and took out a cigarette, which she lit with a plastic lighter next to the box.

Jack couldn't tolerate being in the same room with a smoker, he had said.

"You want to know how it happened," Muire said.

Though she was angular, she might be described as voluptuous. It was the baby, Kathryn thought. The nursing. Perhaps there was just the slightest suggestion of a belly, which would also be the baby.

Kathryn had another unexpected memory then, a picture, really, that Jack had taken. Kathryn was sleeping facedown in a quilted bathrobe on an unmade bed, her arms tucked under her. Jack, who'd been holding the five-month-old Mattie, had placed the sleeping baby, also facedown, on the hump made by Kathryn's butt and the dip of the lower back. Kathryn and Mattie had together taken a nap, and Jack, moved by the sight of the mother and her papoose, had snapped the photograph.

Muire leaned back against a cushion, draped one arm along its back. She crossed her legs. Kathryn thought she might be six feet tall, nearly as tall as Jack. Kathryn tried to imagine what her body looked like unclothed, how she and Jack might look together.

But her mind protested and rebelled, and the pictures refused to form. Just as the image of Jack's body as it may have lain in the ocean had at first refused to form. The pictures would come later, Kathryn knew, when she least wanted them.

"Yes," Kathryn said.

Muire took a pull on her cigarette, leaned forward, and flicked an ash. "I flew with him five and a half years ago. I was a flight attendant with Vision."

"I know."

"We fell in love," the woman said simply. "I won't go into all the details. I could say that we were both swept off our feet. We were together for a month that first time. We had . . . " The woman hesitated, perhaps from delicacy, perhaps trying to find better words. "We had an affair," she said finally. "Jack was torn. He said he wouldn't leave Mattie. He could never do that to his daughter."

The name *Mattie* produced a frisson in the air, a tension that quivered between the two women. Muire Boland had spoken the name too easily, as if she'd known the girl.

Kathryn thought: He wouldn't leave his daughter, but he could betray his wife.

"When was this exactly?" Kathryn asked. "The affair."

"June 1991."

"Oh."

What had she herself been doing in June of 1991? Kathryn wondered.

The woman had delicate white skin, an almost flawless complexion. The complexion of someone who spent little time outdoors. Though she might have been a runner.

"You knew about me," Kathryn repeated. Her voice didn't seem her own. It was too slow and tentative, as if she had been drugged.

"I knew about you from the very beginning," Muire said. "Jack and I did not have secrets."

The greater intimacy, then, Kathryn thought. An intentional knife wound.

The rain slid along the bowed windows, the clouds giving a false sense of early evening. From an upstairs room, Kathryn heard the distant squawk of a cartoon character on a television. Still perspiring, she shed her jacket and stood up, realizing as she did so that her blouse had become untucked. She made an effort to push it back into her skirt. Aware of the intense scrutiny of the woman across from her, a woman who may very well have known Jack better than she did, Kathryn prayed her legs would not betray her. She walked across the room to the mantle.

She took down the picture in its marquetry frame. Jack had on a shirt Kathryn had never seen before, a faded black polo shirt. He cradled the tiny newborn. The girl, the one Kathryn had just seen playing with the construction blocks, had Jack's curls and brow, though not his eyes.

"What's her name?" Kathryn asked.

"Dierdre."

Jack's fingers were deep in the girl's hair. Had Jack been the same with Dierdre as he had been with Mattie?

Kathryn briefly closed her eyes. The hurt to herself, she thought, was nearly intolerable. But the hurt to Mattie was obscene. One could see — how could anyone fail to observe? — that the girl in the photograph was extraordinarily beautiful. A beguiling face, with dark eyes and long lashes, red lips. A veritable Snow White. Had memories that Mattie held sacred been repeated, relived, with another child?

"How could you?" Kathryn cried, spinning, and she might have been speaking to Jack as well.

Her fingers, slippery from perspiration, lost hold of the frame. It slid out of her hands, crashed against an end table. She hadn't meant for that to happen, and she felt the small breakage as an exposure. The woman in the chair flinched slightly, though she did not turn her head to look at the damage. It was an unanswerable question. Though the woman wanted to answer it.

"I loved him," Muire said. "We were in love."

As if that were enough.

Kathryn watched as Muire put out her cigarette. How cool she was, thought Kathryn. Even cold.

"There are things I can't talk about," Muire said.

You bitch, Kathryn thought, a bubble of anger popping to the surface. She tried to calm herself down. It was hard to imagine the woman in the chair a flight attendant in a uniform with little wings on the lapel. Smiling at passengers as they entered a plane.

What were the *things* Muire Boland couldn't talk about?

She put her hands on the mantle, leaned her head forward. She breathed in deeply to calm herself. A distant rage made a sound like white noise in her ears.

She pushed herself away from the mantle and crossed the room. She perched near the edge of the wooden chair, as if she might, at any moment, have to get up and leave.

"I was willing to do whatever it took," Muire Boland said. She fingered her hair away from her forehead. "I tried once to throw him out. But I couldn't."

Kathryn folded her hands in her lap, considering this self-confessed lapse in character. The voluptuousness of the nursing, the slight suggestion of a belly, combined with the height, the angular shoulders, and the long arms, were arresting, undeniably attractive.

"How did you do it?" Kathryn asked. "I mean, how did it work?"

Muire Boland raised her chin. "We had so very little time together," she said. "We did whatever we could. I'd pick him up

at a prearranged spot near the crew apartment and bring him
here. Sometimes, we had only the night. At other times . . ."
Again, she hesitated. "Jack would sometimes bid schedules in
reverse," Muire said.

Kathryn heard the language of a pilot's wife.

"I don't understand," Kathryn said quickly. Though she
thought, sickeningly, that she did.

"Occasionally, he would be able to arrange it so that his home
base was in London. But, of course, that was risky."

Kathryn could remember the months Jack had seemed to
have a terrible schedule. Five days on, two days off, only the
overnight at home.

"As you know, he didn't always get London," Muire continued. "He sometimes had the Amsterdam-Nairobi route. I took a
flat in Amsterdam during those times."

"He paid for this?" Kathryn asked suddenly, thinking: He
took money from me. From Mattie.

"This is mine," Muire said, gesturing to the rooms. "I inherited
it from an aunt. I could sell it and move to the suburbs, but the
thought of moving to the suburbs is somehow rather chilling."

Kathryn, of course, lived in what might be described as a
suburb.

"He gave you money?" Kathryn persisted.

Muire looked away, as if sharing with Kathryn, for a moment,
the particular treachery of taking money from one family to
give to the other.

"Occasionally," she said. "I have some money of my own."

Kathryn speculated on the intensity of love that constant sep-
aration might engender. The intensity that being furtive and
secret would naturally create. She brought her hand to her
mouth, pressed her lips with her knuckles. Had her own love for

Jack not been strong enough? Could she say that she had still been in love with her husband when he died? Had she taken him for granted? Worse, had Jack ever suggested to Muire Boland that Kathryn hadn't loved him enough? She winced inwardly to think of that possibility. She drew a long breath and tried to sit up straighter.

"Where are you from?" Kathryn asked when she trusted her voice.

"Antrim."

Kathryn looked away. The poem, she thought. Of course. *Here in the narrow passage and the pitiless north, perpetual betrayals . . .*

"But you met here," Kathryn said. "You met Jack in London."

"We met in the air."

Kathryn glanced down at the carpet, imagining that airborne meeting.

"Where are you staying?" Muire asked.

Kathryn looked at the woman and blinked. She could not recall the name of her hotel. Muire reached forward and took another cigarette from the box.

"The Kensington Exeter," Kathryn said, remembering.

"If it makes you feel any better," Muire said, "I'm quite certain there was never anyone else."

It did not make her feel any better.

"How would you know?" Kathryn asked.

The outside light grew dimmer in the flat. Muire turned a lamp on and put a hand to the back of her neck.

"How did you find out?" Muire asked. "Discover us?"

Us, Kathryn heard.

She didn't want to answer the question. The search for clues seemed tawdry now.

"What happened on Jack's plane?" Kathryn asked instead.

Muire shook her head, and the silky hair swung. "I don't know," she said. But there was, possibly, an evasive note in her voice, and she seemed noticeably more pale. "The suggestion of suicide is outrageous," she said, bending forward, putting her elbows on her knees, her head in her hands. The smoke curled through her hair. "Jack would never, never . . ."

Kathryn was surprised by the woman's sudden passion, by a level of certainty she thought only she had felt. It was the only emotion the woman had shown since Kathryn had entered the flat.

"I envy you having had a service," Muire said, looking up. "A priest. I would have liked to be there."

My God, Kathryn thought.

"I saw your photograph," Muire said. "In the papers. The FBI is assembling its case?"

"So I'm told."

"Do they talk to you?"

"No. Did they call you?"

"No," Muire said. "You know Jack would never do this."

"Of course I know that," Kathryn said.

After all, Kathryn had been the first wife, the primary wife, had she not? But she wondered then: In a man's mind, who was the more important wife — the woman he sought to protect by not revealing the other? Or the one to whom he told all his secrets?

"The last time you saw him . . . ," Kathryn began.

"That morning. About four A.M. Just before he left for work. I woke up . . ." She left it there.

"You'd been out to dinner," Kathryn said.

"Yes," Muire said, looking slightly surprised that Kathryn knew this. She did not ask how.

Kathryn tried to remember if there had ever been an occasion when she had seriously suspected Jack of having an affair. She didn't think so. How devastatingly complete her trust in him had been.

"You came here just for this?" Muire asked, picking a stray sliver of tobacco from her lower lip. She seemed to have recovered her composure.

"Isn't that enough?" Kathryn asked.

Muire exhaled a long plume of smoke. "I meant will you be traveling on to Malin Head?" she asked.

"No," said Kathryn. "Have you been?"

"I couldn't go," she said.

There was something more. Kathryn could feel it.

"What is it?" Kathryn asked.

The woman rubbed her forehead. "Nothing," she said, shaking her head lightly. "We had an affair," she added, as if to explain what she had been thinking. "I became pregnant and took a leave from the airline. Jack wanted to be married. It wasn't as important to me. To be married. He wanted to be married in the Catholic Church."

"He never went to church."

"He was devout," Muire said and looked steadily at Kathryn.

"Then he was two different people," Kathryn said incredulously. It was one thing to be married in a Catholic church because a lover wanted it, quite another to be devout oneself. Kathryn intertwined her fingers, trying to steady them.

"He went to mass whenever he could," Muire said.

In Ely, Jack had never even entered a church. How could a man be two such different people? But then a new thought entered Kathryn's mind, an unwelcome thought: Jack wouldn't always have been two different people, would he? As a lover, for example. Mightn't some of the intimacies he shared with Kathryn have been the same as those he shared with Muire Boland? If Kathryn could bring herself to ask, wouldn't there be some recognition on the part of the woman sitting across from her? Or had there been an entirely other play? Another script? Different dialogue? Unrecognizable props? Kathryn unlinked her fingers, pressed her palms against her knees. Muire watched her intently. Perhaps she, too, was speculating.

"I have to use the bathroom," Kathryn said, standing up abruptly. The way a drunk might do.

Muire stood with her. "It's just upstairs," she said.

She led Kathryn out of the sitting room and through the hallway. She stood at the bottom of the steps, gesturing with her hand. Kathryn had to pass in front of her, and their bodies almost touched. Kathryn felt diminished by the woman's height.

The bathroom was claustrophobic and made Kathryn's heart race. She glanced into the mirror and saw that her face had taken on a hectic flush and was mottled. She pulled the pins from her hair and shook it loose. She sat down on the toilet lid. A floral print on the walls made her dizzy.

Four and a half years. Jack and Muire Boland had been married in a church four and a half years ago. Perhaps guests had gone to the wedding. Had any of them known the truth? Had Jack hesitated when he said his vows?

She shook her head roughly. Every thought bore with it a pictorial image Kathryn didn't want to look at. That was the difficulty — allowing the questions but holding back the images. Jack in a suit, kneeling in front of a priest. Jack opening a car door, slipping into the passenger seat. A small girl with dark curls hugging Jack's knees.

In the distance, a telephone rang.

How, Kathryn wondered, had Jack possibly managed it? The lies, the deception, the lack of sleep? One day he had left Kathryn and gone to work, and then within hours was standing in a church at his own wedding. What had Kathryn and Mattie been doing on that day, at that precise hour? How had Jack been able to face them both when he came home? Had he made love to Kathryn that night, the next night, that week? She shuddered to think of it.

The questions bounced with tiny pings from wall to wall, repeating themselves endlessly. Then she remembered, her stomach lurching, the twice-yearly training sessions in London. Two weeks each.

If you never suspected someone, she realized, you never thought to suspect.

She stood up quickly, her eyes skittering around the tiny powder room. She splashed water on her face, dried it with an embroidered towel. She opened the bathroom door and saw across the hallway a queen-sized bed. From downstairs, Kathryn could hear Muire talking on the telephone, the words rising and falling in her foreign lilt. If Jack had not been dead, she would perhaps not have had a right to enter the bedroom, but now nothing could matter. This house was hers to see. Knowledge of this house was owed to her. After all, Muire Boland had known all about her, hadn't she?

Kathryn ached to think of that reality. How many details exactly had Muire been told? And how intimate were those details?

She walked through the doorway and thought of the effort she had made to please Jack, of the accommodations she had made for him. Of the way she had created an entire theory of diminished sexual intimacy. Of the way she had once confronted Jack with the fact of his withdrawal, and he had denied it, made it seem beneath his consideration, beneath hers. All of this she had thought normal, within the bounds of a normal marriage. She had, in fact, thought they had a good marriage. She'd told Robert they had had a good marriage. She felt foolish, exposed for a fool, and she wondered if she didn't mind that most of all.

This would be the master bedroom. It was long and narrow, oddly messy, actually extraordinarily messy considering the neatness of the downstairs rooms. Piles of clothes and magazines were strewn about the floor. There were teacups and a container half full of yogurt on a bureau, ashtrays overflowing with butts. Bottles of makeup on a dresser, which was spotted with liquid foundation. One side of the wood-framed bed was not made. Kathryn noted the expensive linen sheets, the embroidered hem. There were bits of lacy underwear on the comforter. The other side of the bed, still intact, had been Jack's — she could see this in the bedside stand with the white noise machine, the halogen lamp, a book about the Vietnam War. Had Jack read other books here than he had read at home? Had he had different clothes? Had he actually looked different in this house, in this country, than he had at home? Looked older or younger?

Home, she thought. Now there was an interesting concept.

She walked to Jack's side of the bed and yanked back the covers. She bent her head to the sheets and inhaled deeply. He was not there; she could not smell him.

She crossed to the other side of the bed, Muire's side. On the bedside table, there was a small gold clock and a lamp. As if conducting a search, she opened the drawer of the table. Inside, there were scraps of papers, receipts, tubes of lipstick, a jar of skin cream, loose coins, several pens, a television clicker, an object in a velvet bag. Unthinkingly, Kathryn picked up the bag and slipped off the blue velvet pouch. She dropped the object as if it were hot. She ought to have guessed simply from the shape. The vibrator fell from her hands and into the drawer with a clatter.

She knelt to the floor, laid her face on the bed. She put her arms over her head. She wanted the questions to stop, and she tried to empty her mind, a futile effort. She rubbed her face back and forth, back and forth against the sheet. She lifted up her face and saw that she had left a smear of mascara on the linen.

She stood up and walked to the mirror-fronted wardrobe and opened the doors.

The clothes were Muire's, not Jack's. Long black pants, wool skirts. Cotton shirts, linen blouses. A fur coat. Her hand felt, in her search, what she thought was a silk blouse. Parting the hangers, she discovered that it was not a blouse but a robe, an ankle-length silk robe with a tasseled sash. An exceptional garment of deep sapphire. Trembling slightly, she lifted the neck of the robe away from the hanger and looked at the label.

Bergdorf Goodman.

She had known that it would be.

She moved through the bedroom to the bathroom, noting everything, as if this were a house she might one day buy.

On the hook by the tub was a man's maroon flannel robe. Jack had not worn a robe at home. Inside the medicine cabinet, she found a razor and a hairbrush. There was a bottle of English cologne that was not familiar to her. Inspecting the brush, Kathryn found short black hairs.

She stared for a long time at the brush.

She had seen enough.

She wanted to get out of the house now. She shut the door to the master bedroom. Downstairs, she could still hear Muire Boland on the phone, the voice somewhat louder now, as though she might be arguing. Kathryn passed the open door of the girl's room. Dierdre lay on the bed on her stomach, her chin in her hands, the same remarkably solemn expression on her face. She wore a long-sleeved blue T-shirt and a pair of overalls. Blue ankle socks. So absorbed was the child in her program that at first she did not notice the stranger in her doorway.

"Hello," Kathryn said.

The girl glanced in her direction, then turned on her side to contemplate this new person.

"What are you watching?" Kathryn asked.

"Danger Mouse."

"I've seen that. They used to show it in America. My daughter used to like *Road Runner*. But she's bigger now. She's almost as tall as I am."

"What's her name?" The girl sat up, more interested in the stranger.

"Mattie."

Dierdre considered the name.

Kathryn took a step forward and glanced around the room. She noted the Paddington bear, almost identical to one that had once been Mattie's. A photograph of Jack in a baseball cap and a white T-shirt. A child's drawing of an adult man and a little girl with dark curls, which might have been done recently. A small white desk covered with scribbles of Magic Marker, blue sky that had gone off the page. What had the girl been told? Did she know her daddy was dead?

Kathryn remembered a basketball dinner of Mattie's when she was eight, and both Kathryn and Jack had wept to see their daughter's nearly uncontainable pride in the dinky little trophy.

"You talk funny," Dierdre said.

"I do?"

The girl had a British accent — no Irish in it, no American.

"You talk like my daddy," the girl said.

Kathryn nodded slowly.

"Do you want to see my Molly doll?" Dierdre asked.

"Yes," Kathryn said, clearing her throat. "I'd love to."

"You'll have to come over here," Dierdre said, gesturing. She hopped off the bed and walked to a corner of the room. Kathryn recognized the doll's wardrobe and trunk from the popular American Girl series. "My daddy gave this to me for Christmas," Dierdre said, handing the doll to Kathryn.

"I like her glasses," Kathryn said.

"Want to see her wardrobe?"

"Absolutely."

"Good, let's sit on the bed, and you can look at all my stuff."

Dierdre brought out dresses, a school desk, a red plastic pocketbook, a blue and red sweater. A minuscule pencil. A steel penny.

"Did your daddy give you all of this for Christmas?"

The girl pursed her lips and thought. "Saint Nicholas left me some of it," she said.

"I like her hair," Kathryn said. "Mattie used to have a doll that was like this, but she cut her hair. You know that with a doll the hair doesn't grow back, and so you shouldn't cut it off. Mattie was always sad that she had done that."

Kathryn had another memory. Mattie, at six years of age, setting off down a hill on a new bike, the bicycle wobbling beneath her as if it were made of jelly, Jack and Kathryn watching helplessly. Mattie, returning, telling her parents with pride, *Well, I've got this handled.*

And another: Mattie falling asleep one night in a pair of glasses with a funny nose attached.

And another: the Thanksgiving that Mattie, who was only four, announced to her father that Mommy had finished cooking the Turkish delight.

Where was Kathryn to put these memories now? She was, she thought, like a woman after a divorce looking at a wedding dress. Could the dress no longer be cherished if the marriage itself had disintegrated?

"I won't cut her hair," Dierdre promised.

"Good. Was your daddy here at Christmas? Sometimes daddies have to work at Christmas."

"He was here," Dierdre said. "I made him a bookmark. It had a picture of me and Daddy on it. I wanted it back, so he said we could share it. Do you want to see it?"

"Yes, I do."

Dierdre looked under the bed for the shared treasure. She brought up a picture book Kathryn did not recognize. The bookmark inside was a strip of colored paper that had been laminated. The photograph was of Jack with Dierdre on his lap. He was craning his neck to see her face.

Kathryn heard footsteps on the stairs.

In the attic at Fortune's Rocks was a box of American Girl doll clothes. Briefly, insanely, Kathryn toyed with the idea of sending the box to Dierdre.

Muire stood protectively in the doorway, her arms crossed over her chest.

"I like your doll very much," Kathryn said, standing.

"Do you have to go?" Dierdre asked.

"I'm afraid I must," Kathryn said.

Dierdre watched her leave. Muire moved to one side to allow Kathryn to pass. Kathryn walked quickly down the stairs, aware that the other woman was behind her. Kathryn reached for her suit jacket. "Dierdre mentioned that Jack was here for Christmas," she said, slipping her arms into her jacket.

"We celebrated early," Muire said. "We had to."

Kathryn knew all about having to celebrate holidays early.

Curious now, she crossed to the bookcase and scanned the titles there. *Lies of Silence,* by Brian Moore; *Cal,* by Bernard McLaverty; *Rebel Hearts,* by Kevin Toolis; *The Great Hunger,* by Cecil Woodham-Smith. A title she couldn't read. She took the book off the shelf.

"Is this Gaelic?" Kathryn asked.

"Yes."

"Where did you go to school?"

"Queens. In Belfast."

"Really. And you became . . ."

"A flight attendant. Yes, I know. The most educated work-force in Europe: the Irish."

"Does your daughter know about Jack?" Kathryn asked, returning the book to the shelf and picking up her coat.

"She knows," Muire said from the doorway, "but I'm not sure she understands. Her father was away so often. I think this just seems like another trip to her."

Her father.

"And Jack's mother," Kathryn said coolly. "Did Dierdre know about her grandmother Matigan?"

"Yes, of course."

Kathryn was silent. Shaken by her own question as much as by its answer.

"But, as you know, his mother has Alzheimer's," Muire added, "and Dierdre has never really been able to talk to her."

"Yes, I know," Kathryn lied.

If Jack hadn't died, she wondered, would he have been in this house right now? Would Kathryn ever have discovered the other family? For how many years might this affair — this marriage — have gone on?

The two women stood on the parquet floor. Kathryn glanced at the walls, the ceiling, the woman in front of her. She wanted to take in the whole of the house, to remember everything she had seen. She knew she would never be back.

She thought about the impossibility of ever knowing another person. About the fragility of the constructs people make. A marriage, for example. A family.

"There are things . . . ," Muire began. She stopped. "I wish . . ."

Kathryn waited.

Muire turned her palms upward, seemingly in resignation. "There are things I can't . . ." She sighed deeply, put her hands into the pockets of her jeans. "I'm not sorry for having had him," Muire said finally. "I'm just sorry for having hurt you."

Kathryn wouldn't say good-bye; it didn't seem necessary.

Although there was something Kathryn wanted to know — despite her pride, had to ask.

"The robe," she said. "The blue silk robe. In your closet."

Kathryn heard a quick intake of breath, but the face gave nothing away.

"It came after he died," Muire said. "It was my Christmas present."

"I thought it might be," Kathryn said.

She reached out and put her hand on the doorknob, as if reaching out for a life ring.

"You should go home," Muire said as Kathryn stepped outside into the rain, and Kathryn thought it an odd and presumptuous command.

"It was worse for me," Muire said, and Kathryn turned, drawn by the slightly plaintive note, a rent in the cool facade.

"I knew about you," Muire Boland said. "You never had to know about me."

IT WAS POSSIBLE SHE WAS CRYING. LATER, SHE WOULD not be able to say when it had started. She had forgotten her umbrella, and the rain soaked her hair, glued it to her head. It ran down her neck, her back, the front of her blouse. She was too exhausted to put her collar up or to wind her scarf around her neck. Passersby raised their umbrellas, glanced at her and then at each other. She breathed through her open mouth.

She had no destination, no idea where she was walking. Coherent thoughts refused to form or to take shape. She remembered the name of the hotel, but she did not want to go there, did not want to be inside with other people. Did not want to be alone in a room.

Briefly, she considered a movie theater as a refuge.

She stepped off a curb and, by habit, looked the wrong way. A taxi squealed. Kathryn stood still, expecting the driver to lean out the window and yell at her. Instead, he waited patiently for her to cross the road.

She knew that she wasn't well and grew nervous, afraid that she might inadvertently walk into a construction hole, might step off a curb again, might be hit by a red bus. She slipped into a telephone booth to put herself momentarily into a safe box. She appreciated being out of the wet, the dryness of the phone booth. She took her coat off and wiped her face with the lining, but the gesture reminded her of something she did not want to think about. A headache claimed her, twisted at the back of her neck, and she wondered if she had any Advil in her pocketbook.

A man stood impatiently outside the phone box, then tapped on the glass. He needed to use the phone, he mouthed. Kathryn put her coat back on and went out again into the rain. She walked along a busy street that seemed as if it might go on forever. Traffic made sprays of water on the sidewalks, hissed along the street. Heads bent against the rain, people passed beside her. Without a hat or umbrella, she had trouble seeing clearly. She thought about finding a department store, buying an umbrella, possibly a raincoat.

At a corner, she saw two men in overcoats laughing. They held black umbrellas and brown leather briefcases. They went inside a doorway. There was a glow behind the door, frosted glass, the sound of communal laughter. It was dark already, night now, and it might be safer to go inside.

Inside the pub, the scent of wet wool rose to her nostrils. She liked the warmth of this interior space. The glasses of the man just in front of her steamed, and he laughed with his companion. A man behind the bar handed her a towel. Someone else had used it before her; it was damp and limp and smelled of aftershave. She toweled her hair as she would do after a shower, and she saw that men were staring at her. They had pints of ale in front of them, which made her thirsty. The men parted slowly, gave her a stool. Across the bar, two women in nearly identical blue suits were chatting animatedly. Everyone was talking to someone else. It could have been a party, except that the people here seemed happier than they normally did at parties.

When the bartender took the towel from her, she pointed to a tap. The ale was bronze colored when it came. Light sparkled from polished surfaces, and men had cigarettes. At the ceiling there was a blue haze of smoke.

She was thirsty and drank the ale like water. She felt it burn in her stomach, which was pleasant. She slipped her shoes, squishy with the wet, off her feet and onto the floor. She glanced down, saw that her blouse was nearly transparent with the soaking, and drew her coat around her for modesty. The bartender turned in her direction and raised an eyebrow. She nodded in answer, and he gave her another glass of ale. Already the warmth, which she decided she had needed, was spreading through her arms and legs to her fingers and toes.

Occasionally, around her, she could make out words, bits of conversation. Business was being conducted. Flirtations.

Her headache tightened, moved toward her temples. She asked the bartender for an aspirin. A man with a mustache glanced sideways at her. Over the bar there was a Guinness sign, and she recognized the black drink in glasses on the bar. Jack had sometimes brought it home. That was another thing she didn't want to think about. The bar was wet with rings of beer, the wood saturated with the smell.

After a time, she needed to use the bathroom, but she didn't want to give up her stool. She thought she should order a third glass of beer just in case she lost her place and wouldn't be able to get another. The bartender ignored her raised hand, but the women across the bar noticed. They spoke to each other as they stared at her.

The bartender, acknowledging her finally, seemed slightly less friendly than he had been before. Perhaps there was a rule of pub etiquette she had failed to follow. When he finally asked her if she'd like a third drink, she shook her head and stood up, catching her coat on the stool. She lifted the wool off the vinyl seat. She tried to walk with a steady gait, moving through the crowd of men and women standing with their drinks. It must be just after work, she decided, and she wondered when exactly that would be in London. She felt something sticky on her feet and realized she had left her shoes at the bar. She turned, but could not see her way back. She had to pee urgently now and could not afford to find her trail. She followed a sign for Toilets. It seemed unnecessarily direct.

It was a relief just to be alone inside a stall.

Afterward, she had trouble with her stockings. She was reminded of having to pull on a wet bathing suit as a child. She struggled in the small cubicle. The soles of her stockings were filthy. She thought of taking them off altogether, that they would be easier to peel off than to pull on, but then she thought, sensibly, that she might be cold if she did that. Her stomach threatened momentarily to revolt, but she held her ground, withstood the queasiness.

She washed her hands in a grimy sink and looked in the mirror. The woman reflected there could not be her, she decided. The hair was too dark, too flat against the head. Half-moons of mascara lay beneath the eyes, a ghoulish makeup. The eyes themselves were pink rimmed, the eyeballs veined. The lips were bloodless, though the face was flushed.

A homeless woman, she thought.

She dried her hands on a towel, opened the door. She passed a phone on the wall. She felt a powerful urge to talk to Mattie. The urge was physical; she felt it in the center of her body, at the place where a woman wants to hold a baby.

She tried to follow the instructions printed on a placard next to the telephone, but gave up after several tries. She asked an older man in a waxed jacket who was on his way to the men's room to help her. She dictated the numbers to him, pleased she could remember them. When he had a connection, he handed her back the phone and looked at her blouse. He walked into the men's room, and, too late, she remembered that she hadn't thanked him.

The phone rang six or seven times. A door shut, a glass broke, a woman laughed in a high register, the shrill laugh pealing out above all the others. Kathryn was dying inside for Mattie's voice. Still the phone rang. She refused to hang up.

"Hello?"

The voice was breathless, as though she had been wrestling or running.

"Mattie!" Kathryn cried, spilling relief across the ocean. "Thank God you're home."

"Mom, what's the matter? Are you OK?"

Kathryn composed herself. She didn't want to frighten her daughter. "How are you?" she asked in a calmer voice.

"Um . . . I'm OK." Mattie's voice still wary. Tentative.

Kathryn tried for a cheerier tone. "I'm in London," she said. "It's great here."

"Mom, what are you doing?"

There was music in the background. One of Mattie's CDs. Sublime, Kathryn thought. Yes, definitely Sublime.

"Can you turn that down a bit?" Kathryn asked, having

already had to stick a finger in her other ear from the pub noise. "I can't hear you."

Kathryn waited for Mattie to return to the phone. The drinkers around the bar crowded at the edges of the tables. Beside her, a man and a woman held pints of beer and shouted into each other's ears.

"So," her daughter said, having returned.

"It's raining," Kathryn said. "I'm in a pub. I've just been walking around. Seeing the sights."

"Is that man with you?"

"His name is Robert."

"Whatever."

"Not right now."

"Mom, are you sure you're OK?"

"Yes, I'm fine. What are you doing?"

"Nothing."

"You sounded breathless," Kathryn said.

"Did I?" There was a pause. "Mom, I can't talk right now."

"Is Julia there?" Kathryn asked.

"She's at the shop."

"Why can't you talk?"

In the background, Kathryn heard part of a sentence, muffled words. A masculine voice.

"Mattie?"

She heard her daughter whisper. A suppressed giggle. Bits of another sentence. A distinctly masculine voice.

"Mattie? What's happening? Who's there?"

"No one. Mom, I gotta go."

Above the phone, on the wall, there were names and numbers written in pen and colored marker. *Roland at Margaret's,* one note read.

"Mattie, who's there? I can hear someone."

"Oh, that's just Tommy."

"Tommy Arsenault?"

"Yeah."

"Mattie . . ."

"Jason and I broke up."

The man beside her was jostled, and he spilled beer on Kathryn's sleeve. He smiled apologetically and tried ineffectually to wipe the spill with his hand.

"When did that happen?" Kathryn asked.

"Last night. What time is it there?"

Kathryn looked at her watch, which she had not yet set to London time. She calculated. "It's five forty-five," she said.

"Five hours," Mattie said.

"Why did you break up with Jason?" Kathryn asked, not acquiescing to the change in subject.

"I didn't think we had that much in common anymore."

"Oh, Mattie . . ."

"It's OK, Mom. Really, it's OK."

"What are you and Tommy doing?"

"Just hanging out. Mom, I gotta go."

Kathryn tried once again to calm herself.

"What are you going to do today?" Kathryn asked.

"I don't know, Mom. It's sunny out, but there's a lot of wet snow out there. You're sure you're OK?"

Kathryn toyed with the idea of saying no to keep Mattie on the line, but she knew that was the worst sort of parental blackmail.

"I'm fine," Kathryn said. "Really."

"I gotta go, Mom."

"I'll be home tomorrow night."

"Cool. Really, I gotta go."

"Love you," Kathryn said, wanting to hold on to her daughter's voice.

"Love you," Mattie said quickly.

Free to go now.

Kathryn heard the transatlantic click.

She leaned her head against the wall. A young man in a pin-striped suit waited patiently beside her and then, finally, took the receiver from her hand.

She crawled under a sea of legs, retrieved her shoes at the bar, and went out into the rain. She bought an umbrella at a news-stand, thinking as she paid for it that the manufacture of umbrellas in England must be an evergreen enterprise. She felt briefly sorry for herself and thought that in addition to everything else, she would doubtless get a cold. It was Julia's theory that if one cried in public, one would catch a cold. It wasn't so much retribution for the display of emotion as it was the irritation of mucous membranes in the presence of foreign germs. Kathryn felt momentarily homesick for Julia, would have liked a glimpse of the woman in her bathrobe, would have liked a cup of tea.

Kathryn marveled at the umbrella's protection (a brilliant design, she thought) and deeply appreciated the anonymity it afforded. If she watched the feet around her carefully, she could hide her face from people as they passed; the umbrella acted as a veil.

All of London in the rain, she thought, while Ely basked in sunshine.

She walked until she found a park. She thought possibly she

should not enter a park at night, although there were lanterns that made pools of light near the benches. The rain was letting up some, seemed merely a drizzle now. The grass had transformed itself into gray beneath the lantern light. She walked to a black bench and sat down.

She was sitting next to what appeared to be a circular rose garden. Lanterns lit the thorns of pruned canes, and the barrier looked formidable. Kathryn thought: It was not just a betrayal of me, but a betrayal of Mattie and Julia. A violation of the family circle.

The rain stopped altogether, and she put the umbrella on the bench. Her chenille scarf, in her travels, had begun to come unraveled at a corner. She fingered the unanchored stitch, gave it a tentative tug. She could fix this when she got home, remake the corner with another strand of chenille. She tugged a bit harder on the yarn, pulled out six or seven stitches, an oddly satisfying gesture. She tugged again, felt the stuttering of the tiny knots giving way.

She unraveled one row and then another. Then another and another. The yarn made a loose and pleasant tangle on her knees, at her ankles. Jack had given her the scarf for her birthday.

Kathryn pulled until she had a mound of twisted chenille as big as a small pile of leaves. She let the last of the yarn fall onto the grass. She stuck her frozen hands into the pockets of her coat.

She would have to recast all her memories now.

An older man in a tan raincoat stopped in front of her. Perhaps he was distressed to find a woman sitting on a wet bench with a tangle of yarn at her feet. Possibly he was married and was thinking of his wife. In the instant before he could ask after

Kathryn, she said hello and bent to retrieve the yarn. She found the end and began to roll the black chenille into a ball rapidly, with practiced gestures.

She smiled.

"Dreadful weather," he said.

"Yes, it is," she said pleasantly.

Seemingly satisfied by Kathryn's display of industry, the man moved on.

When he was gone, she tucked the yarn out of the way under the bench. She thought: I didn't know about my daughter's sexual life, and I didn't know about my husband's sexual life.

In the distance, she could see halos on street lamps, a chorus of brake lights, a couple running across a road. The rain had started again. They had on long raincoats, and the young woman wore heels. They kept their chins tucked against the rain. The man held his raincoat closed in front of his crotch with one hand, had his other arm around the woman's shoulder, urging her forward before the light changed.

Muire Boland and Jack might have done that in this city, she thought. Run to beat a light. On the way to dinner, to a pub. To the theater. To a party to be with other people. To a bed.

Muire Boland's marriage had weight. Two children as opposed to one. Two young children.

And then she thought: How could anything that had produced such beautiful children be thought invalid?

She walked until she saw, from a distance, the discreet marquee, a facade she recognized. The hotel was quiet when she entered, and only a clerk, standing in a cone of light behind the reception desk, greeted her. As she walked to the elevators, her clothes felt heavy and sodden.

She was enormously relieved that she could remember her room number. As she put the key in the lock, Robert emerged from the room next door.

"Jesus Christ," he said. His forehead was furrowed, his tie loosened to the middle of his chest. "I've been out of my mind wondering what happened to you," he said.

She blinked in the unflattering hall light and pushed her hair off her face.

"Do you know what time it is?" he asked. Sounding, in his genuine concern, like a parent with an errant child.

She did not.

"It's one o'clock in the morning," he informed her.

She withdrew the key from its lock and moved to where Robert stood, holding open his door. Through the framed space, she could see a meal, virtually untouched, on a tray at the foot of the bed. Even from the hallway, the room smelled heavily of cigarette smoke.

"Come in," he said. "You look like hell."

Once inside the door, she let her coat fall from her shoulders.

"You're actually dirty," Robert said.

She slipped off her shoes, which had lost their shape and color. He pulled out the chair from the desk.

"Sit down," he said.

She did as she was told. He sat on the bed, facing her, their knees touching — her wet stockings, his gray wool. He had on a white shirt, not the same shirt he'd had on at lunch. He looked a different man, drawn and exhausted, the eyes lined, an older man than at lunch. She imagined that she, too, had aged considerably.

He took her hands in his. Her hands felt swallowed by his long fingers.

"Tell me what happened," he said.

"I've been walking. Just walking. I don't know where I went. Yes, I do. I went to a pub and drank beer. I walked to a rose garden and unraveled a scarf."

"Unraveled a scarf."

"My life, I meant to say."

"I gather it was bad," he said.

"You could say that."

"I gave you thirty-five minutes, and then I followed you to the address. You must have gone already. I walked up and down the street for an hour and a half, and then I saw a woman who wasn't you leave the building. She had two children with her."

Kathryn looked at the uneaten sandwich on the tray. It might have been turkey.

"I think I'm hungry," she said.

Robert reached around, took the sandwich from the tray, and handed it to her. She balanced the plate on her lap, and she shivered slightly.

"Eat some, and then get into a hot bath. Do you want me to order you a drink?"

"No, I think I've had enough. You're being very parental."

"Jesus, Kathryn."

The meat in the sandwich had been pressed so flat that it felt on her tongue like slippery vinyl. She put the sandwich down.

"I was getting ready to call the police," he said. "I'd already called the number where you'd gone. Repeatedly. There was never an answer."

"They were Jack's children."

He didn't seem surprised.

"You guessed," she said.

"It was a possibility. I didn't think about children, though. That was her? Muire Boland? Leaving the building? His . . . ?"

"Wife," she said. "They were married. In a church."

He sat back. She watched the disbelief turn reluctantly to belief.

"In a Catholic church," Kathryn said.

"When?"

"Four and a half years ago."

On the bed was an overnight bag, unzipped at the top. The shirt he'd worn at lunch was peeking out of the bag. Bits of a newspaper had fallen off the bed onto the floor. On the desk, there was a half-empty bottle of mineral water.

She saw that he was examining her, as a doctor might do. Looking at the face for signs of illness.

"I'm over the worst of it," she said.

"Your clothes are ruined."

"They'll dry out."

He held her knees.

"I'm so sorry, Kathryn."

"I want to go home."

"We will," he said. "First thing tomorrow. We'll change the tickets."

"I shouldn't have come," she said, handing him the plate back.

"No."

"You tried to warn me."

He looked away.

"I am hungry," she said. "But I can't eat this."

"I'll order you fruit and cheese. Some soup."

"That would be nice."

She stood up, then faltered. She felt light-headed.

He stood with her, and she pressed her forehead against his shirt.

"All those years," she said, "it was all false."

"Shhhh . . ."

"He had a son, Robert. Another daughter."

He pulled her closer, trying to comfort her.

"All those times we made love," she said. "For four and a half years, I made love to the man while he had another woman. Another wife. I did things. We did things. I can remember them. . . ."

"It's OK."

"It's not OK. I sent him love notes. I wrote things on cards to him. He accepted them."

Robert rubbed her back.

"It's better that I know," she said.

"Maybe."

"It's better not to live a lie."

She sensed a quick change in his breathing, like a hiccup. She drew away and saw that he looked drained. He rubbed his eyes.

"I'll take my bath now," she said. "I'm sorry to have worried you. I should have called."

He put a hand up as if to tell her she needn't apologize. "What matters is that you're back," he said, and she could see the strain of not having known on his face.

"You can hardly stand," he said.

"I'd like to take the bath here. I don't want to be alone in my room. After the bath, I'll be fine."

She saw that he doubted she would be fine.

———————

She ran the water hot and emptied a bottle of shower gel into the tub that made a froth of suds. She was startled, when she undressed, to see just how filthy her clothes were, to see that a part of the hem of her skirt had come undone. She stood naked in the center of the room. She made dirty footprints on the white tiles. On a glass shelf were towels and a pretty basket with toiletries.

She put a foot into the water and winced, then stepped in. Slowly, she sank into the tub.

She washed her hair and face using the soapy water, too tired to get the shampoo. She pulled a towel off a rack, rolled it, and laid it on the lip of the tub. She leaned back, resting her neck on the towel.

A leather toilet kit was perched precariously on the small porcelain sink. The blazer with the gold buttons hung on the hook at the back of the door. Beyond the door, she could hear a knocking, a door opening, a brief conversation, a pause, and then a door shutting again. Room service, she thought. She wished she'd ordered a cup of tea. A cup of tea would have been perfect.

The casement window had been opened a crack, and she could hear street sounds below, traffic noise, a distant shout. Even at one o'clock in the morning.

She felt drowsy and closed her eyes. Despite the buoyancy of the water, it would be an effort to move her body, to climb out of the tub. She willed herself to empty her mind, to think of hot water and soap and nothing else.

When the door opened, she did not move, made no effort to cover herself, though the bubbles had thinned some and the tops of her breasts might have been exposed.

Her knees rose from the suds like volcanic islands. Her toes toyed with the chain of the plug.

He'd ordered tea. A glass of brandy.

He laid the cup and the glass on the edge of the tub. He stood back and leaned against the sink, put his hands into the pockets of his trousers. He crossed his legs at the ankles. She knew that he was looking at her body.

"I'd mix them together if I were you," he said.

She sat up to do as he had suggested.

"I'll leave you alone," he said.

"Don't go."

Behind him, the mirror over the sink was opaque with steam. Near the window, the outside air mixing with the heat created wisps of cloud. She poured the brandy into the tea, stirred the two together, and took a long swallow. Immediately, she felt the heat at the center of her body. The medicinal properties of brandy were amazing, she thought.

She held the teacup with soapy fingers.

His jaw moved. He might have sighed. He took a hand out of a pocket and rubbed the beads of moisture on the lip of the sink with his thumb.

"I'll need a robe," she said.

In the end, she told him everything. In the dark, lying on his bed, she told him every word she could remember of the meeting in the white town house. He listened without saying much, murmuring here and there, once or twice asking a question. She wore the terrycloth hotel robe, and he stayed dressed. He trailed his fingers up and down her arm as she spoke. When they grew chilly, he pulled a comforter over them. She burrowed her head into the space between his chest and his arm. In the dark, she felt the unfamiliar warmth of his body, heard his breathing next to her. She thought there might be something else that she wanted to say, but before she could form the words, she drifted off to a dreamless sleep.

The next morning, she sat on the edge of the bed in the white robe, hemming her skirt with a sewing kit she'd found in the basket of toiletries. Robert had been on the telephone, talking with the airline, changing plane tickets, but now he was polishing her shoes. An oblong of sunlight lit the room from behind the white net curtain. She thought she had probably not moved at all while she had slept. When she'd woken, Robert had already showered and dressed.

"These are almost unsalvageable," Robert said.

"I only have to make it home."

"We'll go down to breakfast," he said. "Have a real breakfast."

"That would be nice."

"There's no hurry."

She sewed patiently and evenly, as Julia had once, long ago, taught her to do, hoping the tiny card of thread would last. She was aware that Robert was watching her intently. Something had changed since the night before, she reflected; her gestures seemed to be taking on a special precision, being so closely observed.

"You look almost happy," she said, glancing up at him.

The insanity of yesterday lurked in the shadows, Kathryn knew, and it would always be there, a dark place in a lighted room. It would nag at her, drag her down when she let it. She thought then that she ought to be able to say she'd had the worst, got it over with. It would be a boon of sorts to know that a nadir had been reached. She could almost feel the freedom of that, to live one's life and not be afraid.

But she knew already that such freedom was an illusion and that there might be more to come. All she had to do was imagine Mattie on the plane that had gone down. It might be Mattie on a future plane. Life could dish out worse than Kathryn had had, and worse than that. In fact, she thought, her life might be all the more harrowing for knowing what was out there.

She put down her sewing and watched Robert buff her shoes. The gestures reminded her of Jack, his foot perched on the pulled-out bread drawer. How long ago was that, exactly?

She rose from her chair and kissed Robert at the side of his mouth, her hands full with the stitching, his with her shoes. She could feel his surprise. She put her wrists on his shoulders and looked at him.

"Thank you for coming with me to London," she said. "I don't know how I'd have gotten through last night without you."

He looked at her, and she could see that he wanted to say something.

"Let's eat," she said quickly. "I'm starved."

The dining room had wood-paneled wainscoting with a sub-dued blue wallpaper above it. There was a red oriental on the floor. They were shown to a table in a bow window framed with heavy drapes. Robert gestured for her to take the seat in front of the window. The table was laid with heavy white linen, nearly stiff from its pressing, and set with silver and a china she didn't recognize. She sat and put her napkin in her lap.

On the walls were architectural prints, and overhead was a crystal chandelier. She saw now that most of the diners were businessmen.

She glanced out the window at her side. The sun glistened on the washed streets. The room reminded her of drawing rooms in old British films, and she thought it might once have been that, a formal space that also conveyed warmth. An effort had been made not to sanitize the room, as would have been done in an American hotel, so that you could never believe anyone ever had, or ever would, live there. A fire burned in a grate. They had ordered eggs and sausages, toast in a silver rack. The coffee was hot, and she blew over the edge of the cup.

She looked up and saw the woman standing at the entrance. Coffee spilled onto the white tablecloth. Robert had his napkin out to blot the mess, but Kathryn stayed his hand. He turned to see what she had seen.

The woman walked quickly toward their table. She wore a long coat over a short wool skirt and sweater. Kathryn had an impression of muted greens and disarray. The woman had drawn her hair up into a ponytail, and she looked frightened.

As she approached the table, Robert stood up, startled.

"I was unforgivably cruel to you yesterday," the woman said straightaway to Kathryn.

"This is Robert Hart," Kathryn said.

He held out his hand.

"Muire Boland," the woman murmured by way of introduction, which he hadn't needed. "I need to speak with you," she said to Kathryn and then hesitated. Kathryn understood the hesitation to refer to Robert.

"It's all right," Kathryn said.

Robert gestured for the woman to sit down.

"I've been angry," Muire Boland began. She spoke hurriedly, as though she had little time. Sitting closer to the woman than she had yesterday, Kathryn could see that Muire had the same enlarged pupils as her daughter, which accounted for the dark eyes. "Angry since the accident," Muire continued. "Actually, I've been angry for years. I had so little of him."

Kathryn was astonished. Was she meant to forgive the woman? Here in this room? Now?

"It wasn't suicide," Muire said.

Kathryn felt her mouth go dry. Robert asked, still operating in a world the women had abandoned, if Muire would like a cup of coffee. She shook her head tensely.

"I have to hurry," Muire said. "I've left my house. You won't be able to get in touch with me."

The woman's face was pinched. Remorse did not produce such features, Kathryn knew. But fear could.

"I have a brother whose name is Dermot," Muire said. "I had two other brothers. One of them was shot by paramilitaries in front of his wife and three children as they ate dinner. The other one was killed in an explosion."

Kathryn tried to process the information. She thought she understood. She felt buffeted, as though someone had knocked into her.

"I'd been a courier since I'd started with the airline," Muire continued. "It's why I went with Vision, for the Boston-Heathrow route. I carried cash from America to the U.K. Someone else would then see that it made its way to Belfast."

Later, it would seem to Kathryn that it was here that time stopped altogether, looped around itself and then slowly began to unwind. The world around her — the diners, the waiters, the vehicles on the street, even the shouts from passersby — existed

in a kind of watery pool. Only her immediate surroundings —
herself, Muire Boland, Robert, the white linen with its coffee
stain — seemed sharply defined.

A waiter came to the table to blot the coffee, replace the napkin. He asked Muire if she wanted to order breakfast, but she
shook her head. The three sat in awkward silence until the
waiter had left.

"I'd be met at each airport, Boston and Heathrow, coming
and going. I had an overnight bag. I was to put the bag down in
the crew lounge and walk away. A few seconds later, I'd pick it
up again. Actually, it was quite easy." The dark-haired woman
reached across for Robert's water glass, took a sip. "Then I met
Jack," she said, "and I got pregnant."

Kathryn felt her feet go cold.

"When I left the airline, Dermot came to the house," Muire
said. "He asked Jack if he would carry on. He appealed to Jack's
Irish Catholic heritage." She paused, rubbed her forehead. "My
brother is a very passionate man, very persuasive. At first Jack
was upset with me because I hadn't told him. I hadn't wanted to
involve him. But then, gradually, he became intrigued. He was
drawn to the risk, certainly, but it was more than that. He began
to take on the cause for himself, to become part of it. As time
went on, he became almost as passionate as my brother."

"A convert," Robert said.

Kathryn closed her eyes and swayed.

"I'm not trying to hurt you by telling you this," Muire said to
Kathryn. "I'm trying to explain."

Kathryn opened her eyes. "I doubt you could hurt me any
more than you have done," she said.

Unlike yesterday, the woman sitting across from her seemed
unkempt, as though she'd slept in her clothes. The waiter came
with a coffee pot, and Robert quickly waved the man away.

"I knew that Jack was in over his head," Muire said, "but he seemed a man who was not afraid to get in over his head." She paused. "Which is why I loved him."

The sentence stung. And then Kathryn thought, surprising herself with the thought: It was why he loved you. Because you offered him this.

"There were others involved," Muire said. "People at Heathrow, at Logan, in Belfast."

Muire picked up a fork and began to scratch the tablecloth with the tines.

"The night before Jack's trip," she continued, "a woman called and told him he was to carry something the other way. Heathrow to Boston. The same procedures would be in place. It wasn't absolutely unprecedented. It had happened once or twice before. But I didn't like it. It was riskier. Security is tighter departing Heathrow than arriving. Much tighter altogether than at Logan. But, in essence, the task itself wasn't that much different."

Muire put down the fork. She looked at her watch and spoke more quickly.

"When I heard about the crash, I tried to reach my brother. I was frantic. How could they have done that to Jack? Had they lost their minds? And politically, it was insane. To blow up an American plane? For what purpose? It was guaranteed to turn the entire world against them."

She put her fingers to her forehead and sighed.

"Which was, of course, the point."

She fell silent.

Kathryn had the anxious sense of receiving important messages in code, a code that needed immediate deciphering.

"Because it wasn't them," Robert said, slowly understanding. "It wasn't the IRA who planted the bomb."

"No, of course not," Muire said.

"It was intended to discredit the IRA," Robert said, nodding slowly.

"When I couldn't reach my brother," Muire added, "I thought they'd killed him, too. And then I couldn't reach anyone."

Kathryn wondered where Muire's children were right this very minute. With A?

"My brother finally called last night. He's been in hiding. He thought my phone . . ." She gestured with her hands.

Around her, Kathryn was vaguely aware that other diners were eating toast and drinking coffee, perhaps conducting business.

"Jack didn't know what he was carrying," Robert said almost to himself, putting it together for the first time.

Muire shook her head. "Jack never carried explosive material. He was very clear about that. It was understood."

In her mind, Kathryn saw the scuffle on the plane.

"That's why Jack doesn't say anything on the tape," Robert added suddenly. "He's just as shocked as the engineer."

And Kathryn thought then: Jack, too, was betrayed.

"It's all coming apart," Muire said and stood up. "You should go home as soon as you can."

She put a hand on the table, leaned down close toward Kathryn, who caught a brief scent of stale breath, unwashed clothing.

"I came here," Muire said, "because your daughter and my children are related. They have the same blood."

Did Muire Boland mean for an understanding to pass between the two women, a elemental understanding? Kathryn wondered. But then, almost simultaneously, she realized that of course the two women were linked, however much Kathryn might wish it not true. By children, certainly, half-sisters and half-brothers, but also by Jack. Through Jack.

Muire straightened, clearly about to leave. Panicky, Kathryn realized she might never see the woman again.

"Tell me about Jack's mother," Kathryn blurted in a rush. An admission.

"He didn't tell you, then?" Muire asked.

Kathryn shook her head.

"I thought he hadn't," Muire said thoughtfully. "Yesterday, when you were there . . ."

Muire paused.

"His mother ran away with another man when he was nine," she said.

"Jack always maintained she was dead," Kathryn said.

"He was ashamed he'd been left. But, oddly, he didn't blame his mother. He blamed his father, his father's brutality. Actually, it's only been recently that Jack could acknowledge his mother at all."

Kathryn looked away, embarrassed for having had to ask.

"I absolutely must go now," Muire said. "I'm putting you both at risk just by being here."

The accent might have done it, Kathryn thought. Acted as a trigger. Or was she simply searching for a reason for the inexplicable: why a man fell in love?

Robert glanced quickly from Muire to Kathryn and back again. He had an expression on his face Kathryn had never seen before — anguished.

"What?" Kathryn asked him.

He opened his mouth, then closed it, as if he would say something but then had thought better of it. He picked up a knife and began to flip it back and forth between his fingers, the way she had seen him do with a pen.

"What?" Kathryn repeated.

"Good-bye," Muire said to Kathryn. "I am sorry."

Kathryn felt dizzy. How long had it been since Muire Boland had walked through the doorway? Three minutes? Four?

Robert looked at Kathryn, then set the knife carefully beside his plate. "Wait," he said to Muire as she turned to walk away.

Kathryn watched as the woman halted, slowly pivoted, and studied Robert, tilting her head in a quizzical manner.

"Who were the other pilots?" he asked quickly. "I need the names."

Kathryn stiffened. She glanced at Robert and then at Muire. She felt herself begin to tremble.

"You know about this?" she asked Robert in a tight whisper.

Robert looked down at the table. Kathryn could see the color coming into his face.

"You've known all along?" Kathryn asked. "You came to my house knowing that Jack might be involved in this?"

"We knew only that there was a smuggling ring," Robert said. "We didn't know who, though we suspected Jack."

"You knew where this might lead? What I might find out?"

Robert raised his eyes to her, and she saw it all, in an instant, pass over his face: Love. Responsibility. Loss.

Particularly loss.

Kathryn stood up, and her napkin fell to the floor. Her movements startled the other diners, who glanced over at her with expressions of faint alarm.

"I trusted you," she said.

She walked from the dining room straight out the hotel door and stepped into a waiting taxi. She had left her coat and her suitcase in her room. She didn't care what was in it.

She would change her ticket at the airport.

During the drive, she stared at her hands in her lap, clasped so tightly the knuckles had turned a translucent white. She could not hear or see anything. But she could feel the rage in her blood, actually feel it pumping and churning inside her. She had never known such rage. She wanted only to go home.

At Heathrow, she moved through the revolving door into an international throng, milling in all directions, as if communally lost. She found the British Airways desk and got in line. She would change her flight and the airline itself, and she didn't care how much it cost.

She felt exposed as she stood in the line, as though she no longer had any insulation at all. Robert might guess her intentions and come looking for her. She would wait for her flight in the bathroom if she had to, she decided.

The line moved too slowly. Her rage began to encompass the inefficiency of the ticket agents.

She wondered if she'd fly over Malin Head, if she'd fly a route similar to the one Jack had flown.

And then she began to feel the gravitational pull. The pure force of it surprised her. She put a hand to her chest.

The pull grew stronger as she moved closer to the beginning of the line.

When it was Kathryn's turn, she laid her ticket on the counter. The agent looked at her, waiting for her to speak.

"What's the closest airport to Malin Head?" Kathryn asked.

HER ARMS ARE FULL OF DIRTY LAUNDRY — WET towels, crumpled sheets, and sprung socks that keep slipping from her arms and falling to the floor. She bends to retrieve an errant washcloth, thinking that if she'd brought the basket upstairs first the laundry wouldn't be so frisky. She hugs the damp bundle even more tightly and walks toward the stairs. As she passes the entrance to their bedroom, she glances in.

It is a fleeting tableau, so brief it barely registers. A subliminal picture, no different from the thousands of subliminal pictures that enter the brain but fail to interest the consciousness. Like seeing a woman in a camel jacket selecting oranges at the supermarket, or seeing but not noticing a locket around a student's neck.

Jack is bent over his carry-on, packing for a trip. His hand moves quickly, tucks an item out of sight. A shirt, she thinks, blue with yellow stripes. A shirt she has never seen before. Perhaps a shirt he bought in a pinch at an airport kiosk.

She smiles to show that she hasn't meant to startle him. He straightens and lets the lid of his small suitcase fall closed.

— You need a hand with that? he asks.

She stands for a minute, admiring the way the afternoon sun falls on the old floorboards of the house, setting the pumpkin stain aglow.

— When are you leaving? she asks.

— Ten minutes.

— And you'll be back when?

— Tuesday. Around noon. Maybe we'd better call Alfred Zacharian, get him in to take a look at the leak. It's worse today.

She notices that his hair is still wet from the shower. He's slimmed down some, she observes; there's hardly any sign of a stomach now. She watches as he crosses to the closet, takes his uniform jacket from a hanger, and slips it on. She has never failed to be moved by the sight of Jack in his uniform, at the immediate authority that drapes itself over his shoulders, that clarifies itself as he fastens the three gold buttons.

— I'll miss you, she says impulsively.

He turns and steps into a block of sunlight. Around the eyes, he looks tired.

— What is it? she asks.

— What's what?

— You look worried about something.

— It's just a headache, he says, shaking his head and rubbing his eyes.

She watches him relax his features, smooth his brow muscles.

— You want some Advil? she asks.

— No, I'm fine, he says.

He zips the suitcase shut, grasps the handle, and pauses. He seems about to say something to her, then appears to change his mind. He swings the bag off the bed.

— Just leave the dry cleaning until I get home, he says, walking to her. He holds her eyes for a second longer than he might have. Across the bundle of dirty laundry, he kisses her. The kiss slides off the side of her mouth.

— I'll take care of it on Tuesday, he says.

SHE WAS TRYING TO READ THE MAP WHILE REMEM-
bering to drive on the left, a challenge that taxed all of her concentration, so that it was some time before she realized the
irony of being on the Antrim Road as it led west, away from the
Belfast airport. The flight had been uneventful, the car rental
straightforward. She felt an almost physical urgency to get to
her destination.

By landing west of Belfast, she'd missed the city altogether,
had seen none of the bombed-out buildings and bullet-scarred
facades she'd heard about. Indeed, it was difficult to reconcile
the pastoral landscape spreading out before her with the unsolv-
able conflict that had claimed so many lives — most recently
one hundred and four persons in an airplane over the Atlantic
Ocean. The unadorned white cottages and pastureland were
marred only by wire fences, telephone lines, occasionally a satel-
lite dish. In the distance, the hills seemed to change their color
and even their shape, depending on how the sun shifted through
the fair-weather clouds. The land looked ancient, trespassed

upon, and the hills had a worn and mossy look, as though they had been trampled by many feet. On the ridge of hills closest to the road, she could see the scattered white dots of hundreds of sheep, the plowed and furrowed bits of patchwork, the low green hedgerows that bordered the crops like lines drawn by a child.

This would not be what the bloody struggle had been about, she thought as she drove. It was something else she'd never fathom, never understand. Though Jack, in arrogance or love, had presumed to do so, had involved himself in Northern Ireland's complex conflict, thus causing even Kathryn and Mattie to be peripheral, if unwitting, participants.

She knew few facts about the Troubles, only what she'd absorbed, like everyone else, from headlines and from television when events occurred that were catastrophic enough to make news in the United States. She'd read or heard about the sectarian violence of the early 1970s, the hunger strikes, the cease-fire of 1994, and the breakdown of the cease-fire, but she knew little about the *why* of it all. She'd heard of kneecapping, of car bombings, and of men in ski masks entering civilian homes, but she had no sense of the patriotism driving these terrorist activities. At times, she was tempted to think of the participants in this struggle as misguided thugs cloaking themselves in idealism like murderous religious zealots of any age. At other times, the cruelty and the sheer stupidity of the British had seemed positively to invite a frustration and a bitterness that might lead any group of people to violent action.

What baffled her now, though, was not the reason for such a conflict, but Jack's participation in it, a reality she could barely absorb. Had he believed in the cause, or had he been drawn by its seeming authenticity? She could see the appeal of that, the instant meaning given to a life. The falling in love itself, the romantic idealism, the belonging to a righteous organization, and even the religion would have been part of the whole. It would have meant a total giving over of oneself to a person or an ideal, and in this case the two would have been inextricably linked. Just as the cause would have been part of the love affair, the love affair would have been part of the cause, so that you couldn't, later, have one without the other. Nor could you leave one without the other. Seen in this light, she thought, the question wasn't so much why Jack had taken up with Muire Boland and married her in a Catholic church, but rather why he hadn't left Mattie and Kathryn.

Because he loved Mattie too much, she answered herself at once.

She wondered then if Jack and Muire had actually been legally married. Did a wedding in a church automatically confer legal status? She didn't know how it worked, or how Muire and Jack had specifically worked it. And she would never know. There was so much now that she would never know.

Just outside of Londonderry, she showed her passport at the checkpoint and passed into the Republic of Ireland, simultaneously entering Donegal. She drove north and west through countryside that became noticeably more rural as she went, the number of sheep beginning vastly to outnumber people, the cottages becoming even more rare. She followed signs for Malin Head, Cionn Mhalanna in Irish, through the heavy aroma of peat. The land grew rugged, wilder, with long vistas of cliff and jagged rock, tall sand dunes capped in green and heather. The road narrowed to barely a single lane, and she realized she was driving too fast when she came upon a sharp curve and nearly put the car into a ditch.

Of course, it could have been the mother, Kathryn thought. A desire to recapture the mother, have the mother he'd been denied. Certainly this might have been the case with his having fallen in love with Muire Boland, and even Muire had seemed to understand that. But beyond this speculation, Kathryn thought, the territory grew murky: Who could say what a man's motivations were? Even had Jack been alive and with her in the car, could he have articulated his own Why? Could anyone? Again, she'd never know. She could only know what she imagined to be true. What she herself decided would be true.

As she drove, certain memories pricked at her, nagged at her, and she knew it might be months or years before they stopped: The thought, for example, that Jack might have taken money from her and Mattie to give to another family was insupportable, and she could feel her blood pressure rising in the car. Or the fight, she remembered suddenly, that horrible fight for which she'd blamed herself. The gall of him, she thought now, letting her believe her own inadequacies had been the cause, when all along he was having an affair with another woman. Was that what Jack had been doing on the computer all that time? Writing to a lover? Is that why he'd been willing to escalate the hostilities so quickly when he'd asked her if she wanted him to go? Had he been flirting with the idea?

Or the lines of poetry, she thought. Had Jack relaxed his vigilance and allowed bits of his relationship with Muire Boland to seep into his marriage with Kathryn? Had Kathryn's life been invaded in ways she'd never noticed? How many books had she read or films had she seen that Muire might have suggested? How much of the Irish woman's life had leached into her own?

Again, Kathryn would never know.

She turned off the main road, following the directions she'd been given to the most northwesterly point in Ireland. Astonishingly, the road became even narrower, no wider than her driveway. She wondered as she drove why she had never imagined an affair. How could a woman live with a man all that time and never suspect? It seemed, at the very least, a monumental act of naïveté, of oblivion. But then she thought she knew the answer even as she asked the question: A dedicated adulterer causes no suspicion, she realized, because he truly does not want to be caught.

Kathryn had never even thought to suspect; she'd never smelled a trace of another woman, never found a smear of lipstick on the shoulder of a shirt. Even sexually, she'd never guessed. She'd assumed the falling off she and Jack had experienced was simply the normal course of events with a couple who'd been married for a decade.

She rolled down her window so that she could breathe the air — a curiously heady mix of sea salt and chlorophyll. The land around her, she realized suddenly, was extraordinary. The texture of the landscape — its rich green hues, its density — gave a feeling of solidity she'd not felt in London. The confluence of ocean and rocky coast, albeit wilder than her own New England shore, struck a responsive chord. She breathed evenly and deeply for the first time since Muire Boland had appeared at the hotel dining-room door.

She entered a village, and would have passed through but for a sight she'd seen before: Only the old fisherman was missing. She slowed the car and stopped. She sat parked along a common ringed by shops and homes. She could see where the cameraman must have stood, where the reporter with the dark hair and umbrella had conducted her interview in front of the hotel. The building was white and smooth and clean. She saw the sign above the door: Malin Hotel.

She thought she should get a room for the night. Her flight back to London didn't leave until the morning. Maybe she ought to get something to eat as well.

It was several minutes before her eyes adjusted enough so that she could make out the scuffed mahogany of the traditional bar. She noted the scarlet drapes, the stools with beige vinyl tops, the dreariness of the room alleviated only somewhat by a fire at one end. Along the walls were banquettes and low tables and perhaps half a dozen people playing cards or reading or drinking beer.

Kathryn sat at the bar and ordered a cup of tea. Almost immediately, a woman with blond sculpted hair claimed the stool next to hers. Kathryn turned her head away and examined the signs above the register. Too late, she understood that the people in the bar were reporters.

The woman's face was reflected in the mirror behind the bottles. She was flawlessly made up and looked distinctly American. Their eyes met.

"Can I buy you a drink?" the woman asked, speaking quietly. Kathryn realized immediately that the hushed voice was because the blond didn't want anyone else in the bar to know that Kathryn was there.

"No, thank you," Kathryn said.

The woman gave her name, the call letters of her network. "We sit in the bar here," she explained. "The relatives sit in the lounge. Occasionally a husband or a father will wander in here and order a drink, but in terms of conversation, we've pretty much exhausted each other. We're all bored. I'm sorry if that sounds callous."

"I imagine even a plane crash can grow tedious," Kathryn said.

The bartender set down Kathryn's tea, and the journalist ordered a half pint of Smithwick's. "I recognized you from the photographs," the reporter said. "I'm sorry for all that you've had to go through."

"Thank you," Kathryn said.

"Most of the bigger networks and news organizations will keep someone in place until the salvage operation is abandoned," the woman said.

Kathryn made her tea strong and sweet and stirred it to release the heat.

"Do you mind if I ask why you're here?" the journalist inquired.

Kathryn took a tentative sip. "I don't mind," she said. "But I can't give you an answer. I don't know why I'm here myself."

She thought about her rage and the gravitational pull, about the newfound knowledge of the morning. About how easy it would be to offer to the blond all she had learned. How excited the reporter would be to have what would undoubtedly be the biggest story of the entire investigation, even bigger than the leak of the tape. And once the story was printed, wouldn't the authorities find Muire Boland? Arrest her and send her to jail?

But then Kathryn thought about the baby who looked like Mattie, about Dierdre, who had a Molly doll.

"It wasn't suicide," she said. "That's all I can tell you."

Robert would have known all along, Kathryn thought. He'd have been briefed before he ever came to the house. The union had suspected Jack and had asked Robert to keep an eye on her. Robert would have watched and waited for some sign that she knew about her husband's activities, could name the other pilots. Robert had used her.

She no longer had any interest in her tea. The urgency to reach her destination had returned. She got up off her stool.

"Look, can we at least talk?" the reporter asked.

"I don't think so," Kathryn answered.

"Are you going out to Malin Head?"

Kathryn was silent.

"You won't be able to get out to the site. Here."

The blond removed a card from her wallet, turned it over, and wrote a name on it. She handed it to Kathryn. "When you get there, ask for Danny Moore," she said. "He'll take you out there. This is my card. When you're done, if you change your mind, give me a call. I'm staying here. I'll buy you dinner."

Kathryn took the card and looked at it. "I hope you get to go home soon," she said.

On her way out of the hotel, as she passed the lounge, Kathryn glanced in and saw a woman sitting in an armchair with a newspaper on her lap. The paper hadn't been opened, and the woman wasn't looking at the type. Kathryn thought the woman could not see anything at all in front of her, so vacant was her gaze. By a fireplace at the far end of the room, a man with a similar look stood with his hands in his pockets.

She recrossed the common and got into her car. She looked again at the card in her hand.

She already knew what she would do. She could not control what actions Robert Hart might eventually, or even immediately, take. But she could control what she herself would do. Indeed, she felt, in a quiet way, more in control of herself than she had been in years.

To reveal what she knew about the reasons for the plane's

explosion would mean that Mattie would discover Jack's other family. And Mattie would never get over that. Of this, Kathryn was certain. She ripped the card into pieces and let them fall to the floor.

Knowing her destination was not far, Kathryn once again followed signs for Malin Head. She passed ruined cottages, no more than toppled stones, the thatched roofs long fallen in and rotted. She saw velvet grass bunched along a cliff — an emerald green even in the dead of winter. On ropes strung from pole to pole, clothes stiffened in the sun, the abstract art of wash on the line. Good drying weather, she thought.

As she rounded a corner, the horizon line of the North Atlantic surprised her. In the middle of that horizon line was a dark gray shape, a ship. A helicopter circled overhead. Brightly colored fishing boats hovered near the larger ship, like pups with a mother seal. The salvage boat, she thought.

This, then, was the place where the plane had gone down.

She parked the car and got out, walking as far as she dared toward the edge of the cliff. Below her were three hundred vertical feet of rock and shale descending to the sea. From such a height, the water looked stationary, a scalloped border on a distant beach. The spray hit the rocks below in star-bursts. A red fishing boat was headed in toward shore. For as far as Kathryn could see, the water was a single color, gunmetal blue.

She doubted she had ever seen a more theatrical piece of coastline — raw and deadly, wild. It put a disaster in perspective, she thought, if anything could. There had probably been many disasters here.

She followed the fishing boat with her eyes until it disappeared behind the jutting peninsula that was Malin Head itself.

Starting up the car again, she drove the narrow road, keeping the boat in sight when she could catch glimpses of it. It pulled into a small harbor formed by a long concrete pier. She stopped the car and got out.

The boats tethered to the pier were shiny with primary colors — orange, blue, green, and yellow — making her think more of Portuguese vessels than of Irish ones. The boat she'd been watching maneuvered around the pier and then threw out her mooring line. Kathryn walked toward the pier. There were uniformed guards at one end, and beyond them groups of men in civilian dress. As she walked, the fisherman aboard the red boat unloaded a piece of silver metal the size of a chair and placed it on the pier, where it immediately captured the attention of the men in civilian dress, who crowded around it. One of the men stood and beckoned to the driver of a truck, which backed onto the pier. The metal shard, presumably a piece of Jack's plane, was loaded onto the truck.

At the entrance to the pier, a guard stopped her. "Can't go beyond this point, miss."

Perhaps he was a soldier. A policeman. He held a machine gun.

"I'm a relative," she said, eyeing the gun.

"Sorry for your loss, Ma'am," the guard said. "There are scheduled trips for the relatives. You can inquire about them at the hotel."

Like a whale watch, Kathryn thought. Or a cruise.

"I just need to talk to Danny Moore for a second," Kathryn said.

"Oh, well then. That's him there," the guard said, gesturing. "The blue boat."

Kathryn murmured a thank you and walked briskly past the man.

Avoiding eye contact with the officials in civilian dress, who were beginning to notice her, Kathryn called out to the fisherman in the blue boat. She saw that he was preparing to leave the pier.

"Wait," she cried.

He was young, with dark hair cut close to the head. He wore a gold earring in his left ear. He had on a sweater that had probably once been ivory colored.

"Are you Danny Moore?" she asked.

He nodded.

"Can you take me out to the site?"

He seemed to hesitate, perhaps also about to tell her of the scheduled trips for relatives.

"I'm the pilot's wife," Kathryn said quickly. "I need to see the place where my husband went down. I don't have much time."

The fisherman reached up and took her hand.

He gestured for her to sit on a stool in the wheelhouse. Kathryn watched as one of the men in civilian dress strode toward the boat. The fisherman untied the mooring, came into the wheelhouse, and gunned the engine.

He said a word she couldn't understand. She leaned forward, but the noise from the engine and the wind made conversation difficult.

The boat, she saw, had been scrubbed clean and bore no signs of fishing. Why fish when there was this task to be performed, this work for which those in charge might pay good money? "I'll pay you," Kathryn said, being reminded.

"Ah, no," said the man, looking shyly away. "I don't take money from family."

As soon as the boat rounded the pier, the wind began in earnest. The fisherman smiled slightly when she made eye contact.

"You're from here," Kathryn said.

"Yes," he answered, and he again uttered a word Kathryn could not make out. She thought it must be the name of the town where he lived.

"Have you been doing this since the beginning?" she shouted.

"Since the beginning," he said and looked away. "It's not so bad now, but at first . . ."

She didn't want to think about what it had been like at first. "Pretty boat," she said to change the subject.

"It's grand."

She heard in his accent an uncomfortable reminder of Muire Boland.

"Is it yours?" she asked.

"Ah, no. It's my brother's. But we fish together."

"What do you fish for?"

The engine made a steady grinding sound through the water.

"Crab and lobster," he said.

She stood and turned, facing the bow. Beside her at the wheel, the young man shifted his weight. She teetered some in her shapeless heels. "You fish now, in this cold?" she asked, clutching her suit jacket around her.

"Yes," he said. "All weathers."

"You go out every day?"

"Ah, no. We'll make away on a Sunday evening and return on the Friday."

"Hard life," she said.

He shrugged. "It's fine weather we're having now," he said. "There's always mist at Malin Head."

As they drew closer to the salvage ship, Kathryn observed the other fishing boats engaged in the operation — gaily colored boats, such as the one she was in, boats too festive for their ugly task. On the deck of the salvage boat, divers stood in wet suits. The helicopter continued to hover overhead. The debris, of course, would have gone down over a large area.

Behind the fisherman's head, Kathryn noted the shoreline, the cliffs with their shalelike geological exposure. The landscape was gothic in its shape, atmospheric even in the good weather, and she could easily imagine this forbidding landscape in a mist. So very different from Fortune's Rocks, where nature seemingly had subdued herself. And yet, on either side of the Atlantic, reporters had stood, facing each other across the ocean.

"This is the loran reading where they pulled up the cockpit," he said.

"This?" she asked. And began to tremble. For the moment. For the proximity of death.

She left the wheelhouse and walked to the port railing. She peered over the edge at the water, at its surface, constantly shifting, though seemingly still. A person was not who he had been the day before, Kathryn thought. Or the day before that.

The water seemed opaque. Overhead, gulls circled. She didn't want to think about why the gulls were there, either.

What had been real? she wondered as she studied the water, trying to find a fixed point, which she couldn't. Had she herself been the pilot's wife or had Muire Boland? Muire Boland, who had been married in the Catholic Church, who knew of Jack's mother and his childhood. Muire, who knew of Kathryn, whereas Kathryn had not known of her.

Or had Kathryn been the real wife? The first wife, the one he had protected from the truth, the wife he wouldn't leave?

The more Kathryn learned about Jack — and she had no doubt now that she would learn more, would find, among Jack's

things when they were returned to her, other references to M —
the more she would have to rethink the past. As if having to tell
a story over and over, each time a little differently because a fact
had changed, a detail had altered. And if enough details were
altered, or the facts were important enough, perhaps the story
veered in a direction very different from its first telling.

The boat rocked from another's wake, and she braced herself on the railing. Jack had been, she thought, only another
woman's husband.

She glanced up briefly at the circling helicopter. Once she had
seen a wide-body hovering just off Fortune's Rocks. The day
had wanted to be sunny, and an early fog was just lifting. The
plane flew low over the water, and the fat silver slug had seemed
too heavy to stay aloft. Kathryn had been afraid for the plane,
awed that flight was possible.

Jack would have known his fate, she thought. In the last several seconds, he would have known.

He had called out Mattie's name at the end, Kathryn decided.
She would believe that, and it would be true.

Again, she studied the water. How long had the fisherman
been circling? She had lost the ability to perceive the passage of
time as it was actually unfolding. When, for example, had the
future begun? Or the past ended?

She tried to find a fixed point in the water, but couldn't.

Did change invalidate all that had gone before?

Soon she would leave this place and fly home and drive to
Julia's. She would say to her daughter, We're going home now.
Kathryn's life was with Mattie. There could be no other reality.

She took her wedding ring from her finger and dropped it
into the ocean.

She knew that the divers would not find Jack, that he no
longer existed.

"You all right, then?"

The young fisherman leaned out of the wheelhouse, one hand still on the wheel. His forehead was creased, and he looked worried.

She smiled briefly at him and nodded.

To be relieved of love, she thought, was to give up a terrible burden.

HE PLACES THE RING ON HER FINGER AND, FOR a moment, holds it there. The justice of the peace intones the sentences of the simple ceremony. Kathryn looks at Jack's fingers on the silver, at the gleam of the silver itself. He has bought a suit for the occasion, a gray suit in which he looks handsome but strange to her, in the way of men who do not normally wear suits. She has on a flower-print rayon dress that nips in at the waist and doesn't show the baby. It has short sleeves and small shoulder pads and falls just below her knees. She can still smell the store in the fabric. She has on a hat as well — peach, like the dress, with a dusty-blue silk flower at the brim, a blue that matches the flowers in the dress. In the corridor, another couple speaks in hushed, impatient tones. Kathryn lifts her head for a kiss that is oddly chaste, prolonged and formal. The wide-brimmed hat slips from her head.

— I'll always love you, Jack says.

They drive to a ranch in the mountains. The temperature drops nearly forty degrees. Over the peach dress, she has on his leather jacket. She can still feel the wedding smile on her face, a smile that hasn't faded, as if it had been captured in a photograph. Her head jostles some when he shifts. She wonders what it means to have a wedding night if they already live together, and if they will feel different to each other in the bed. She wonders what it means to have a wedding in front of a man neither of them had ever met and who won't remember them. The dry air of the west makes her hair feel thinner than the humidity of Ely does. It tightens the skin on her face.

Still they climb higher. Dark now and clear, the night sky draws white lines on scrub and rock and makes shadows of small boulders. In the distance, they can see a light.

A fire has been lit in the cabin. She wonders if the wattle between the logs is real or for show. The bathroom has a metal shower and a pink sink. Jack seems abashed by the modest furnishings, as though he had planned for something else.

— I love it here, Kathryn says, reassuring him.

She sits on the bed, which sags and gives a loud metallic creak. Her eyes widen, and he laughs.

— I'm glad it's a cabin, he says.

They undress in the firelight. She watches as he pulls his tie to the side, unbuttons his shirt. The way he tugs his belt buckle slightly to release the tongue. He slides his legs from his suit pants. Men's socks, she thinks. If they knew how they looked, they wouldn't wear them.

Naked, he is cold and dives into the bed. They glide against each other like dry silk. He pulls the comforters, piled high and weighty, the only luxury in the room, over their shoulders.

The bed squeals at the slightest shift in weight. They lie side by side, their faces not three inches apart, and touch each other as they never have before: slowly, with an economy of movement, as if executing an ancient dance, ritualistic and intent. When he enters her, he moves with exquisite care and patience. She sighs once quickly.

— The three of us, he says.

three

MATTIE'S ARMS TREMBLED, JERKING THE REEL WITH
the strain.

"Hey, did you see that?" Mattie cried.

"It looks huge," Kathryn answered.

"I think I've really got him."

"Bring the line in away from the rocks or you'll cut it."

Kathryn could see the black and silver stripes tumbling just
below the surface of the water. For forty minutes now, she'd
been watching Mattie fight the fish with her father's oversized
rod, letting the line spin out, setting the drag, grunting, and then
reeling in the fish, anchoring the pole in her armpit for leverage.
Kathryn waded out with the net, scooped and missed, tried
again. Finally, she held the striper aloft for Mattie to see.

Jack should be here, Kathryn thought automatically.

Mattie put down the rod, took the fish from her mother, and
laid it on the sand. The doomed striper flipped its tail. Mattie got
out the measuring tape, and Kathryn crouched with her to get a
better look.

"Thirty-six," Mattie said with pride.

"Yes!" Kathryn said, scratching the top of Mattie's head. Her daughter's hair had gone a lovely coppery color over the summer. She wore it natural, let it wave where it wanted to. She was nearly naked but for the two thin wisps of ice blue that were her bathing suit.

"Are you going to eat it or release it?" Kathryn asked.

"What do you think I should do?"

"If it weren't your first, I'd say release it. Did Dad ever teach you how to clean a fish?"

Mattie stood up, hoisting the fish with muscles that were all but spent.

"I'll get the camera," Kathryn said.

"Love you, Mom," Mattie said, grinning.

Kathryn walked across the lawn and listened to the halyards on the flagpole sending out an arrhythmic beat of hollow notes. It was a day as fine as any they had had this summer, already a long string of fine days saturated with rich color. Just this morning, she had seen a nearly miraculous sunrise, the low clouds of daybreak giving way to a neon pink all along the horizon, with swirls of rising vapor that looked like lavender smoke. And then the sun had popped, a detonation on the sea, and the water had turned, for a few glorious minutes, a flat, rippling turquoise, reflecting the mackerel pattern of the neon. It was the paradoxical beauty of a nuclear bomb, she had thought, or of a fire aboard a ship. A conflagration of earth and sea and air together.

It was her only complaint, the rising early, like a spinster or a widow, which, of course, she was. The early risings suggested a lack of night excitement that might require sleep. In these often ghostly mornings, Kathryn read, pleased that she could read a book through now. She could also read a newspaper in its entirety, as she had read the one on the porch, read particularly the article on the front page about the cease-fire.

The story of the bomb planted on Vision Flight 384, with the unwitting though not blameless assistance of Captain Jack Lyons, had broken on New Year's Day in the *Belfast Telegraph*. Also reported was the long-term history of crew-assisted smuggling on airliners, the names of the other pilots involved, and the effects of the attempt on the part of the Loyalist splinter group to discredit the IRA and sabotage the peace process. Among others, Muire Boland and her brother had been arrested, and a connection with Jack Lyons established. There had been no mention yet of a marriage or of another family, and for months now Kathryn had dreaded this final word. She had gambled with Mattie, deciding to say nothing to her daughter unless this knowledge was made public. It was a large gamble, and who could say how it would end? Mattie knew only what the rest of the world knew, which was enough.

Kathryn didn't know what had happened to Muire Boland's children. Sometimes she imagined them at A's.

In the spring, Kathryn had read books about the Troubles in an effort to better understand them. She could say that she knew more facts than she had in December, but she thought this knowledge only made the saga more complex. Over the last several months, she'd also read, in the newspapers, of prison riots, paramilitary executions, and car bombings. Now there was again a cease-fire. It was possible that one day there would be a resolution, although Kathryn didn't think it would happen soon.

But it was not for her to say. It was not her war.

Most days, it was all that Kathryn could do to manage the day in front of her, and, as a consequence, she required little of herself. She lived in her bathing suit, worn under a faded navy sweatshirt. She was knitting a tank top for Mattie in confetti cotton, and she wanted to try one for herself. This seemed to be the limit of her ambitions. Most days, Julia came by, or Kathryn stopped in town. They ate meals together, trying to re-create a family threesome. Julia had taken the news of Jack's infidelity particularly hard. It was the first time Kathryn could remember her grandmother at a loss for words, unable to give advice.

Kathryn jogged up the porch steps, passed through the front room and the kitchen. She thought the camera was in a windbreaker in the back hall. She turned the corner into the hallway and stopped short.

He was standing at the back door, having already knocked. She could see his face through the glass panes. She put a hand out to the wall to steady herself. Between herself and the door was a pungent memory, a reprise of another time she'd walked the length of the hall and opened the door to him, a moment when all her life had changed, had altered its course for good.

She moved the six or seven steps to the door as if in a trance, and opened it.

He leaned against the door frame with his hands in his pockets. He had on a white T-shirt and a pair of khaki shorts. He'd cut his hair, she saw, and had some color. Beyond that, she couldn't make out much because the sun was behind him. She could feel him there, however, in the curious mix of determination and resignation that seemed to emanate from his body. She thought he must be waiting for her to shut the door or to ask him to leave or to demand of him, curtly, what it was that he expected from her now.

The air seemed crowded between them.

"Has enough time passed?" he asked.

And she wondered, as she stood there, exactly how much time would be enough.

"Mattie has a fish," she said, coming to, remembering. "I've got to get the camera."

She found the camera where she thought it was. She put a hand to her forehead as she passed through the house. Her skin was hot to the touch and abrasive with layers of beach sand and sea salt. Earlier, she and Mattie had gone bodysurfing, crawling from the undertow on their hands and knees like two ship-wrecked sailors.

She crossed the lawn again, preoccupied now with the man she'd left in the doorway. She wondered, briefly, if she had dreamt him there, only imagined that he stood backlit by the sun. She took a dozen pictures of her daughter and the fish, wanting to prolong the moment, to give herself some time. Only when Mattie grew impatient did Kathryn put the camera around her neck and help Mattie haul the equipment and the fish to the porch.

"You're sure you want to do this?" she asked Mattie, referring to the filleting of the fish. But Kathryn thought it was a question she might well have asked herself.

"I want to try," Mattie said.

Mattie had the keener sight and saw the man on the porch just before her mother did. The girl stopped and lowered her fish slightly. Her eyes flickered with a warning, the memory of a bad dream.

The messenger, Kathryn thought.

"It's OK," she said quietly to her daughter. "He's just come."

The woman and the girl crossed the lawn together, walking in from fishing as countless others had done before them, the parent carrying the rod, the child carrying the trophy, the first of many fish caught in a lifetime. Last week, Mattie had found Jack's fishing pole and tackle in the garage and had methodically set out to recall what Jack had taught her the previous summer. Kathryn had not been able to help her much, never having liked fishing herself. But Mattie was determined and had learned to manage the oversized equipment, developing some skill along the way.

The wind shifted to the east, and immediately Kathryn felt the faint chill in the air that came with an east wind. In a few minutes, there would be whitecaps on the ocean. She thought of Jack then, as she always did, and she knew that she would never again experience an east wind without remembering the day she had stood on the porch, the day Jack had told her of the offer on the house. It was one of hundreds of triggers, small moments: There it is again, the east wind.

She had these moments often. She had them about Jack Lyons, about Muire Boland and about Robert Hart. She had them about airplanes, about anything Irish, about London. She had them about white shirts, and she had them about umbrellas. Even a glass of beer could trigger a splintery recollection. She had learned to live with them, like learning to live with a tic or a stutter or a bad knee that occasionally sent a jolt of pain through the body.

"Hello, Mattie," Robert said when the girl had reached the porch. He said it in a friendly manner, but not overly so, which would have put Mattie on alert, made her even more uneasy than Kathryn could see she already was.

And Mattie, well brought up, said hello in return, but turned her head away.

"It's a beauty," Robert said.

Kathryn, considering Robert and her daughter in the same frame of her vision, said: "Mattie's been teaching herself to fish."

"It's thirty-four, thirty-five?" Robert asked.

"Thirty-six," Mattie said, and not without a note of pride.

Mattie took the tackle box from her mother. "I'll do it over here," she said, pointing to a corner of the porch floor.

"As long as you hose it down afterward," Kathryn answered. She watched as Mattie laid the fish at the porch's edge. The girl studied the gills from different angles, then took a knife from the tackle box. She made an experimental cut. Kathryn hoped the fish was dead.

Robert walked to the other end of the porch. He would want to talk, she thought.

"This is beautiful," Robert said when she had drifted in his direction. He turned and leaned against the railing. He meant the view. She could see his face now, and she thought it looked sharper than she remembered it, more defined. Which would be the color, the tan. "I've imagined this," he added.

Both simultaneously hearing the painful reminder of things imagined.

Robert's legs were also tanned and had tiny golden hairs. Kathryn thought she had probably never seen his legs before. Hers were bare, too, which he took in.

"How is she?" he asked, his gaze as she remembered it: intent and acute. Observant.

"Better," Kathryn said quietly so that Mattie couldn't hear. "Better. It was a rough spring."

For weeks, she and Mattie had borne the brunt of a collective anger. *If Jack hadn't been involved . . .* , some said. *It was your father who carried the bomb . . .* , others said. There had been threatening calls from strangers, anguished letters from relatives, a platoon of reporters at her gate. Simply driving to work had occasionally been harrowing, but Kathryn had refused to leave her home. She'd had to ask the Town of Ely to post a security detail on her property. The selectmen had called a town meeting, put it to a vote, and the unusual appropriation, after much debate, was inserted into the budget. It was listed under a section called Acts of God.

The need for security had abated with the passing months, but Kathryn knew that neither she nor Mattie would ever recover a normal life. This was now a fact, a given, of their existence with which they struggled daily to come to terms. She thought of Robert's comment about the children of crash victims: *They mutate with disaster and make accommodations.*

"And how are you?" he asked.

"I'm all right," she said.

He turned, put a hand on a post, and surveyed the lawn and the garden.

"You grow roses," he said.

"I try."

"They look good."

"It's a fool's enterprise near the ocean," she said.

In the arch of the garden, she had buff Friars and thorny Wenlocks; in the oblong were the Cressidas and Prosperos. She thought she liked the St. Cecilias best, however, for their shameless blush centers. They were easy to grow despite the sea air. Kathryn liked extravagance in flowers, wasteful luxury.

"I should have told you the very first day," he said, and she was unprepared for this so soon. "And then later, I knew that if I told you, I would lose you."

She was silent.

"I made the wrong decision," he said.

"You tried to tell me."

"I didn't try hard enough."

And there, it was said. It was done.

"Sometimes I can't believe any of it happened," Kathryn said.

"If we'd found them sooner, it might not have happened."

Found Jack and Muire sooner, was what he meant.

"The bomb was supposed to go off in the middle of the Atlantic, wasn't it?" she asked. "Meant to go off where there would be little evidence."

"We think so."

"Why didn't they just call in right away and say the IRA had done it?"

"They couldn't. There are codes between the IRA and the police."

"So they simply waited for the investigation to find its way to Muire and Jack."

"Like a long fuse."

Kathryn took a deep and audible breath.

"Where is she?"

"The Maze," he said. "In Belfast. Ironically, the Loyalist terrorists are there as well."

"You suspected Jack?"

"We knew it might be someone with that route."

She wondered, and not for the first time, if a woman could forgive a man who'd betrayed her. And if she did, was that an affirmation? Or was it merely foolishness?

"Are you over the worst of it?" Robert asked.

She fingered a mosquito bite on her arm. The light was clarifying itself, sharpening in the sunset.

"The worst is that I can't grieve," Kathryn said. "How can I grieve for someone I may not even have known? Who wasn't the person I thought he was? He's gutted my memories."

"Grieve for Mattie's father," Robert said, and she saw that he had thought about this.

Kathryn watched Mattie make a serious cut from behind a gill to the backbone.

"I couldn't stay away," Robert said. "I had to come."

She realized that Robert, too, had gambled. As she was doing now with Mattie. Not revealing something when she might.

And then, turning slightly, so that she saw her garden from the porch's edge, so that she was looking down upon it as she seldom did — or perhaps it was only this year's particular configuration of roses — she saw it.

"There it is," she said quietly.

Mattie, hearing the hushed surprise in her mother's voice, glanced up from her surgery, scalpel in her hand.

"The chapel," Kathryn said, explaining.

"What?" Mattie asked, mildly bewildered.

"The garden. The arch there. The shape. That marble thing I thought all this time was a bench? It's not a bench at all."

Mattie studied the garden for a moment, seeing, Kathryn knew, only a garden.

Whereas Kathryn could see the Sisters of the Order of Saint Jean de Baptiste de Bienfaisance kneeling in their summer-white habits. In a chapel made of wood in the shape of an arched window. A chapel that had perhaps burned down, leaving only the marble altar.

She walked closer to the garden.

Seeing things for what they were, she thought. And had been.

"I'll get us something to drink," she said to Robert, privately pleased with her discovery.

She walked into the front room, meaning to continue into the kitchen, to put iced tea into glasses, to cut a lemon into slices, but she instead paused to look out one of the floor-to-ceiling windows. In the frame of the window, Mattie struggled with the fish, and Robert watched her from the railing. He might have shown her how to angle the knife, but these were Jack's tools, and Kathryn knew that Robert would bide his time.

She thought about Muire Boland in a prison in Northern Ireland. About Jack, whose body had never been found. She thought it might be easier to bear if she could say that it had been his mother's leaving him when he was a boy, or his father's brutality. Or that it had been the influence of a priest at Holy Name, or the Vietnam War, or middle age, or boredom with the airline. Or a search for meaning in his life. Or a desire to share risk with a woman he loved. But she knew it might be all of those reasons or none of them. Jack's motivation, which would always remain unknown to Kathryn, was made up of bits of all his motivations, a baffling mosaic.

She found the piece of paper where she had recently left it, tucked under the clock on the mantelpiece. She had thought, some weeks ago, that she might do this.

She unfolded the lottery ticket.

On the porch, Mattie lifted up a fillet and slid it into a plastic bag that Robert held open for her. In London, there was a silence, as Kathryn had known there would be.

"I just wanted to know if the children are all right," she said across the sea.

ACKNOWLEDGMENTS

This is an entirely fictional story about a woman whose husband goes down with his plane. The characters are not drawn from life and do not resemble anyone I know or have ever heard about.

I would like to thank the following people at Little, Brown and Company: my editor, Michael Pietsch, for his sharp eye, his love of editing, and his quiet wisdom; my publicist, Jen Marshall, for the ease with which she appears to be able to solve any problem that comes her way; and Betsy Uhrig, for the clarity and care she brought to the task of copyediting this book.

I would like to thank as well my daughter, Katherine Clemans, for helping to shape the portrait of Mattie; Alan Samson of Little, Brown and Company, U.K., for reading the manuscript and for his continuing support; and Gary DeLong, for sharing with me details about the harsh reality of the grieving process.

As ever, I am grateful to John Osborn, who always has first look at any manuscript and who consistently manages to steer me ever so gently in the right direction.

And finally, though certainly not least — indeed, she is the linchpin of all my books — I would like to thank my agent and friend, Ginger Barber, for her excellent criticism and unwavering graciousness.

BACK BAY · READERS' PICK

Reading Group Guide

The Pilot's Wife

A NOVEL BY

Anita Shreve

A conversation
with Anita Shreve

Four years after the initial publication of *The Pilot's Wife*,
the author talks with Sue Fox of *The Independent* about
the novel's origins and about her life as a writer

It comes as something of a relief to meet Anita Shreve in person. All around the world, on planes, trains, and beaches, you can't avoid someone reading one of her bestselling novels: *The Pilot's Wife, Fortune's Rocks, The Weight of Water, The Last Time They Met*. There she is again — the author photograph on the cover, looking unbelievably perfect. Expensive black jacket, classic white blouse (a discreet gold bracelet under a designer cuff), subtle blond highlights, flawless makeup, and an enigmatic gaze giving nothing away.

"Airbrush and lighting," Anita Shreve says, shooing away the dog and seeing to her son, Christopher, a charming, chatty twelve-year-old who has just come home from school. We are sitting in the kitchen of her newly renovated, to-die-for, large, white, sun-filled turn-of-the century house in Longmeadow, Massachusetts. "The photographer who took it usually works with models."

Away from the airbrush and lighting, Shreve doesn't look anything like her photograph. But even in jeans and not much makeup, she is quite lovely. She has a natural, lived-in beauty, entirely appropriate for a happily second-time married, fifty-five-year-old mother of two (her husband, John, who is in insurance, has three children from an earlier marriage). She looks exactly like a wife and mother whose books — written in longhand, in her bathrobe, in a corner of the living room — have been so successful she probably never needs to work again. "But I'm very driven and can't imagine not writing. It's my work. You don't stop just because you've finished a book. No one would think of saying to an architect, 'Will you create another building?' but it's something writers are asked all the time."

Shreve has written nine novels in eleven years. She writes love stories, told in eloquent, painterly prose and compelling dialogue. They are filled with shocking emotional tidal waves that take place in exquisitely drawn locations.

Her latest is *Sea Glass,* set in New Hampshire in 1929. Honora Beecher and her husband, Sexton, are settling into marriage when they suddenly find themselves rocked by the stock market crash of 1929. Penniless, they are forced to adapt to new circumstances.

Shreve, exploring how lives are interconnected, tells their story by returning readers to the house central to both *The Pilot's Wife* and *Fortune's Rocks.* It's loosely based, she says, on a real house she once saw from the outside that, for some reason, she couldn't get out of her head. "But the details are all made up. The house is straight out of my imagination; it's just another character, like Honora and Sexton. In *Sea Glass,* I make a reference to a painting by Claude Lugny, an artist I mentioned in *The Pilot's Wife.* It was just me having fun, but some readers are convinced he's real and want to know where they can go to see more of his paintings."

Shreve constantly returns to the New England coastline, using innovative devices to invent recurring characters and places, compelling flash-forwards, flashbacks, and deeply unsettling endings. Two novels have been adapted into screenplays. *The Pilot's Wife* was a film for American TV. *The Weight of Water,* starring Liz Hurley and Sean Penn, was shown at the London Film Festival. "It's quite similar to the book except that in the film the child doesn't die. Hollywood would never make a movie with that ending."

Oprah Winfrey catapulted Shreve to huge commercial success, selecting *The Pilot's Wife* for her TV book club. Her titles automatically sell over a million, propelling authors to national and, frequently, international fame. "Oprah has encouraged a whole new audience of readers, so publishers love her. The odds against being chosen are huge. I was very lucky." *The Pilot's Wife* gave Oprah "the idea to do a program about women who've discovered their husbands have other families somewhere else. I was invited onto the show, where she had five women come and tell their stories. Each story was much worse than anything I'd written. Real life is invariably worse than novels."

Writing fiction is, says Shreve, a wonderful career for any woman with children. "I work all morning, as soon as Chris has gone off to school, and finish around lunchtime. At certain stages, when I'm totally preoccupied by what's happening, I spend a lot of time living in my head. It's sometimes hard to come back into the real world — especially in the beginning, when there are so many unanswered questions. Which character is going to tell this story? What tense will I use?"

In her new house, Shreve no longer sits in her bathrobe. She has a room of her own: an office above the bedroom in the adjoining guesthouse. She also has a swimming pool with a device that, at the touch of a button, creates currents so you feel you are swimming in the sea. The pool is her one luxury. "The room where I write is like an empty schoolroom. Just a desk and blank walls. I don't listen to music and I don't have any photographs because I don't want life to invade. My writing has to be created out of deprivation, not excess."

Asking questions used to be Shreve's stock-in-trade. A journalist for fifteen years, she didn't much care for that part of the job. "I always felt anxiety around asking questions, but I loved library research and finding creative ways to put all the material together." Journalism was good training for a novelist, though. "I could never write an article until I knew what my last line was going to be. It's the same with my books. I have to know the ending, although I don't necessarily have any idea how I'm going to get there. That's part of the pleasure — the sense of a story developing." Although she doesn't have time now, for the past few years Shreve taught creative writing classes at Amherst College, using journalism techniques to encourage her students to make up their own stories.

Growing up in Dedham, a middle-class Boston suburb, she dreamed of being a writer. "I majored in English at college, but my father was a child of the Depression and very practical. He insisted that after graduation, I could do anything as long as I qualified as a teacher first and had a profession. I taught high school for five years before quitting to write short stories and discovering that my father was right. It's difficult to earn a living from writing." Some of Shreve's stories were published in magazines and one won her an O. Henry Award.

Marriage and a daughter (twenty now and at away at college), journalism, and time in Kenya make up Shreve's personal story, but she is reticent about giving away her private life. "I enjoy meeting people at book clubs, discussing the text, or doing readings, but that's all. Part of me wishes I could write anonymously. Of course that's impossible if you want anyone to buy your books. My stories are invented. The characters are imaginary. They're not about me or my life. Early on I learned to put everyone I knew — parents, friends, even readers — out of my mind so that I wouldn't feel intimidated, and there was no one to interfere with my daydreams."

Shreve describes writing novels as daydreaming: "A delicious way to have imaginary conversations." She started writing fiction in secret. "It was a bit like trying to give up smoking. You don't want people to know you're doing it in case you quit and don't make it. It takes such a leap of faith to write something nobody has asked for and may not want." Despite her success, she is still very secretive. "The universe I'm trying to create is so fragile, it's easier not to reveal anything — even the title. I don't want my editor or anyone to know what I'm writing about until I'm ready."

As a journalist, Shreve was an editor for *Us* magazine and freelanced for *Newsweek* and the *New York Times Magazine*. She spent a couple of years based in Nairobi, where she edited an African magazine, "doing everything from writing recipes to interviewing the president." Two of her articles were expanded into nonfiction books. "By the time you've written a piece for the *New York Times Magazine,* you've collected so much research material, expanding . . . isn't very difficult. It gave me the impetus to expand beyond the journalistic restriction of a certain number of words, but nonfiction made me realize that I'd much rather be writing stories."

An aspect of journalism that never lit up Shreve's life was the golden rule that a journalist has to be concerned with facts. "You just can't go into someone's head and make assumptions about people," she says. "Oddly enough, I think it's much easier to 'tell the truth' when you write fiction."

The complete text of Sue Fox's interview with Anita Shreve originally appeared in The Independent *on March 30, 2002. Copyright © 2002 The Independent. Reprinted with permission.*

Questions and topics for discussion

1. The complex relationship between secrecy and intimacy is an important theme of *The Pilot's Wife*. Consider the secrets kept by the following characters: Kathryn, Jack, Mattie, Robert, Muire. In each case, what motivates the deceiver? Who is protected and who is harmed by the secret? Can deception ever be an expression of love? Examine the conversation between Kathryn and Mattie on pages 118–119, especially Mattie's question: "But how do you ever know that you know a person?" Is there a more satisfactory answer to this question than the one Kathryn offers?

2. Does Shreve's use of flashbacks to Jack and Kathryn's marriage reveal the changes occurring between them? In what way did Jack and in what way did Kathryn each contribute to the marital problems? How did each of them react to the difficulties?

3. Was Robert's betrayal the worst of all, as Kathryn thinks to herself? Who betrayed whom in this novel? Can you ever love someone who has betrayed you?

4. When Kathryn throws her wedding ring into the ocean, she thinks to herself: To be relieved of love is to give up a terrible burden. Do you agree?

5. Regarding Jack's religion or lack of it, he appeared to be quite divided. Was he assuming religious beliefs just to please the women he was with? How does his religious division give us clues to his character?

6. How do the memories and thoughts Jack and Kathryn each have about their respective mothers influence their views of marriage?

7. The theme of disaster is central to the story. Not just the physical disaster of the crash, or even the disaster to the family that Jack's death produces, but the disaster that unfolds as Kathryn learns the truth about Jack's double life and many secrets. How does the passage from the bottom of page 13 relate to the disasters?

8. "And she thought then how strange it was that disaster — the sort of disaster that drained the blood from your body and took the air out of your lungs and hit you again and again in the face — could be, at times, such a thing of beauty" (page 13). Could this passage also be used at the end of the book? Is there beauty in disaster?

9. What devices does Shreve use to make her novel such a compelling read? Consider the flashbacks, the action, the style of language and word choice, and character painting.

10. Do you think the reason Jack couldn't be honest with Kathryn about his mother and his life with Muire was not so much because of his love for Kathryn, but more because he didn't want to repeat what his mother did and subject his child to what he went through? In what ways do Kathryn and Jack repeat their respective mothers' mistakes?

11. Muire revealed the whole truth to Kathryn about Jack's secret life. How did this confession help Kathryn find the answers to her questions about how "real" her marriage was? Who is the "real wife" (page 275)? What constitutes a "real wife"? Do we continue to think that Kathryn is the "real" wife, because this is her story, or Muire for accepting the truth about Kathryn?

12. As the story progresses, Kathryn gradually pieces together mysteries of her husband's life from the facts that come to light following Jack's death. At the same time, she is trying

to understand the pieces of her own life. Does Kathryn and Jack's house, originally inhabited by nuns retreating from the world, play a significant part in this story? In what way was the house that Kathryn and Jack lived in for eleven years a metaphor for their relationship? Discuss the significance of Kathryn's discovery of the site of the Sisters' Chapel at the end of the book.

13. At what point in the story did you figure out that Jack was having an affair? Were you suspicious when Kathryn found the receipt for the bathrobe or the note in his pocket? Did you want to believe Kathryn's suspicions?

14. Discuss the differences between Kathryn's relationship to Jack and Mattie's to him. Which relationship seemed more honest? Which relationship seemed stronger? As a mother, is Kathryn obligated, at some future time, to share full knowledge of Jack with Mattie?

15. Do you think *The Pilot's Wife* would make a good film? If so, why? Who would you cast as the major characters in the film version? Why?

Booksellers who contributed questions
to this reading group guide to The Pilot's Wife:

Melissa A. Frazer, Lake Country Booksellers, White Bear Lake, Minnesota
Susan Avery, Ariel Books, New Paltz, New York
Justine Morgan, The Bookstore, Hollister, California
Lucy Crane, Bookworks, Albuquerque, New Mexico
Kristin Kennell, Elliott Bay Book Company, Seattle, Washington
Peggy Baldwin, Bookworks, Aptos, California
Heidi Gunter, Magnolia's Bookstore, Seattle, Washington
Kristin Brackett, Key Chain Books, Tavernier, Florida
Ettabelle Schwartz, The Learned Owl, Hudson, Ohio

ABOUT THE AUTHOR

Anita Shreve is the author of several internationally praised and bestselling novels, among them *Body Surfing; A Wedding in December; Light on Snow; All He Ever Wanted; Sea Glass; The Last Time They Met; Fortune's Rocks; The Pilot's Wife,* which was a selection of Oprah's Book Club; *The Weight of Water,* which was a finalist for England's prestigious Orange Prize and for which the author received the New England Book Award and the PEN / L. L. Winship Award; *Resistance; Where or When; Strange Fits of Passion;* and *Eden Close.* She lives in Massachusetts. For more information, visit AnitaShreve.com

. . . AND HER NOVEL *TESTIMONY*

Following is a preview from the novel's opening pages.

IT WAS A SMALL CASSETTE, NOT MUCH BIGGER THAN THE PALM OF HIS hand, and when Mike thought about the terrible license and risk exhibited on the tape, as well as its resultant destructive power, it was as though the two-by-three plastic package had been radioactive. Which it may as well have been, since it had produced something very like radiation sickness throughout the school, reducing the value of an Avery education, destroying at least two marriages that he knew of, ruining the futures of three students, and, most horrifying of all, resulting in a death. After Kasia brought Mike the tape in a white letter envelope (as if he might be going to mail it to someone!), Mike walked home with it and watched it on his television — an enormously complicated and frustrating task since he first had to find his own movie camera that used similar tapes and figure out how to connect its various cables to the television so that the tape could play through the camera. Sometimes Mike wished he had just slipped the offensive tape into a pot of boiling water, or sent it out with the trash in a white plastic drawstring bag, or spooled it out with a pencil and wadded it into a big mess. Although he doubted he could have controlled the potential scandal, he might have been able to choreograph it differently, possibly limiting some of the damage.

Much appeared to have happened before the camera in the unseen hand focused on the quartet. One saw the girl (always *the girl* in Mike's eyes) turning (twirling, it seemed to be) away from a tall, slender boy who still had his jeans on, and toward a somewhat shorter, more solidly built naked young man, who caught the young girl and bent to suck on her right nipple. At that point in the tape, no faces were visible, doubtless a deliberate edit on the part of the person behind the camera. Also, at that moment in time, Mike, who was then headmaster of Avery Academy, did not recognize the setting as a dorm room, though he would soon do so. The shorter boy then turned her to face the first boy, who by then was unbuckling his belt, his jeans sliding off in one go, as if they were cartoon pants, too big for the boy's slender hips. The camera panned jerkily, instantly causing in Mike the beginnings of motion sickness, to a narrow dorm bed on which a third boy, entirely naked and appearing to be slightly older than the other two boys, lay stroking himself. And Mike remembered, among other images he wished he could excise from his brain, the truly impressive length of the young man's empurpled penis and the concentrated tautness of the muscles of the boy's chest and arms. The camera slid back to the center of the room, producing a second dip and rise in Mike's stomach, to the two standing boys and the now kneeling girl.

It was at this point in the tape that Mike realized there was sound attached, for he heard a kind of exaggerated groaning from the side of the room where the bed was, as well as hard-pounding music (though the latter seemed to be, for some reason, muted). Meanwhile, the tall boy with the slender shoulders was holding the blond head of the girl to his crotch. She appeared to know what to do — even to have, at some point prior to the event, *practiced* what to do — for Mike couldn't help but notice a certain expertise, a way of drawing the standing boy's engorged penis toward her so that it seemed she might painfully stretch it before gently swooping forward and seeming to swallow it whole. The slender boy came with an explosive adolescent sound, as if taken by surprise. The cameraman or -woman (it was difficult to picture a girl behind the camera) swung the lens up to capture the boy's face, which, with a start, Mike Bordwin recognized. He had assumed, when Kasia had solemnly handed him the tape just an hour earlier, saying to him in an extremely sober tone, *I think you should take a look at this,* that the tape was simply confiscated pornography (not that the tape *wasn't* pornographic) — something a dorm parent might have dealt with. The idea that there would be recognizable people attached to the action — students he had seen in hallways, in the cafeteria, and on the basketball court — did not really occur to him until he saw the face of the boy, contorted as it was in a paroxysm of pleasure and therefore somewhat grotesque to the outside observer. He thought, *Rob,* and *It can't be.* The Rob he had known was a polite, hardworking student who also happened to be an outstanding forward on the basketball team. And was that how Mike had seen his students, he wondered then, even as he was observing the moment of coming on Rob's face, as *excellent student* or *promising actor* or *pretentious brownnoser* or *good arm?* Because it was perfectly apparent that such descriptive tags were entirely inadequate. The Rob whom Mike had known seemed to be but an embryo of the full-fledged sexual being on the tape. There was a kind of seizure then in Mike's chest as he suddenly, from different parts of his brain, received alarming and unwanted bits of information, not unlike an air traffic controller watching several blips on his radar screen inexplicably about to collide. The girl hardly seemed to come up for air when she turned to the other standing boy, whose face had not been visible during the first pan but which now clearly was, jolting the headmaster and causing him to cry out the name of the boy —

Silas — and to emit a groan of his own, entirely unsexual. Silas and the girl lay down on the floor with Silas on top and went at it in an old-fashioned though frenetic way, the girl's body thudding lightly onto what was clearly now a dormitory floor, dotted with a half-dozen beer cans. Mike closed his eyes, not wanting to watch this particular boy have his own paroxysmal seizure. When he opened them again, the camera was on the face of the girl, who was either experiencing the heights of pleasure or giving an excellent imitation of same. It was then that he saw the girl was very young — very, *very* young: the number *fourteen* floated through his brain — though he didn't at that time know her name. It was not unusual for the headmaster not to know all of the students by name, particularly the underclassmen who hadn't yet distinguished themselves, which Mike was pretty certain she had not. He suddenly wondered how many other persons — faculty or students — had watched this performance on the tape, this particular worry marking perhaps the worst moment of his life to date (though far worse was yet to come).

Groping for the camera, he found and pressed the *pause* button. He was on his knees in his empty house, his breath tight, causing him to put his hand to his chest as if an angina attack might be coming. That any number of people might already have seen the tape was creating in Mike what felt like a temporary heart stoppage but what was really a temporary brain stoppage, his neurons refusing to fire, or whatever they did — *connect* — because he couldn't process another thought, the last having been too awful to contemplate, with its attendant images segueing into the words *police* and *rape* and *alcohol* and *press,* none of which any headmaster wanted in any sequence in any sentence. It seemed important then to focus on the girl to determine how willing a participant she had been in this . . . this *thing* that he was witnessing. Since he didn't have the heart to rewind and review what had gone before, he poked *play*, wishing he could slow down the action, not so that he could enjoy it more — Lord, no — but so that his whole being could catch up to what was inevitably going to be a difficult future. To ease into it, so to speak.

The tape started again with what felt like a snap, once more zooming in on the girl's face. Mike saw, to his dismay, that no matter how experienced she had seemed earlier (and also seemed now, in her fairly convincing expression of ecstasy), she was, in fact, as he had suspected, very young indeed. A freshman, there could be no doubt about it. He thought he could almost retrieve the face and body in a uniform — field hockey? soccer? JV? thirds? — and he was certain that she was a boarder, not a day student like Silas, who seemed to have collapsed upon the girl, who was smiling now, actually smiling. *Is this good or bad?* Mike wondered.

There seemed to be a great deal of chaos. Perhaps the unseen hand had lowered the camera for a moment. Mike narrowed his eyes to keep the nausea at bay while the lens momentarily came to rest on the perfectly innocent corner of a desk leg, with a boy's dirty white sneaker, its laces untied, leaning against it. Mike felt an ache in his throat at the sheer innocence of that image, since it seemed to represent, at that moment, a universe of loss. In the background, there were sounds — none of them very articulate. Mike was fairly certain he heard *Hey* and *Go for it* and *Your turn* (and not necessarily in that order), and then the lens, with a sudden, wild swoop, settled upon the body of the third boy. (*Boy*, Mike thought, *isn't at all accurate in this case.* There was a subtle moment in time when boys turned into men, and it had nothing to do with age or facial hair or voice timbre. It had to do, he had decided — and he had seen this happen hundreds of times over the course of nearly twenty years in a secondary-school setting — with musculature, the set of the jaw, the way the male held himself.) The young man was quite literally holding himself, masturbating over the supine body of the (Mike had to admit) heartbreakingly lovely girl, who appeared to be urging the young man on with rhythmic movements and even various contortions, doubtless learned from watching movies. The unseen person behind the camera had moved his or her vantage point, and one saw now, saw all too clearly in fact, the utter determination on the face of the young man, who was, Mike instantly recognized, a PG (postgraduate) brought to the school to take the basketball team to the play-offs. It was then that Mike quickly calculated and arrived at the number *nineteen* just before the PG, whom the other students called J. Dot (as in *J.Robles@Avery.edu*), came all over the chest and neck and chin of the girl who was *at least* four years younger, causing Mike to reach forward and push *stop,* the way he wished he could push a *stop* button on the future long enough to figure out what to do with this very unwanted piece of celluloid now poised to explode inside his camera.

He sat back against the sofa in the TV room. Mike had tried, in the early years of their residence in the impressive Georgian, to refer to the room as a *library,* as befitted his position in life, but in fact Meg and he had spent more time there watching television and DVDs than they had reading, and so they had started calling it what it really was. Mike was panting slightly, his mouth dry. That there was probably more to the tape seemed unthinkable. (And, after all, hadn't all three boys come within minutes of one another? But then again, these were teenage boys.) He doubted that he could watch any more. He was both glad and sorry that Meg was not in the house, glad because he needed to think about what to do, and sorry because it was just conceivable she might have comforted him, though probably not. Would Meg have been as shocked as he? Was she closer to the kids? Did she understand them better?

Mike immediately wondered when the event had taken place and in what dorm. It seemed likely that the incident had followed a drinking binge, to judge from the number of beer cans on the floor. Perhaps there was a clue on a desk or a date marked on a calendar. It almost certainly had to have been on a Saturday night, because students had to be present for study hall in their dorms at eight p.m. weekday evenings as well as on the Friday night before a Class Saturday. There had been a school dance the previous weekend. Geoff Coggeshall, the dean of students, had mentioned that there had been the usual number of kids who had been caught drinking or who were suspected of it. The abuse of alcohol was impossible to stop and was at the top of the list of worries for nearly every headmaster or principal of every secondary school in the country. Though there had been many assemblies and seminars on the subject, it was Mike's opinion that the problem was more severe than it had been in previous years. He sometimes wondered if all the focus on alcoholism, meant to promote awareness of the dangers of drinking, had not, in fact, subtly brought it to the fore in a way it had not been so blatantly *important* before. Every generation of students had done its share of binge drinking, but it was pretty clear, from all the data he had seen, that the drinking was starting at an earlier age and was both more habitual and more intense than it had been just a decade earlier.

He lay his head back against the sofa and closed his eyes. The house was empty and quiet. He could hear the wind skidding against the windows and, from the kitchen, the sound of ice cubes tumbling in the Viking, recently installed. Tasks now needed to be accomplished, students queried, the Disciplinary Committee convened, and all of this conducted beneath the radar of the press, which would, if they got wind of the story, revel in a private-school scandal. In this, Mike thought that private schools had been unfairly singled out. He doubted that such a tape would have been of any interest to the press had it surfaced at the local regional high school, for example. The tape might have circulated underground, students might have been expelled, and meetings might have been held, yet it was likely that the incident would have been greeted with indifference not only by the local newspaper, the *Avery Crier* (its editor, Walter Myers, could be talked down from just about any story that might cause embarrassment to local kids and parents), but also by the regional and national press. Mike thought the national media would scoff at the idea that sex and alcohol, even sex and alcohol involving a fourteen-year-old girl in a public-high-school setting, was news of any sort; *whereas* if the same set of facts, but in a private-school setting, were to pass across the computer screen of a reporter at the *Rutland Herald* or the *Boston Globe*, it was entirely possible that the reporter would be dispatched to Avery to find out *what was going on*. In such a story, there was juice, there was heat, there was blood. There was also, if this tape had been copied in any way, *footage*. Was it because private schools were held to higher standards, according to which such an incident ought to be nearly unthinkable? Or was it because everyone loved to see the elite (even if that elite involved a local farmer's son on scholarship) brought down and ridiculed? A little of both, Mike guessed, with emphasis on the latter.

More troubling, however, was the thought of police involvement. Though Mike felt nothing but revulsion when he thought of the Silas and Rob he'd just seen on the tape (boys whom he had previously much respected and even, in Silas's case, been quite fond of), the idea of them being led away from the administration building in handcuffs was appalling. (Did police routinely handcuff boys suspected of sexual assault, which was what this particular crime, in the state of Vermont, was deemed?) *Police* in this case meant either Gary Quinney or Bernie Herrmann, neither of whom would find any satisfaction in the arrest; Gary was, after all, Silas's uncle. Would the boys then appear some months later in the dowager courthouse across the street from the gates of Avery, the building itself smug in its self-righteousness? Mike's job would be at risk, and any number of teachers who were supposed to be supervising either the dance or the dorm that evening might be fired, for one could not expect the trustees to view the incident and its attendant legal fuss lightly. Would the boys then go to jail, to the Vermont State Prison at Windsor, where almost certainly they would be raped in turn?

Mike reined in his thoughts. He was getting carried away. No, he had to get a grip and act quickly. Three boys were in trouble, and a girl . . . well, presumably, if it did turn out to be a case of sexual assault, the trouble had already occurred to the girl, though the fallout for her might be endless.

Mike got up off the floor and sat on the sofa while he loosened his tie and unbuttoned the top button of his shirt, as if increasing blood flow to the brain might help solve his problem. And it was then that the word *containment* entered his mind. And with that word, moral, ethical, and political choices were made, though Mike would realize the implications of these only later, when it occurred to him that he might have chosen at that moment another word, such as *revelation,* say, or *help.*

Look for these other novels by Anita Shreve

Body Surfing

"Deceptions abound in this engrossing page-turner. The embittered family drama has unforeseen plot twists and character tiffs galore."   — Alexis Burling, *Washington Post*

A Wedding in December

"Engrossing. . . . An excellent novel about new beginnings threatened by old memories that ultimately reveal uncomfortable secrets from the past. . . . By book's end, lives are drastically changed, and Shreve has made readers care that they have."
     — Tasca Robinson, *Fort Worth Star-Telegram*

Light on Snow

"An evening's entertainment that will linger at the edges of your mind for days. . . . Shreve's writing is spare, neat, and crisp, yet the principal characters are fully formed, and their lives worth caring about."   — Lynn Hopper, *Indianapolis Star*

All He Ever Wanted

"Anita Shreve is up to her old page-turning tricks. . . . There's something addictive about her literary tales of love and lust. . . . She is a master at depicting passion's ferocious grip."
     — Jocelyn McClurg, *USA Today*

Back Bay Books
Available in paperback wherever books are sold